A BRIEF STAY WITH THE LIVING

by the same author

PIG TALES
MY PHANTOM HUSBAND
BREATHING UNDERWATER

MARIE DARRIEUSSECQ

A Brief Stay
with the Living

translated by Ian Monk

faber and faber

First published in France as *Bref séjour chez les vivants* in 2001
by P.O.L éditeur
First published in Great Britain in 2003
by Faber and Faber Limited
3 Queen Square London WC1N 3AU

Typeset by Faber and Faber Limited
Printed in England by Mackays of Chatham plc,
Chatham, Kent

The right of Ian Monk to be identified as translator
of this work has been asserted in accordance with
Section 77 of the Copyright, Designs and Patents Act 1988

Lines on page 156 from Frank Kuppner,
Second Best Moments in Chinese History (1997) are reprinted
by permission of Carcanet Press

A CIP record for this book
is available from the British Library

ISBN 0–571–21494–0

2 4 6 8 10 9 7 5 3 1

Cast of Voices

Madame Johnson, divorced mother of three daughters, now remarried and living in the South of France with Momo.

Jeanne, the oldest of the girls, now living in Buenos Aires with Diego.

Anne, the second daughter, now living alone in Paris.

Éléonore, or 'Nore', the youngest daughter, staying with her mother and stepfather.

The Mother

Summer is drawing to a close. There are fewer roses, fewer buds. On the old white bush, the Madame de Sévigné, there are two little green-helmeted flower heads, pointing stiffly upwards, like tiny soldiers among the thorns. Snips from the secateurs clip away the abandoned blooms. Watch you don't catch tetanus. Momo tells her that summer is drawing to a close and there is perhaps no point in hosing down the patio today; they'll be able to read there without suffocating, the summer heat has evaporated. The spoon chinks in the cup. A smell of coffee. She cuts a beautiful rose, only two of its petals have uncurled from the bud, it isn't even a proper flower yet, not with just two open petals. She thanks God knows who or what for this morning's reprieve, the flow of breath, happiness so huge and liquid.

Anne

In the courtyard . . . Is this really the place? I've been waiting ages. Someone else could turn up, someone other than him. Unless he's in disguise . . . A recruiting agent. Someone who'll give me something. A mission. Money up front. How must that feel? Close your eyes. Vulgar thoughts. Just plain vulgar period. Back in primary school, *and what's this young lady's name?* Anne. *Anne what?* Just plain Anne period. The number of times John or Mum has told me that in English or in French . . .

He could come now. He could . . . Meet you in the courtyard outside the library. The big sundial. The large towers, or one of them, casting a shadow around me. Send it flying. The shadow cast by the west tower at a quarter past nine . . .

At the foot of the west tower. He said *nine o'clock at the foot of the west tower*. Not east. Not south. There's no one at the feet of the other towers. West towards the sea, the way the Seine meanders. The west tower which casts its shadow westwards, *quarter past nine, knickers on the line*. Courtyard outside Paris's *Très Grande Bibliothèque*. It's like a sundial with four needles, four large tall towers shaped like open books. Such a massive, naïve, assertive idea. A kid's idea four times over. Like me making houses of books with Jeanne. Four stacks for the walls, an open album for the roof. When we were five or seven. Playing at Hansel and Gretel. And, in the middle of the courtyard, between the four towers, they've planted a forest. A real one. They cut it out, all in one lump, from a real forest . . . earth and trees with it . . . plus shrubs and undergrowth all in one go. From Fontainebleau the oak and the willow. Is the hole still there? A large ditch, a big rectangle in the earth. Then they transported it and placed it like a bit of Lego, click, in a rectangular hole just the right size, in the right place, between the four towers of the library. Must have panicked the rabbit population. Now they have to hold up the trees with rubber straps until they take proper root again. Imagine the rabbits and badgers leaping off at the last moment as the rectangle took off . . . like James Bond when the phone box is hiked up by a crane's hoist, off he jumps . . . My name is Bond. My word is my name. Twenty past nine. Like in the dream I had last night. Black ribbons, the slanting shadows of tree trunks on the dark ribbons of the criss-crossed straps. Around the neck of Olympia des Pins. Maybe they took the burrows up with it too, burrows full of leverets and bunnies, suddenly shifted between these massive childish books. Hansel and Gretel, in the forest, the perilous house of gingerbread. The west tower casts its shadow westwards. The sun's pale. But Hansel and Gretel still had parents. And the witch. In those days . . . once upon a time there lived . . . and then they lived happily ever . . . Nothing . . . The sun . . . No one . . . The sun on the courtyard . . . The shadow of the east tower . . .

2

Impeccably upright above the impeccably rectangular patch of forest . . .

The recruiting agent will come and recruit her. Or maybe she'll answer an ad . . .

PHARMACEUTICAL COMPANY
is recruiting for laboratory tests

No, they won't say 'laboratory' tests . . .

is recruiting for tests
to test new products/drugs
young women aged 25–35 who are single/free/nulliparous
That word . . .
highly sensitive highly moral with great personal qualities
emotional sensual very affective very

They won't say . . .
Picture madrepores, sea sponges, just brush past them and they blink, large underwater eyes, coral animated by itself, you'd think it was the undersea current, but it isn't . . .
Very sensitive, like flowers, like plants

Like that TV film, when little . . .
An arm in the form of a spray, a seed which people breathe in, then a tree grows inside them, comes out of their mouths, slits open their guts, but they're still alive, planted there, if you touch their green branches, like ghastly membranes, they writhe in pain, their screams smothered by the foliage, the forest grows, engulfs them . . .

Sensitive young woman
For experiments

She'll be recruited . . .

Her legs give way . . .

Twenty-five past nine. The library spins round the sun. The shadows of its four towers on the teak courtyard, like a ship's

3

sheltering bridge as it turns. She lets herself be sliced in two, one cheek warm, the other cold, one dazzled eye, the other fixed on the hull, sun and shade. One step away it's full daylight. He isn't coming.

Nore

Italianate domes, yellow and pink in the sunlight, a large sun, motionless, sun and city all handed down. She emerges on to a square, surrounded by domes. She isn't alone, there are two or three of them, like members of a club, the club that often surrounds her in her dreams, attached to indistinct members, or rather, as she wakes up as the light breaks over the bed, as she sinks back a little, between dreams and recalling dreams – just time enough to emerge on to that square and realize, with no fear, no dismay, no surprise or revulsion, that the square is suspended halfway up towards the domes, with no way down to the city, no steps, no slope, no gangway. It's a detached section of the city, deposited there, rotating just beneath the sun. If there's enough time, she'll understand, just a second, to go back to sleep, into her dream, catch the end of the story . . . The fixed sun slices the bed in two . . . No, the ray has shifted already, towards the pillow, she's awake, *the earthquake that struck Turkey yesterday* . . . if now the walls shook too, the earth with them, on Richter's scale, which is apparently exponential, the higher you go the worse it gets, a bit hard to grasp . . . *The serial killer would single out his victims amid the crowd* – if she stays put, in two minutes' time, she'll have just one eye in the sunlight, with differently coloured eyes, such pretty eyes for no one – *the little boy locked up in a cellar for the first three years of his life* . . . No one's listening to the radio, they're already having coffee on the patio, watching the grass and the roses grow, should go downstairs and turn it off, *Hurricane Mitch has ravaged Honduras* – the sun slides on the curve of the eye. With a bit of patience you can feel the gentle flow of the sun's motion, or rather the slow roll

4

of the earth, ever westwards, chasing what? Falling, ever onwards, turning, an imperceptible and spinning shadow on the barrier of your eyelids, what was that dream . . .

The floorboards feel granular beneath her feet, dusty, *plane crash in Manaus, five survivors*, the sunrays arrive intermittently, full of molecules spinning in suspension – an image, the sun, a spinning disc, domes, the image fades – every morning such an effort, a leak, a flow of waste, night spent in such and such a place with certain people, sensations, worries. And all that's left in the morning is a sense of having been inhabited . . .

Yes, inhabited, used, exploited in such and such a way by a dream, reconstituted by the dreams for which she was just the means . . .

As though dreams were floating, on high, scattered over the world's surface, then they wrapped themselves up in her head at night, spreading out inside her, before fleeing when she wakes; unless there's just one dream for everyone, the entire planet, and that's the dream you have to recover, write down, paint, when you get up, decidedly unconvinced and turn off the radio . . .

The Mother

There's a postcard from Jeanne. She hands it to Momo. He hasn't seen much of Jeanne. She just couldn't bear the move, the divorce, this house. As for their childhood home, they'll have to sell it now – don't keep on about it. He looks at the photo, the Tigre delta, Rio de la Plata, with its clumps of wild cinnamon, spices, gigantic fig trees gobbled up by wisteria, a maze of ponds and canals, and on the back it says, *It's like Normandy here, everyone has a holiday home, ours is fantastic, it's already spring, I hope you're all well. Love, Jeanne.* Here autumn is coming. The roses are wilting. The Tigre is half an hour from Buenos Aires, like the sea from here. Jeanne must be asleep right now, it's one or two in the morning. Every day it's the same story, piece the family back together again: Anne in Paris, Nore here still in bed, Jeanne out yonder. The earth's like a timer for boiling eggs, shaped like a hen, a golf ball, a grain of sweetcorn, or something like that, sliced in two by the equator, into the southern hemisphere, northern hemisphere, each rotating its way, with everything going in opposite directions, the seasons, the quarters of the moon and the minutes of course, but also the growth of plants, the circulation of currents . . . He gives her back the postcard. She goes to stick it on the fridge along with the others under the magnet. She just can't understand how Jeanne could have moved there for good, with her Diego. She was born here, after all. And all those efforts to get pregnant. Put the secateurs on the table, wipe your hands. Nore will be down soon. For cereal and tea. The blue and green patch of Jeanne's card beneath the magnet, yonder, on the far side of the world, head downwards, like a bat. She never says anything personal. What does she send cards for, just to say she's alive?

Jeanne

The sun's immense, as large in the yellow sky as the yellow esplanade beneath it. I must go to fetch that very, very important thing, down there, in the road with the same name as it had last time. We're all walking together, three or four of us, looking for a way out from the esplanade. Under the sun, the shadows are dipping in the same direction. It's all completely coherent. Short shadows, high sun. All's well, despite the strange layout of this place, as though suspended, enclosed by the air, it doesn't really matter. We'll end up finding a way. Basically speaking, it's beautiful. Those pink domes under the yellow sun. Powdered rock, sandstone buildings. There's no panic. There's no hurry, despite our mission drawing us towards that point. A point of convergence. I'm going down slowly. I'm stretching in the sunlight. It's like Italy. I'm very tall. Growing from my head and my toes, as I approach the point. Going quite normally and calmly towards the meeting place. Where someone's waiting for us. The police sirens blare ever closer. Through the double glazing, there are blue lights in my room, blue neon on blue night . . . Go back to sleep. All's well. I'm dreaming. I'm far away. In Argentina. With Diego . . .

Anne

He isn't coming. What a stupid date at the library. What's to become of me? It's spinning. My body's now completely in the sunlight. A light pressure, the sun isn't holding me, isn't enveloping me, I'm detached, that's what. All's not well. The large disc of the courtyard is coming with me, that's what. The long slats of teak are curling up and coming with me. The first step of the stairs, security rail, anti-skid notches, the sharp angle of the Inca pyramid, the four regions of the court-yard of the library with four childish books as open as ram-parts, as angles of attack, my foot flat on each step, two escape routes stretching behind me, like a bridal train, and the Seine, a moat, with the ghastly green pyramid on the other side of the water, beside the majestic ministry, and the warehouses still left standing, and the garden centre, I ought to buy some, some compost, green fingers in this family . . .

The lightship they've towed here, bright red, visible in a storm, and turned into a restaurant where people I don't know go, is particularly colourful today. The pyramid oppo-site particularly green, and the library's teak deck was, I'd say, particularly beige-grey. It's the morning light, I don't see morning light that often, a late riser like my sisters, like my mother used to be, like *toda la familia*, this morning the light is, *I strolled as the light beat down like rain* . . .

I hadn't gone for a stroll, I was coming back from being stood up, from an amorous let-down, probably from the beginning of the end, and the light was, maybe it was just normal morning light . . .

7

Coming down from the *Très Grande Bibliothèque* with its numerous names, *Bibliothèque François-Mitterrand*, *Bibliothèque Nationale*, *TGB* instead of the old *BN*, coming back from being stood up, a wallflower, planted there, an uprooted tree . . .

Maybe it was just morning light, I don't get to see it that often being a late riser, like my sister, now asleep in a country where they sleep all the time, stuck between two time zones the precise size of our waking hours, which means when Jeanne's asleep I'm awake, and vice versa, two a.m. because it's nearly ten and I'm walking beside the Seine where light splits, falls, splits, then leaps back in two distinct bursts – one hitting the glass sides of the library and bouncing back into my left eye, the other reflected by the ministry into (if I aim correctly) my right eye. And the sun, no longer a soppy pink, is colourless above my head, making the shadows turn and shorten . . .

The air's yellow now, diffused with violent light, trapped in a triangular cage: the left-hand slab of the sky, then the right-hand slab of the sky, and the Seine. Here's my position: in the middle of a triangle, whose three sides concentrate the yellow air into a single point of fusion, where light burns, where, maybe, it's being produced, in millions of particles . . .

The barge's sluggish motor beneath the bridge, like a conveyor belt, is slap slap slapping between the piles, up to my feet, I could slip along it too, if I was something else, different from this body linked to this consciousness, which waited this morning dumbly in the courtyard, the slap slap slapping of water and then, a silk cut, a satellite photo of some coastline or other – Holland, polders – with criss-cross wakes of unseen boats, too small or out of shot, wakes forming networks, lingering there, lingering long after the boats have gone, white on blue water, seen from above – but the Seine apparently closes up again without a trace, it's the air maybe, the quality of this yellow, shattered, dense air, you shift it around in lumps between your hands – behind me the void closes up and I suppose I'm visible to the satellite, the recruiting agents leaning down above the air I'm swimming through, through morning's dense liquid – fishing-rod, fisherman – *sorry, sorry, I didn't see you there*, people are so edgy, just look where you're going, can't you, OK, OK . . .

The Mother

The fragrance floating in the air is like honeysuckle, but it's already autumn. The last roses sag, blossom less fully. The late-blooming Forever gives off a violent yet bland odour of death, raw meat, like a large layered organ, with alveoli and ventricles. They fill your palm with their swollen petals. The fragrance floating in the air in this early autumn is like honeysuckle, maybe it's the bindweed starting to rot in the grass it colonized and which will in turn gobble it up in humus and moss. Bindweed grows fast and dies young. Winter is creeping into the grass, you can sense it in the cool of the morning, as the sun warms up in steam and autumn mists. Momo comes out of the kitchen with the cordless phone, he lays it on my lap, the voice of my daughter Anne, cordless phones, there's progress for you . . .

Anne, via a satellite link, before they used to lay cables, didn't they? under the sea, dropped from heavy boats in more or less straight lines between the whales, above the troughs, the agile giant squids, aquatic sounds could be heard between two continents, transatlantic conversations . . .

Jeanne in Buenos Aires, Nore here at home, and Anne, swallowing back her sobs, as usual, *whatever's the matter this time*, only calls when something's wrong, in other words all the time, in other words at certain times and practically hourly since her recent acquisition of a mobile, variant of the cordless phone . . .

She plucks a white dahlia in her free hand, crushes it slightly. Whatever next? Anne in tears, what can I do about her

9

constant crises? Live for yourself a bit at your age, three daughters and four births, Nore's still living with us, occupying territory, so little intimacy, they've never really accepted Momo, John's like a god, a lost god, their Daddy. Anne reckons she's the only one who's miserable, the only one who suffers, has suffered, will suffer . . .

Kisses, hang up, sit on a large block brought back from the beach, a lump of seventeenth-century dressed stone, washed up by the sea, with saxifrage growing in its cracks, quite a success. With her nail she snips away a wilting carnation, shrugs off what's still weighing down on her – a deep breath to recover the scent of the roses, that's what they're there for, like semicolons, pauses in time, stains of broken time; don't think about Anne, the closest likeness, the same, my best, just plain Anne period, still a little girl, *Oh, Madame Johnson, you give birth like you're shelling peas*, the wet fur of a little creature . . . at the time people named them Anne-Lise, Anne-Marie, Anne-Sophie, depending on your social status. Handed down from A to Z in one go. Then with Éléonore we turned original – an artist, a princess. I must sell the house, I can't stop thinking about that house. Nore is the one who's most attached to it, even though she hardly ever lived there. Pure innocence. Pure ignorance. After all, she had to be protected. Then there were Anne's absences, how to explain them to her? Touch wood – lumpy ancient oak bark. Just hope there'll always be someone to put her back on her feet, she's a big girl now, someone to pick up the pieces . . .

Nore

Since the phone rang, you can hear the garden. A contrast. The poplars rustling. The air full of soughing and brushing, and occasional smells, coming down like birds. The precision of roses right under my window. Mum absent-mindedly crushes a white flower, the roses cry out like jays. Try to catch what she's saying, her neck is twisted over the receiver, it must be Anne who's calling, you can tell by the tense, pained look on her face – I can hear her, caught in the midst of air-waves, in the layered density of the air, a low frequency, the same as the background hum which, when you home in on it, could be either the motorway or the sea, who knows? It's always there, beneath the noise of the birds, trees, insects . . . Mum is saying, what? Nothing, neither yes nor no, she's going to suggest once more . . .

Stupid spluttering, stupid backfiring lawnmower, only nine in the morning and he's already attacking the garden, out to decapitate the earwigs, *it's so lovely and quiet in the country*, he told Anne, *how on earth can you live in Paris?* Mum's leaning against the old oak tree, not leaning, just putting her hand there, feeling it, I can't hear a thing, airport din of the lawn-mower over my mother's petal-coloured face . . .

Elephants when I was little, circus in the square, five fettered elephants, the mahout let me touch them, their leathery skin, like dead bark, you had to hit them to stroke them, except the extremity, pink trunk, a hand with soldered fingers – the mahout's circus, I was just a little girl, ten or eleven, Jeanne in Africa, Anne already in Paris, I learned my price, a ride on the elephants for being touched up, they were fettered, almost immobile, big feet of oak cork, I was scared of being crushed between the barrels of their ribcages – she's hung up . . .

Lift one foot on to a stool, wobble, ears like flounces and that massive skull, crammed full, chains clanking . . .

When you close the window you can hear the background hum and nothing else. Momo says it's the sea, when the wind's up maybe it is, crashing, at night, as far as our beds. But in summer, in the hollows of August, or now in autumn after the equinoctial tides, a moment of calm in Europe's most dangerous gulf – Jeanne by Mar del Plata, the east coast, flat sea beneath a metal sun, backwaters of lianas . . . I reckon it's the motorway, since it was built, there are too many trees

11

between the sea and us, and the hills and the ferns and even the sheep's wool must deaden the sound. And the wind, it's often the wind you can hear at night above the roof, or else whistling in the grass . . .

It's always disgusting beneath the shower mat, silver fish, like millipedes below an upturned stone, each going its own way, armoured caterpillars, close-knit chain mail, attention focused on tiny things by the machine which produces them, and mites, thriving, huge miniature monsters teeming in the carpet, on our skin, the harvest bugs must already have laid their eggs for next year, you'd need a microscope to get a constant seamless view of the world, drops of water, particles, troughs in your skin and all the creepy-crawlies, germs, flies, spiders, their honeycombed eyes . . .

On the pampas, clouds of locusts rain down from countries that don't exist . . .

In the shower, late as usual, relax and think, appointment at a quarter past ten, be realistic, materially I just don't have enough time . . .

Jeanne

She's back in that empty square, but this time she feels alone. Maybe there's still an aura by her side, a vague set of presences, hardly any denser than the air, like dust, grains of consciousness or of memory. She walks on. The aura distorts itself as she advances, then it apparently recedes. But this isn't what the dream's about, what it's all about. The distant sirens become incarnate, the sound stands out in her bedroom. She knows she's dreaming, walking on amid the sirens, pushing them back, slipping in between their soft, elastic shapes . . . when she breaks through, the sun's still there, both on her and inside her. It fills her mouth. She opens her lips as hot energy pours out of it. What an effort to close it again, to cast that damp, internal shadow once more – she swallows her saliva, she's thirsty, her tongue is sticking to the roof of her mouth with a fine nocturnal secretion. Beside her, he turns over and mutters something in Spanish. The police sirens are back, louder now, she grabs the bottle of water . . .

In France sirens have two notes and, through the windows of the airport, this is one of the first signs that she's back, when she goes back home waiting for a new assignment – elsewhere, sirens go up and go down, *uuu-iii-uuu*, throughout the entire world, New York, Shanghai, Buenos Aires, everywhere except where she was born. There they have two distinct notes, *ti tam ti tam*, the soundtrack of nights in France . . .

The water trickles into her mouth, water from the Andes, *directamente de las sierras a tu cuerpo*, tongue and roof unhitch, she turns towards him: *¿quieres?* While the water slips down the long column inside her, directly from the mountains to her body, making the air she breathes unravel like wool. *¿Quieres, hombre?* She softly whispers in his ear, calling him *hombre, guapo, hijo*, between rolled 'r's and harsh *jotas*, scraps of Arabic in the back of her throat, shifts in her mouth producing other syllables. Her nightly folklore when he's asleep, when it becomes so utterly obvious that she isn't home, she's elsewhere. When that heady nocturnal lucidity leaps up before her and, happily, she turns towards him: *¿hombre, quieres?* He takes the water from her to make her shut up, to sleep, the bottle is dangerously open, he's unprotected now. She embraces him and laughs into his neck. Because with him, here, everything is possible. Because what is so utterly obvious is that stiffness inside her, that solid column which holds her, especially at night, when all that is left are their differences, and the perception of those differences. Then, that gleaming stiffness rises up inside her, abruptly, it must be mounted, shared or else it will split her in half. He says, in French, he whispers to her that she's *chiante*, he learned that word fast enough, how to tell her that she's pissing him off, she grabs his hand and places it on her warm, swollen sex. His body is stretched out, his member pressed against her,

13

arms and legs erect too, his face and hands – the sudden
arrival of his stiff penis, not there before – then quick, dry
love, tearing the skin from the night, when the fluids later
flow into the bed's laterite . . .

Anne

I remember how everything seemed clear, then vanished. On
the bridge, emerging from the shadow of the west tower. I
should have retraced my steps. It had something to do with
verticality. It was all perfectly clear. Of course, Mum didn't
understand a word. As for Laurent, who knows? I've tried to
call him half a dozen times, I've tried to get hold of him,
meanwhile, everything remains recorded in those memories,
the slightest bleep, wrong button, the slightest remorse, mistake, slip-up, it's all there, in numbers, sparkling on the
screen of my mobile . . . On the bridge, what I wanted to tell
him was how clear and plain it all was. But I must have called
my mother by mistake, at that moment I could have told him
everything, but he wasn't there . . . as a motorist, I've already
been through that, the car that stops or needs repairing, an
interruption, hard to concentrate, it was even harder on the
bridge, in that clarity, that . . . experience I've already had,
they spot you on the bridge, standing dead still or pretty
much so, staring into space, and they think they're going to
save you, it's the red of a lifebuoy, fireman red, emergency
red, pompom red, because they've driven so many times past
these lifebuoys, through a red light. SAVE HER. Yes, that's
exactly what happened, and my mind went blank, I was
interrupted, so difficult, they do it on purpose so you can't
concentrate . . . to repeat that word, to think back over the situation, yes . . . I should have stayed at the library, got some
work done, progressed a bit . . . It's because of these experiments, which are so tiring for the mind, and also because of
what Jeanne told me, what she's seen during her travels, her
thoughts and reactions – but her story is only a parable, a way

14

of speaking, a metaphorical description of my existence, with creepy similarities with my life: a village of genociders, or that lake island, or those fields of cinnamon in her last post-card between the arms of the Rio de la Plata, and her ultra-modern block of flats, and her penthouse in beautiful BA, as she puts it, because she does absolutely everything better than everyone else, with her rich man she met on a plane, naturally, higher up than everyone else, better than everyone else at love, death, cooking, languages, cycling, stronger than everyone else, brave, generous, balanced, my sister the champion of the world . . .

But that wasn't what I was thinking about. No, not that. I must already have been recruited. That's what I have to concentrate on. To spot them. With their urban-camouflage techniques. Trained to disappear. Because, on the surface of the world, and probably even beyond, there is just one consciousness floating there, changelessly, only split into individuals. Among them, agents are selected who are sufficiently sharp to be able to penetrate the worldwide consciousness – or else, it's the opposite, you must be sufficiently open, empathetic, that's the word, porous, permeable, to be able to float in unison with the great consciousness and perceive its desires, and then they spontaneously lodge themselves in any perceived disturbances. If I've been recruited, it's as much for my exceptional ability to concentrate as for my extraordinarily open mind. But such things aren't mutually exclusive. Allowing yourself to drift requires a firm hand. I've been trained in intensive sessions and through successive selections. When I was little, with Jeanne, we played at not thinking, at thinking of nothing, in our woolly way . . . But you still think about thinking nothing, you reproduce yourself, that's the snag in exercises like this, you see yourself thinking and so no longer think. Like pain management in hospitals, place all your suffering in one single point, a circle on a sheet of paper, then slowly take your eyes off it . . . a metaphorical cure . . . In the same way, they taught me to rank my feelings of imminent death from 1 to 10. I never gave myself 10. That would mean death. Just like some teachers never give full marks. Right now, I'd say it was 5 or 6, because of Laurent, I suppose – think back over it, so there was a thought, floating around in the world's blue head, as in all heads, with me as a traveller, I mean having first successfully passed all the tests, got through all the trials, recruited to float and surf across this worldwide consciousness . . .

So, while waiting for Laurent at the foot of the west tower at nine in the morning, suddenly, there was a recruiting agent standing there beside me, he must have come from behind the tower, from the east, and he said to me (in code), *we've been looking for you* (sure enough, during the previous few days I had spotted a similar-looking person on a number of occasions and had wondered whether to confront him or not, was he really following me, was he really that bad at his job – hanging around a second too long at the crossroads, coming too quickly out of a phone box where, disguised as a woman, he had been waiting for me, or else dressed up as a street-sweeper, his anxious stare allowing no possible room for doubt), saying to me, when he at last approached me in the courtyard in front of the library, after trailing me for so long and realizing that he had been spotted, *we've been expecting you*, his voice so calm, so cool, almost affectionate, though also a touch threatening, they know me so well, but I wasn't afraid, because I didn't want to have a choice, I had already chosen, long ago, to accept my destiny, my task, my duty, I know that I'm up to it – and I had been playing at losing him, at throwing him off my trail, only in order to see if it was really him, by testing him, sometimes by running, elbowing my way through the passers-by, to check that he was really the man I had been expecting. His insistence wore down my final reservations. I had already been convinced when I welcomed him in the courtyard:

I'm ready.
We'll start straight away.

I know what these travels mean, but not the price I'll have to pay, because of course there is one – the little mermaid was racked with pain when walking on her feet – and what I now fear is that my exceptional ability to concentrate has already suffered, been worn down by these travels and exercises – but I'm still ready. I won't have to plant bombs, I simply have to use the power in my mind or, rather, in thought to exploit my abilities for

1) openness
2) concentration

to slip into the shell of the world like a hermit crab or, rather, given that space isn't empty, to slip over from one consciousness to another, like an egret ridding a hippopotamus of its parasites, always in motion, helping them in their work . . .

The Mother

All the same, the day did start well enough. Ten o'clock, coffee and a postcard from Jeanne. And then Anne called. The slightest phone call from Anne always sets me off and now here I am, in a state again. But the day did start well, with roses, and that hint of a cool morning breeze, that first chill getting into the trees, the sounds in the air, branches, the gate banging, and even Nore was in a good mood and didn't complain when Momo got the lawnmower out. She's got an appointment. Three daughters and three mysteries. Then Anne on top of it all. I lent Nore the car, she could have given me more warning, now all I have to do, the bowls are dirty, dishwasher full, Nore driving along narrow, slippery roads, the first dead leaves piling up in the bends, only passed her test two months ago, I won't be able to stand it, it will be the death of me, and Anne all alone in the city, alone on that bridge, maybe still there, looking at the water, like when she

17

was little, lying flat on her bed instead of doing her home-work, *but I am working!* Spending so much time daydreaming we had to take her to see Dr Waterlot, so unhappy, in any case, what happened was nobody's fault, not even Jeanne's – don't say it, don't even think it – the mason should phone soon, should already have phoned, I won't call Anne back, anyway, mobiles are so expensive. *You must think of yourself, Madame Johnson.* Jeanne must be asleep now, peacefully asleep, I hope, I'm always quiet at this time, but Jeanne has always got on with her life, always a survivor, even when everyone thought she was dead and gone in Africa, or God knows where, yes, Jeanne must be sleeping now, her postcard there on the fridge, I must clean the floor, Rio de la Plata, like in books. Just think, those giant fig trees really do grow there, now, on the other side of the world. Nore's favourite green bowl is cracked. She never takes care of her things, everyone's at her beck and call, a real little princess, the youngest child has all the faults, ah, he's calling to me . . . he never knows where his things are either . . . that smell in the air, cut grass, green juice, sap stopped dead as autumn arrives, he's going to wind up injuring himself. I'm tied to them all, and they'll be the death of me, even John, I'm long over him of course, but if he died, I'd . . . Waterlot said it wasn't the divorce which was killing this family, he told Maïder, who passed it on to me. Confidential information. When they were little, I never let them out of my sight, I would even have liked to have a third eye, in the back of my head, or on the sides, like hens. No one in this house ever picks up crumbs except for me. I used to run upstairs to their rooms. Nore still in my womb, Anne here, Jeanne there, no wonder they left. Even though no one's less of a prison warder than me. Crushed peanuts now. They think I'm their skivvy. What was I saying? Out of sight, out of mind. I hope it won't rain, with Nore out in the car. They never think of clearing anything up and I'm supposed to think of everything. One side lies anxiety, the other, depression. Too much meaning or none at all. Charybdis and

Scylla. In the straits of Messina between Italy and Sicily, and not Gibraltar, like people used to think. Ulysses leaving his native sea, heading for the Atlantic. Among savages. I was thirty and thought I was going to die, almost as old as Jeanne is now, when you think about it, it's incomprehensible . . .

Nore

Close eye contact. Does that do anything for him? Or are my eyes just objects? Does he look into women's eyes in a purely medical way (searching for cataracts, glaucoma, conjunctivitis)? Or does he see our stares? *Half an hour late, Mademoiselle Johnson, the next time I'll have to cancel.* The eyes of octopuses and pigs are the closest to mankind's – do they see the world as we do, with its lines and colours? A mask and a snorkel to breathe under water, see waves upside down and fish like the back of your hand, so big and clear . . . At Daddy's place in Andalusia, the school of sardines that formed one huge, jagged, silvery sardine, suddenly exploding, then reforming . . . – The sweetness of his gestures, *comme ça?* . . . – Lean slightly on the chin and look up, look down. I must look a real sight, one eye missing, and my chin stuck in this thing. But my eyes are green. Statistically, he can't see that many green eyes. I take after Daddy. With gold spangles around the pupils. Remember how Arnold explained in his last lesson the way ancient philosophers believed in how things peeled: a lens comes free, then fixes itself on the eye, and if the eye isn't smooth and curved, it doesn't stick on properly and your vision is blurred. Or, to put it another way, the eye actively fits into its peelings and explores their ups and downs with more or less attention (scale models for the blind at the entrances of public buildings which can be taken apart, floor by floor, each door, each awkward step, each twist and turn to be learned by the fingertips; at the entrances of department stores, scale models of the products, hats, scarves, dresses and shoes; at the entrances of brothels too, animated figurines

19

to hold in your hands – *look right . . . look left . . . straight on . . .* – and beside beaches, dunes, high and low tides, dangerous currents, but the sound of the waves must be enough to make the sea visible; and at the entrances of pyramids, the models themselves will be booby-trapped or else be precise repro-ductions of the labyrinth as a memory test . . .)

Been short-sighted for a few years, two or three, I can't remem-ber . . .

The families of grave robbers knew which pyramids were cursed, from father to son, they knew which ones to avoid, and the explorers who laughed at them, such silly supersti-tions, died from the arsenic they picked up from the frescoes, or just from breathing in the air of the sarcophagi, from inhal-ing the cement of the crumbling seams . . . *Ninety-nine ways to kill an archaeologist . . . An ophthalmologist . . .* The walls Jeanne had in Africa, smeared with chilli powder to stop the children from getting lead poisoning. And her neighbour treating her stretch marks with leather grease, and her blue, swollen, cretinous baby sucking in the poison every day from her sat-urnine breasts . . .

Le pré est vénéneux et joli en automne
Les vaches y paissant
Lentement s'empoisonnent . . .

You read a lot of reports, don't you? So, what happens is that you lean down and your eyes are drawn towards the page, by attraction, by the pull of gravity, if you follow me, hence your short-sighted-ness. The eyes become deformed like a falling drop of water, and the pupils which receive the light beams move further away from the backdrop where the images are cast. It thus becomes necessary to trick the eyes by using a filter (spectacles, lenses, a piece of glass or any other transparent object) which bends the light beams that fall on to it in such a way that those which originate from a given object are redistributed while passing through it, so that they appear to come from a different point, which, in your case, would be nearer to you, let's see now . . .

```
        R  V  S  K  A  O
     N  L  T  A  N  R
     O H S V E
     M  C  F
     Z    U
```

His hand is soft and firm, placing the frame on my nose, adjusting the side-pieces behind my ears, changing the lenses, concentration, application, will I ever get over such hands, depths of the soul, *a slight, almost stabilized myopia* . . .

His hands changing the lenses again, fingers on my chin, on my temples, slow and soft, yes, a soft sensation, a wave rising up along my skull, shrinking my scalp . . . a process of head-shrinking . . . my head, my brain, tingling skin, his fingers, letters . . . the absolute calm of the surgery, a smell of vinyl and carpets, there aren't any . . . *Now read this, please*, a small printed card . . .

> As for me, I have never presumed that my mind was in any way more perfect than is usual; I have even on frequent occasions wanted to have wits as quick, an imagination as vivid or a memory as capacious and accessible as some other person. And I know of no other qualities than these which serve to perfect the mind; as for reason, or sense, which alone makes men of us and marks us out from the beasts of the field, I would say that it is entirely present in each of us, and I here follow the common opinion of philosophers who state that there are individuals of the same species only in terms of accidents and not in terms of forms or natures.

Good close vision, how old are you, eighteen, or twenty?

He's writing, sitting behind his desk, you can make the feeling last, hypnotically, by following the tip of his pen, anything will do . . . A soft, regular motion, something unbroken,

21

which goes on, swinging, sleepy, to and fro, rocking . . . When I was little, at school, the teacher's voice, in my absence, creeping into the very top of my skull, my limp hands . . . To have a healthy body, all there, but only there for this pleasure – Anne taught me to vanish, to think of nothing, just a game, thinking of thinking of nothing is still thinking, my first circular thought, swings and roundabouts . . .

Body and soul, back and forth, the body with its ball of thought up there, around it and below it – Mum taking tango lessons with Momo, each to his own . . .

The swift, regular tip of the pen, him reading out loud, which also draws out the charm, rocked by your own voice, the parade of syllables or the pen's swift, regular tip, the whole point is not really to converse, not to think about a thing, to let yourself go on the beat of your heart, the air you breathe . . .

How's your mother, and your stepfather, and your sisters, do you have health insurance, frames at a reasonable price?

Ages since I've seen Jeanne and Anne, the last time with Daddy in Paris – has he at least noticed my eyes, now it's finished, over, end of the consultation, must find Mum's chequebook, I've got a lesson with Arnold in ten minutes' time and I'll never make it – Jeanne thinks Anne's ill, maybe Anne experiences her mind like I do my body, what a mess in this bag, only the body is present, our sole companion, *Is the Death of Sardanapalus also the Death of Romanticism?* It had completely slipped my mind. To be handed in by the 26th, so in two days' time, *ah, here's the cheque* . . .

Something to do with metabolism, the shape of the idea not fitting the shape of the mind, like educational toys with babies putting triangles into triangular holes, and not circles into squares. I don't even know who Sardanapalus was. Momo might know, what with all the crosswords he does . . .

Goodbye, goodbye . . .

So if I've lost another tenth in each eye, and the sea is at the end of the street, I must convince myself that it is more . . . that the waves are less . . . that the vision is blurred, more blurred than last time, a blurred sea without any surrounding contrast, because the town's blurred too, when the waves in reality are – for other passers-by or some bionic creature – as sharp as blades, clear cut against the blue sky, because colours too are going pastel and the first time I wore my glasses everything seemed bluer, redder, yellower, every-thing *was* bluer, redder, yellower, royal blue, royal red, royal yellow, the sea, roofs, sun and the map of the continents in geography lessons, only white didn't change . . .

There are sick, sad people for whom the sea is just a stack of parallel blue, white and grey lines, but having sound, smell and motion. But they can't make the connection, unfortunate-ly their illness makes them incompatible with this idea, not so much as far as the sea is concerned, but with vision, the coherency of the world . . .

A lion with a bear's paws
A bull with a cat's tail
A dolphin with a woman's breasts – a siren
A sphinx, a mammal with a fish's blood, covered with scales
An armadillo, a duck-billed platypus, an otter with a duck's beak that lays hen's eggs, Jeanne's slides of Australia and Africa, hybrids . . .

Where the hell did I put that prescription?

Just imagine grafts, you can transplant hands, or eyes, they play around with the DNA of flies, feet instead of eyes, eyes instead of feet, six eyes along the abdomen, two feet in the eye sockets wiggling about above the skull, get that idea thor-oughly into your head: it really exists, right now, monsters like that exist in some lab somewhere . . .

Four little ducks went out one day
Over the hills and far away
Sad mother duck said, 'Quack quack quack'
But only three little ducks came back . . .

Wales, Wales, bloody great fish that swim in the sea, as Daddy used to say . . .

Maybe Mum also senses her mind sometimes, as a physical presence, like a blood vessel on the verge of popping, an epileptic fit . . .

Apollinaire I can place, but the death of Sardanapalus?

Where did I park the car?

The idea of waves being blurred, with no adjacent points of comparison . . .

That man with the transplanted hand, the hand of a painter, pianist, thief, or the cat-in-boots' boots, transplanted speed, if they transplant dead people's eyes, what do we then see, what ghosts, what waking dreams? A third one in the middle of the forehead, staring at what? Through a ghost's eyes, you can see what was hidden . . .

I came this way, I went by here and the sea was on my left, so the car must be . . . Let's see, it wasn't that far away . . .

Anne

Anne, ma sœur Anne, ne vois-tu rien venir? All I can see is the sun sparkling and the grass greening. My mission. My solution. The serial killer started by singling out his victims in the crowd and then he followed them for days on end. *You have to die, my lady. At first she saw nothing, because the windows were closed. After a while, she began to notice that the floor was covered with blood and that, in this blood, there lay the dead bodies of several women, who were tied up and lying next to the walls.* Beauty and the Beast. Bluebeard. Following them, for days on end, becoming devoted to them, his next chosen victim, considering that it was an honour for them. First of all noting their comings and goings, their daily rounds, their habits – by satellite, everyone's lives and tics seen as points moving around space. Jeanne, for instance, seen as traipsing about seventeen years in a tiny area of south-west France, blocked against the ocean, then suddenly winging away, first southwards to Africa, to traipse around by the Great Lake, then a decisive flight across the earth to Australia and back again, then finally across the Atlantic, south-west once more, thoroughly south-west, to Buenos Aires – Jeanne's cartography is a constellation of spider's webs linked by straight lines . . .

A rapid reading of the diagram, a bug-free recording, comings and goings already noted, connections and routines; from the edge to the centre, a student going every day to her lessons (e.g. Nore), easy to follow, easy to trap, going there every day, coming home every day, journeys piling up and thickening the killer's mental diagram. From time to time, an exceptional excursion, a visit, mother in the provinces, father in Gibraltar, sister, maybe, in Buenos Aires (money required, though). I too would be fairly easy to kill, even though I'm on my guard. They didn't recruit me for no reason, I alter my daily round, from the lab to the library, with a rational disturbance of my schedule; a probabilistic modelization, Brownian motion applied to my habits . . .

No longer keeping your eyes peeled = murder . . .

I know, we all know that only too well . . .

All they'd need would be some maps, showing everyone's comings and goings, in order to be able to intervene at a given statistical moment in a journey, marking the interruption with a cross. Otherwise, how could they have spotted me? How could they have recruited me? My movements sketch out a figure I can't see, determined by laws I don't understand, which are programming even my wanderings, ruses and zigzags. Recruiting agents – trust them for that – know how to decipher such maps, each life is locked in a pathway marked out by a string of routines, like a fugue – even if I don't personally know the names of the streets I'm walking along, except for my own one and a couple of neighbouring ones, and I sometimes forget my address, which is the first thing the emergency services ask you, along with your date of birth and what day it is . . .

Then the killer interrupts the journey, swooping down on his prey as though from the heavens, from where he has been observing her tiny territory, after absent-mindedly raping her, carefully cutting out a window in her belly and pulling out her intestines, unrolling them end to end, unravelling their knot, all in one piece, because the alimentary canal in fact goes straight down, despite all its twists and turns – and so emptying out, *I've been doing that all my life*, the young lady's long, bluish, stinking sausage, and maybe trying out some daring operations, surgical feats, soldered vaginal connections and posthumous digestion of the uterus (his fingers are prickling, attacked by still-living enzymes), then getting fed up, sitting down, a blow-up doll, a corn dolly, all my life I've dreamed of being an air hostess, emptied out, completely out . . .

(Laurent, I'll eat your brains out, I'll obliterate them, I'll fuck your brains with my two bollocks in your eye sockets and shoot my own grey matter . . .)

The *Amnesty* newsletters Mum used to get when we were young, Argentina/Chile/Paraguay/Uruguay: a map of torture seen from the condor's nest. Momo never talks about his war, but then there's his face . . . The white-hot chains against the Maghrebin's belly, the abdomen splitting open and spilling its contents, an envelope under a guillotine – I can imagine that, not that they're my memories: imagine having that in your memory . . .

Harden myself up for the mission. List my psychological

points of resistance. Note down my mental blocks and barriers, spot them and toughen myself up, list chronologically my stupefying discoveries, find the origin of evil, locate the weaknesses in me, the basic flaw, cut it out, extract my squeamishness . . .

Chronological List of Stupefying Discoveries
- 1973, cannibalism in *Robinson Crusoe*
- prostitution, at the same age, that girl in the street and John not letting us see
- 1974, Mum out of control
- 1978, Auschwitz in a history book, and around the same time Hiroshima
- 1981, human cloning, in science fiction and teenage magazines
- 1983, snuff movies, irony, the cinema turned inside out like an octopus

Let's be clear, before Robinson I have no memories, or else, maybe, though hard to date, Jeanne and me behind a door, them making love, audible proof, they do do it, John and Mum, our parents, Pierre was too small for us to talk to him about that, then no one to talk to at all . . .

Of course, reasons to be astonished become more and more complex in time, the mind opens, with forceps, a mental Caesarean: put yourself in the place of the gutted Maghrebin, in the place of the gobbled-up brains, in the body of a clone. My grown-up task, as they've recruited me, bug-free sequences from A to Z all in one go, without recourse to notes or mental discourse. Yes, I can do it. I've been trained for that. $1 + 1 = 2$ and $2 + 2 = 4$, I can telepathically open the sluice gates and make my reports without any material support, they can film the inside of my mind, directly from me to them, I can think purely, with pure concentration, no fading away – an overview from zero to infinity, my consciousness in one rush . . . despite the nausea, the vertigo . . . the worst bit of all is Bluebeard's politeness: *Well, my lady, in you go and sit down with the other ladies you have seen . . .*

Nore

Holding her prescription, she decides to buy a new pair of glasses rather than go to her lessons, her curiosity is so great – well, let's call it plain curiosity, but it's more like scientific interest, more like a right, or at the very least a necessity: what it's all about is being able to take in, right now, the state of the sea, now that the car's been relocated after she'd quite simply plugged her brains in – who said girls lack a sense of direction? A nice job would be to produce a daily programme, a sea forecast of the shapes of the waves, the height of the swell, not to mention of course the times of the tides, which everyone wants to know, there'd definitely be an audience for it. *Is the Death of Sardanapalus also the Death of Romanticism?* Get that out of your head. Forecasting is a matter of dates. Observations made at the same time every day. She could do .that, allot herself responsibilities, study the ways of the wind and, even from cliff tops, the chances of setting up wind generators – which way to point the blades, enter the directions, short- and mid-term forecasts – the largest of the turbines in Gibraltar, where her father lives, only switches on when there's a storm, you can hear it from down on the shore, the wind whistling in a rush from above, then it suddenly creaks once, twice, heavy and breathless, blade after blade raising its helicopter mass, then lift-off, too quick for your ears because, unless you keep them pinned back – a fleeting human voice – the virtually ultrasonic whistle merges with the swell of the wind . . .

When the neighbours, the small and medium-sized coleopterans, squirm on their backs and snore . . .

Who's been drinking in my bowl? asks baby bear. Who's been sitting in my chair? asks mummy bear. Who's been sleeping in my bed? asks daddy bear.

A first-year literature course isn't the best opening into a career in meteorology – *Is the Death of Sardanapalus also the Death of Romanticism?* while running a wind farm, or anything else for that matter to do with the wind, the sea, the sun, dizziness of rotating bodies . . .

If you were big enough to sit on the earth, with your feet on the moon, elbows dangling in the ocean, you'd feel the stellar wind whistling in your hair, sparkling sand from the rim of the universe . . .

The sea is rising, dragged up by the moon's pull, astrology determining our lives, Capricorn, love social life good health and a bad star, Daddy loves his job, shame he lives so far away, seeing the world's limited does his head in too, some day she . . .

Waves curled into a ball violently unravelling, inevitable ignition, my father, John, my sister Jeanne, with Anne we played at staying as long as possible by the water's edge before the swell covered our ankles. That is to say, when Anne deigned to play with me. That is to say, with her rolling her eyes and arms, making me think there was a tidal wave coming, and me only four or five, a twelve-year gap, too small to judge, always faster than the waves or my shadow, and the entire fretful family circulating around Anne . . .

In a sulk, I played at having no shadow, feet wet, I went off to play further out, you can spot vampires by their lack of . . . right in the middle of dinner time, the entire family would scream out my hidden identity: *look, no shadow!* Unmasked, fork in hand, mouth full, and my shadow would be waiting at the door, *this way, come on, this way,* gesturing to me with its long broken arms, its long hand fractured by the angles of the walls, gesturing with a *ttttssstt, this way,* my shadow would be waiting for me at the door like a faithful mount, and in one leap, one decisive bound, off we would go . . .

That wave there above the others pins down high tide, I've

seen that, hand pierced by the sun, Mum waving bye-bye, when who was going now, with five sunbeams moving to say goodbye to . . .

Long tidal blades coming towards her, since the day they all moved in with Momo. Anne always saying that she'll move back down there, to their childhood home, but she won't, *the family all together*: Daddy Mum Jeanne Anne and she, Nore. It's her house, she's the only one who really likes it. Anne's problem is that she lives too far away from the sea. When she used to live here, she may have been a bit sad, but she was still in with the rhythm – the memory of games with Anne, the brief span she stayed with Momo before going to Paris, a chronology like a heap of clothes (the little striped pullover, the lace mobcap and the skirt with a heart-shaped pocket in front, sun, rain, and the Irish wellies Daddy brought back, green with frogs' eyes). Anne tall and skinny, in the photo, on the edge or in the middle, Jeanne out of shot – long blades coming, gliding down in precisely parallel lines on the sand, slithering . . .

Then back with them; rolled up, a constant exposure of transparencies, taken away, thrown away, then put back on, tulle satin velvet brocade, the great body of the sea turns on tirelessly, revealing nothing in its successive horizons, she could stay there for hours, wave after wave, their date . . .

Jeanne

She's dozing, then something suddenly drags her up to the surface of sleep. She wakes up with an effort, holding the silence at arm's length, with maybe, far away in the distance, on the other side of the double glazing and heavy air, the hesitant flickers of some emergency, cops, *bomberos* . . . It isn't the sirens that are stopping her from sleeping, or from going back to sleep. It's the quality of the nights here, even though she's a great traveller, but she's been here for two years and that's two years of still being unused to it. In constant transit, jet-lagged for the past two years, something topsy-turvy which breeds dreams . . . The quality of nights here, superimposed across the days, never flat, letting glints of light break through, gaps in their blue shades and their pavements, letting in daylight which is not completely shut off, night with a backdrop of stars. She feels that all she dreams at night is a dream even more absent than her daytimes. A wake and awake, etymological certainties, sudden revelations blocking her path back to sleep. Nocturnal syllogisms. This lucidity when both the inside and the outside of things are revealed. Wet dreams dripping sperm down her thighs, vagina of various derivations opening and closing at various times of the night, sluice gates mounting up to the base of her belly, from her sex to her belly, to her throat, to her brain, a luminous reassurance – her insides are also her outside. A continuity you can follow like a Möbius strip. Down a slide. She exists constantly, without a break or gaps. And if a child was growing inside her and multiplying, she would be nursing a being outside her straight from the start . . .

She turns towards him (how calm and clear it all is!), embraces him, his heat is immediate. A hand placed on the small of his back, tentative with sleep, *querido*, sentimentally at night under the single sheet that marries them, it's your tongue, *mi amor*, that makes me think this way, that pays me what it owes me. Songs come back and make the bed lilt, *solo sé que una noche fuiste hundamente mía*, abruptly awake, and if I pulled away from you, they'd find a single gory body, gutted under a red sheet, a male and a female body . . . She sleeps against him in a lyrical sleep that keeps her awake, aware of the intonations of his breathing, the inflexions of the night and her own mutual pathways, outside and in . . . Tomorrow, she'll go by Flórida to have lunch with Jimena, she'll have time after her lessons at L'Alliance Française (only three students tomorrow, an advanced class for executives, the Aguas Argentinas contract), and buy some *foie gras* at Bouvier's,

31

Rossini tournedos is something they have no idea about here, even though their meat's wonderful, especially the *churrascos*, that's it, *foie gras* and *churrascos*, the marriage of the century . . . She rolls up in the sheet, a gun dog, a slide . . . A landscape of water, a plain ribboned with streams, confluents, islands amid branches, lagoons amid mangroves and budding hills, one of them offers a foothold, her skin dries at once, she was supposed to think of something, but what? *Sus ojos se cerraron*, the air is soft *com'un beso*, but she stays leaning over the water, under the weight of this slight concern that's bugging her, the water is limpid and silent, soft, green, something she should think about and this thing that's bugging her wakes her up . . . Or the slight burning sensation against her thigh which, when examined, turns out to be red and inflamed, covered with nodules, spots or jellyfish blisters, a whale's forehead pushing through just there and about to burst open, whalebones, flesh gnawed by parasites. She jumps. She's in bed, against him, she's too hot, the night is endless, something's missing, something's here and unwanted, all through her sleepy days, in the purr of the air conditioning, sudden awakenings, the certitude of being in the heart of the matter, she's here, whole, with him, perfect reasoning – if, in dreams, we're all characters in dreams, then she's either all alone among the islets or else (they're fading already) everything all at the same time, herself, this body, and the atolls and arms and the whale's body, the animal forming a cyst in her leg, both the tropics and Europe, this city and over there, the temperate zone of her birth . . .

The Mother

Noon. The sound of that old clock. Momo and his furniture. The first, the oldest, is still asleep. The second, I hope, is back home. The third, the youngest, is at her literature class, with a bit of luck. All those bodies out of her own body. And so many others, or so it seems, now shifting around outside her.

John and Momo. Light green strips roll out as he mows. Good to see the morning glide by. The spiders swinging on their threads, *chabada bada*, the spider song. I should sweep the floor, clean up, beneath the panels. House too big. Dust everywhere. Endless work. And what for? Tiles and masonry. But this morning started well. Then Anne phoned. List them: Nore here, Anne there, Jeanne out yonder . . .

Ding dong bell
Pussy's in the well . . .

My first is Jeanne, my second is Anne, my third is Nore and my answer is . . . One missing. Sonny Jim who stopped shining. What's left? Just memory techniques . . . mnemonics . . . It's good to think that Jeanne's still asleep. Anne calling me on her mobile and me stuck here at home. That film on TV . . . the mother caught in a traffic jam and following live the rape and murder of her daughter via the phone receiver which has fallen on to the floor, the screams, then the dying gasp . . . What put that into my mind? It's that business about time zones. Before starting to cook I'll make the beds. Mnemonics. And Anne's favourite story, about the hermit crab. Anne always wanting to be read books, with *real stories*, while I always pretended. The one about the king who lost his memory. I had premonitory dreams. I should have paid attention to them. Steam on the glass. With their fingers, they drew on the car windows

funny faces.

It's all greasy. I must clean this window with Ajax. Jeanne in her hemisphere where the moon tells no lies . . .

P as in *premier quartier* and d as in *dernier quartier*. As they used to say, *King Hector doesn't usually drink cold milk*. But what was that to remember? *Sir, I send a rhyme excelling in sacred truth and rigid spelling*, for pi. *Thirty days hath September, April, June and November, Remember, remember* . . . The story of the king who lost his memory. Where did I leave the Ajax? He puts up posters in town which say, 'Wanted! The king's memory.' And when they eventually find it, he no longer remembers that it's his memory. So they cut his head off. Or else, his memory strayed from one mind to another, with everyone dipping into it a bit, so that when he got it back at last, it was as empty as an old walnut. The king couldn't remember the address of his castle, or where he'd left his crown (*it's on your head, your majesty*). The king couldn't remember his laws any more, or the name of his kingdom, or even that he was the king. Or else, they found a memory which fitted him, but it belonged to someone else. So he could now remember memories which were new to him. A shoemaker's memories. A woman's memories. A cicada's memories. An elephant's memories. The king sings, the king trumpets. The king orders new clothes. The king wants to have children. Momo will listen to my stories just once, but not ten times over, not the variants, I have some old recipes in this notebook somewhere, from the days of margarine. Rabbit and prunes to be marinated overnight. John's friends, what was their name? The wife broke a tooth on a stone. The expression on her face! Momo says John left me because of my cooking. I say that I was the one who left John. This cat's hungry . . .

Here you go . . .

34

Ten past twelve. Make the beds. The unmade beds left open to air in the afternoons, in the days when, that summer when . . .

Pollen hanging motionlessly in the sunbeams, crossed by the light which shifts and rolls itself up even though nothing's moving. Maybe the cat, all rolled up beneath the sheets, sighed or flicked its ears . . . Pollen and dust dancing, light cast like a blanket, to the south, from southern windows . . . Unmade beds in those old summer days. Straight, precise beams, here and then there. Lie down and wait. That summer was an endless nap. No longer to see the sun silently slice up the walls. Escape from it, from the patterns of light. The angles of the white walls placed on the white sky, the two-dimensional flatness of summer; the claustrophobia of summer, the torment of summer . . .

Thank heavens it will soon be winter. There's just a little of that golden-yellow light left, a yellow that refuses to go away. The thinking is simple. Dying is a legitimate thing to want, but she didn't die that summer. In the old days, people died of a broken heart or gave up the ghost. Death was common-place. Did they feel less sorrow? The horror of life goes on. Manage to make the beds, all the same. No more unmade beds at three in the afternoon, when there was nothing to be done but get into those awful rumpled sheets, still damp and warm from a sleepless night . . .

One of life's greatest pleasures is tormenting cats. Cats with full bellies, crammed with certitudes. She thinks back over her reasoning. Her simple thinking. Rather than kill yourself, leave, drop everything. Car. Airport. Plane to Paris. Taxi to Roissy. Don't call by to see Anne. Take the first flight. To Havana. Buenos Aires. No, not Buenos Aires. Or to be rein-carnated as a cat. Land in the centre of a cat's mind. See the wild in black and white with red spots. Look for warmth, avoid the rain. Chew grass as a purge. Hunt parasites. Stop thinking. No one can. Momo behind his mask of a face.

35

Momo always thinking pussy. She thinks about thoughts being precisely superimposed, all non-proposed thoughts being instantly available. She smiles. Superimposed memories. What she mustn't think about. What no one must know that she still thinks about, every minute, mingled up with all the rest. She goes back to the bedroom and glances down the corridor. She's alone apart from the irritated cat. With a magic wand, make my mind go still like a cat's eyes. If a sentence has a verb, subject and predicate it is still no more or less true than the rest. Excessive love of logic . . .

Outside, the trees are speaking, *chchchch*. Come and sit below our boughs and dream. On the highest branch, a nightingale is singing. *Chchchch, calm down*, the oak, the hornbeam, the elm and the poplar. Beds to be made. The sun hitting the beds sliced with light at a constant speed. That summer. Don't cry. Thank heavens it will soon be winter. Nore will be on holiday. Anne will be down for Christmas. We'll be sleeping closer to Jeanne once it's winter. The fireplace at five in the afternoon, it will be dark, we will breathe in the air crisp with frost and sparks. We will breathe. And the clocks will turn like tops in the breathable cold of the beginning of the year, when time at last speeds up and runs, after the death of summer. Jeanne and John clinging on to each other, Jeanne redolent with summer and youth, John napping, beds of wrinkles creased between his eyebrows. The other house. The dog and the cat of another life. Anne upstairs crying. In the torment of summer, in the suppliant death of summer. Think about it every day. Think about it all the time. The background of the picture, the frame of it all, of everything that is less important. Does John think about it? Does Jeanne, on the far side of the ocean, think about it? Transatlantically casting the bridge of this sad thought from coast to coast? Does this thought go round the world every day, from coast to coast, from night to day? Does Anne remember? She was five, Jeanne was seven. Do the sisters talk about it? I was hot, overcome by gleaming childhood. Jeanne with her rosy cheeks.

Anne in my arms and John, napping all summer, burnt by the summer sun, eyebrows bleached white. Nore came so much later, seven years later, that desire again, as if she could have given us back the importance of it all . . .

But the day did start well, the fresh roses and first autumn breeze, clear, light and fragrant. The line of dusk passes across the earth from coast to coast, casting its shadows, day and night, closing the eyelids of the earth on the sea, on this land that looks so flat when seen from a height – a calming hand gliding over my eyes, a cosmonaut's helmet visor . . . But this morning, all was well when I woke up. Before the sun hit the angles of the walls. The mingled rivers, embracing beneath the wings of the plane. A shot partridge on the ground, flapping its wings. I was hot, Anne with her pink cheeks in my arms. What's the point of keeping on about it? Incapable of going back on board or of serving (with a smile) the trays to the passengers, making in-flight safety demonstrations and seeing the tiny fragile children in their mothers' arms . . . Dolling myself up. Make-up. It was John who chose the name, Pierre, and we both agreed. Not the same with the eccentricity of Éléonore. We agreed, totally agreed, to have lots of children and live by the sea. Rub, rub, rub. A binge of housework. What am I going to do now the beds are made? Light a cigarette, here, on the edge of the bed. To have lots of children and live by the sea. Pierre because it was unpronounceable in English. Pierre for the two of us. Just the two of us. Jeanne, Anne and Pierre, a girl, a girl, a boy. We thought we had all our lives in front of us. John used to sing, *toute ma vie j'ai rêvé d'avoir les fesses en l'air* with his terrible accent, while I was more into, how did it go? *La vie était jolie Suzette, on est heureux Nationale 7*. The world champion in the world championship of pregnant air hostesses. But, Madame Johnson, there are ways and means. Drown them like kittens . . .

The most incredible part is still to be alive afterwards, and that this life goes on, how long? Twenty-five years now. A blazing summer, a heat wave, dying in the heat because I was still alive. John, Jeanne, Anne and me, veins beating in our brows, all having to eat again, and crap as a result, and breathe and drink, life making plain its hold on us. In bed most of the time. Anne stopped walking. And I hoped I'd die, but every morning, in the damp sheets, we ended up falling asleep, when we should have, at the very least, stayed up for him all our lives . . .

The thinking is simple: rather than killing yourself, because death will come anyway, rather than killing yourself, drop everything and disappear. People used to die of a broken heart. The suffering will, of course, follow me to Cuba, but that's not the point. Rent a bed and lie on it. Owe nothing to anyone. Stop everything. But the neighbours will wonder what's going on. Rumours will start up again. A tiny world. Feet on the bed's crossbar, heat and the fan. There would inevitably be a man, but there'd be no more children. The thinking is simple – she toys with the cat's ears, she'll have to go down for an ashtray . . .
   – rather than suffer, kill yourself
   – rather than kill yourself, run away and disappear
   – rather than run away, stay and play the departed, in bed, silent, waiting
   – since death will come, participate as an absentee
   – rather than be an absentee, fake your presence
   – rather than faking . . .?

The innumerable bodies that have emerged from her body, who emerged, surrounded her when she was little, chorusing around her the same endless thinking with no solution since that summer. Twenty past twelve. The sun has stopped high in the sky . . .

Anne

Going back home, noon, empty streets, Rue Saint-Paul leading to Rue Saint-Pierre leading to Rue Sévigné leading to Rue

Quatre-Fils leading to Rue des Archives, the sun above Paris flips over from its zenith like a pole-vaulter. The sky spread out between two tides. Go back there, for a rest perhaps, will they leave me alone? The house as empty as a shell. The story about the hermit crab who grows and grows, until its shell is too small, then the other crabs, lobsters and creepy things with feet, claws and snappers are on the lookout: he'll be out soon, just has to be, he's a smothered, soft, transparent little thing, I'd have liked to see one bare, hours spent over rock pools in green wellies from Ireland. Dr John's little women: Anne, Jeanne and then Nore Johnson, the Johndaughters, six green boots, small, medium and large around a hole full of water, haunted by a hermit crab suffocating in its shell but refusing to come out, no way . . . If the sea was there, at the end of the street, I could breathe better, the sea flying its ensign at the end of the quay on Rue des Archives . . . Once at the crossroads, I'd say to myself, still as a lake, or else, a bit choppy today. Or maybe, fine lines pointing south, so rain tomorrow. It would keep me busy, every day, I'd be eager to see the sea, because there would be, as there is this morning, except now every day, at the end of Rue des Archives where the sea stops dead, a strong humid breeze, ample and blue, my cheeks and hair slightly moist, and I'd say, *Good morning, half a baguette, please, the sea's choppy we're in for a storm*, or else, *My Johnny was a shoemaker and dearly he loved me, My Johnny was a shoemaker but now he's gone to sea, And when he has a gallant captain's sword he'll come home and marry me* . . . And the full wind will bathe us every morning, at noon, in the afternoon, and I'd go to the lab with a lighter step, carried by the wind, a wind that turns at the corners of buildings, a wind that keeps you company, the sea wind when it enters the city. We had no coats, just a mac was enough, an anorak, it was always mild. Only Nore still doesn't know what the cold is. As soon as I got to Bordeaux, then Paris, I bought a coat – I always had Jeanne's old macs. A coat of my very own, new, my mouth full of steam. I was in Paris. Of course,

39

Jeanne was already in Ushuaia or at one of the other ends of the earth. Fifty degrees in Africa, a specialist in temperature variations, a microclimate with an ego. *All's well here, the renovation of our house on the delta is almost finished, when are you coming to stay? Love, J. Un abrazo, D.* Never picks up the phone to ask me, even just once, how I am. What is it? An Indian camp? A blue parrot in some sort of cage? A view from the terrace? *Querida. Un abrazo fuerte, un beso fuerte.* The hermit-crab knight without his helmet, lying pathetically at the bottom of the pool. Soft, defenceless and pitiful. We tried to pull them out of their shells, but they resisted, preferring to let themselves get torn in two rather than give up, disgusting, translucent, soft flesh . . .

For the invisible man too, it started with his skin, the best book in the world, see all of him, like with shrimps, his brain, his guts, when cooked he goes opaque and pink . . .

No messages, of course, a red zero flashing, and no mail, a card from Jeanne and a bill . . . zilch. And this, what's this? The electricity board. *You have chosen to take out an easy meter reading contract. Please accept our congratulations* . . . And this . . .

GREAT CLAIRVOYANT! GREAT MEDIUM!
Monsieur NaBa
Possessor of powerful hereditary gifts
BEWITCHED? UNDER A SPELL? NO PROBLEM
WITHOUT A SOLUTION BAD LUCK DOGGING YOU, IN
SERIOUS DIFFICULTIES, WHEN DESPERATE A PHONE
CALL WILL DO TO SOLVE EVERYTHING. DON'T HESI-
TATE TO PHONE A GENUINE AFRICAN MARABOUT,
MONSIEUR NABA, AT ONCE.
Monsieur NaBa can reveal your past, present and future.
Love, luck, work, exams, taxes, evil eye, travel, rapid return
of loved ones, don't worry, call Monsieur NaBa's office.
WORK CARRIED OUT BY POST
PLEASE ENCLOSE SAE

Invisible, first the skin, the epidermis, a thin coat, with the roots of the hairs, then the fatty tissue, a woman would have far more of it, at least around her hips, but right now we're only interested in his hands, I mean, what he could see of himself outside his clothes, the blue star of his veins and then the red star of his arteries, the comings and goings of his blood stripped bare, then the veins vanishing, the clumps of blood floating in his hands disappearing, while the tendons appeared, white cords whose structure made him feel queasy – no, just a shock perhaps, maybe even a hint of joy – white when folded, grey when at rest, then the pulse could be seen in his muscles, his hands emptying, a white squid, then flooded with blood, in a purple flash, pigments flickering, going out . . . Finally, the muscles disappeared, fading to white, standing out more and more next to the bones, then no more skeleton. For one violent second, he saw himself as a vulnerable and mortal being. Then fading, a shadow, a tiny bird's claw. Finally, nothing at all, an empty sleeve . . .

X-rays, the skeletal hands of Marie Curie, mother of us all, dead from radium. Laurent the other day in the lab, saying that, at the time, they used to send each other 'sources', to see who could enrich the largest radioactive sample, sent through the post all round the world in infested packages or envelopes, the excitement when they reached one gram, *Dear Colleague, Please find enclosed a source weighing one gram* – without pressing the point, such elegance, such triumph – *I hope it will find you and your husband in good health and that I shall hear from you soon.* At the beginning of the century, on either side of the ocean there are still letter boxes which could explode a Geiger counter. The Curies lived on Rue de la Glacière, every evening they went home and took off their explosive gloves, hats and coats. The building's still there, and the local post office took their parcels, those vibrant grams, *Dear Professor*, a gram and a hundredth, a gram and a quarter, a gram and a half. Ping, pong, across the ocean.

Incandescent cargo holds, relays and stage coaches. And, in postal museums today, the badges, caps and bikes of deserving postmen who mysteriously died young. Pierre Curie asking for the hand of Marie Sklodowska, and radiography was born, X-rays around that hand whose bones had been exposed, she'd taken off her wedding ring for the shot, unless it's her right hand. The ring must still be pulsating on her skeletal hands in the Panthéon. If Laurent left his wife and married me, what would be born? Him, a physicist. Me, a linguist. The future, the future will tell . . .

It's so sad straight after lunch. At two p.m. At the zenith. When the sun cuts out the building opposite into big white squares. Flat structures against the blue sky. A round eye amid the sky. Through the windows, over the coffee cup, through the windows and the whorls, the check pattern of the building opposite. The family on the fourth floor whose sofa is positioned exactly parallel to the sofa of the family on the first floor, the perpendicular passing through the couch of a psychoanalyst, who draws his curtains during consultations, and also the ever-present white-haired woman sitting with her back to the window, the only permanent resident among the squares that empty out for the day, for school, for work, with binoculars I could read over her shoulder, the book held out at arm's length, all that changes is the lighting, someone brings a lamp and puts it down beside the dummy . . . It's the hour of the cleaning ladies . . . cleaning ladies in empty flats, smoking melancholically out of windows and looking towards me, my flat, and the street. Some put on the TV. Others start by making coffee. The enormous melancholy of empty flats. Dusting. Busying themselves, moving their arms and making household appliances purr, before the sheets are spun for placing over things, the dusty display of absence over things, the linen ghosts wear. But we aren't there yet, no, not there yet. A scarecrow in a field of crows. In the evening, the paintings I can see on the far walls thanks to the electric lights, pale green shading, a pond, a dress, a stretch of sea-water, nineteenth-century details . . .

The hour when the sun opens wide its eye, up in the sky, whatever have I done with my cigarettes?

My cigarettes . . .

Mum always threatening to go away to Cuba, scuba-diving, take a ticket for a gap in space-time, if I took shelter there, in our childhood home, it would be Cuba cubed . . .

In Cuba, rid of us, of her trappings, but not of what's gnawing her insides, the inside of her brain colonized by hermit crabs, thoughts snapping their tiny pincers . . .

And the more stubborn than the rest, panicking (so they say) at the moment of death – *saw my entire life pass before my eyes*, the survivors say – panicking at having to put a stop to her painful, painstaking undermining of us, to her tiny double, to her quadruple voice, her dead ends, her traipsing around, her toings and froings, to the song she never stops singing, to her musical saw in the hollow of her ear, in the depths of the lobes of her brain – that tweeting never stops, Faraday's cage of parrots when lightning strikes around them, a moment's surprise, then off they go again – *my life before my eyes*, the survivors say – drip, drip, drip in their heads, water torture, *plick*, *plock* between their eyes, the horrific endless migraine of thought, those who have returned, who have seen, who shall see again, recruiting agents have always favoured them, that's right, I know a few who've had near-death experiences, returning from the dead, spared from a coma, an accident, murder, slaughter. The light they see at the end of the tunnel, the light that comes on to show the way out, is what you see on the other side of the vagina, a buried memory or, as John used to say, *the lights of a train that's about to hit us. I'm beginning to see the light* . . .

I'll stay sitting in the big green armchair in the house down there. Put my body someplace for good. For a while. To keep my eyes peeled. Not to miss the agent's glance, not to be trapped in the web of other stares. To sort them all out with vigilance and concentration. Detect any interference and eliminate the irrelevant. A straight line of steps and thoughts, as calm as today, barring the panic attack this morning. Slow down, I can do it. Progress towards perfect agreement, tend towards being exemplary, professional cover and thorough work. My ability not to make babies cry. Anne Johnson. I'm always the one they ask for. The gentlest, the most experienced, the most maternal, even . . .

I'd move in, I wouldn't disturb a thing, I wouldn't cost them a cent, I'd just have to convince my mother. Then I'd stay sitting in the big green armchair, most of the time . . .

London Bridge is falling down, falling down . . .

Sitting most of the time, that's right, nothing on my mind or in my mind, or in my eyes, a permanent holiday, moulded in silence . . .

In the state of Tennessee, Dr William Bass is scientifically studying the decomposition of bodies: under water, lying on grass, under tarpaulins, in the boots of cars . . . Paths of black mud run between the bodies, which are stored and studied in a farm for as long as necessary. How quickly does a four-year-old decompose? Dr Bass knows. Clear answers, science out to help justice, the citizen. Who is struggling against obscurantism, uncertainty, the vagueness of the Middle Ages? Bill Bass is! Me too. Inside my brain, they'll find cocoons of those larvae which gnaw at the flesh, hatch out twenty-one days after death. Thus allowing us to date . . .

Put my body someplace, be in charge of myself, as though of the mothership. Technical control. Autonomy. Down there, in the house. Or in Cuba. Or Buenos Aires. The problem is the habitat. Especially at night, more than ever, you float around your body, not knowing what to do with it. Momo laying tiles and mixing concrete, always more concrete, a Chernobyl sarcophagus, and then it starts leaking, his

horrible face behind his trowel – stop, disgusting thought . . .
Pizza Face, giggling away with Jeanne . . . Right now, she's
asleep. Far away. We made houses with the bed linen draped
over the table, a long tablecloth or sheets hanging down to the
floor, cushions and bolsters, piles of books for windows and
crates for furniture. Jeanne and spectacular departure, a
Cannes princess, spangles, false eyelashes and crocodile tears
. . . In the Philippines, she lived off rice and fish for a year. In
Africa, they started a mass grave beside her house, like they
were opening a garage, a handy place to park your dead. In
Australia, the empty desert, jerry cans of petrol and water in
the boot. All those stories thrown together, fireworks, dust in
your eyes . . .

Pourquoi Anne est-elle partie?

Suppose that a voice, just one, one day asks that question.
*Anne, my sister Anne, why did you leave? Can't you see what's
coming?* Then I'd climb to the top of the tower and say, *no, I
can't see anything coming.* Sun and sea from the top of the lighthouse. The earth, from the bridge of the mothership. A glance
at the blue sphere through the porthole. Sitting most of the
time, stuck in my armchair. The pull of gravity. That's it, not
to mention accommodation. Without mentioning accommodation and the night when you have to put your body someplace, out of the rain, safe from predators, while we're all
elsewhere. London Bridge is falling down. While we're elsewhere, connected to our supine bodies only by the thread of
our dreams . . .

Experience shows that there are slip-ups, errors, mistaken
directions when (as though on winter holidays you put on
your skis) it comes to finding again the right box of brains.
It's obvious that some people are going round in other folks'
shoes, and no one notices, except them, as they silently move
around us, knowing everything that's inside us. They
recruited me. Experience shows, the very experience they
gave me, when you think you're connecting with a given
brain, but it's another one that receives you. Replaced in

45

your sleep, swapped over at birth . . .

The coffee's gone cold, the tree beneath the window is swaying its leaves slowly and making its noise, hand on my forehead, a large, calm, green hand, there were poplars in front of the . . .

Sitting in the big green armchair. Mum would presumably agree to feed me. We're alike. She'd understand. A direct link. Handed down. To stop and have a rest. No plans, nothing, except staying there, sitting in front of the trees of our house. Because there's no escape. Sitting most of the time. In the big house where I was scared at night. Leave your body there in the big empty house where no one hears you. Body in the armchair. The shell of the house all around, then pilot your thoughts. Be at your thoughts' dashboard, be in unfiltered control of your thoughts' joystick. Home sweet home . . .

Nore

Stick thrown, stick back, stick thrown, and back. He's sitting, playing on the sand, with the dog playing tricks. Taking it a bit far – then the hand cracks down: *here!* the master on his buttocks, grabbing the stick, throwing it – or else the dog, looking playful, delighted, in charge, keeping its prey in its jaws and growling – she's seen him here a few times now, at lunch time, he parks his 4L up there by the dunes, no surf-boards – the wind is soft, she lets her hair loose, puts her clip in her bag – even supposing the dog's eyesight is focused on itself, even supposing it can see the difference between itself and the world (its master, smells, this great stretch of water) – or else it may have a pleasant tendency to confuse itself with the world, who knows? – something's been washed up over there, the tide's pushing it onwards, turning it over and over as it slithers up the beach – the dog sniffs, weaves about, four paws and snout to the ground, smell/piss/undertow watch your paws/spin-dry flap flap flap the ears/smell where from

46

where is it/last trace/forgotten/master: throw the stick, throw! The dog's incredible joy, from the tips of its paws to its snout, racked by the muscular thrill of the game, by the world giving itself up, which recedes/routine return of frustration, hunger, loneliness, the master has turned his eyes towards another creature, a human . . . there are still the fleas, scratch, scratch, scratch, and that thing floating in the water . . .

He stands up, elegant, supple, dressed in corduroys, what she likes on a man are big corduroys tumbling down nicely (Momo, it has to be admitted, wears them to perfection), long vigorous legs, large shoes, big sweater, aged thirty or thirty-five, single (spaniel). He looks at her. The thing that's floating in the waves like a buoy, washed up, whisked up again, like a bundle of clothes, or a large knotted bag (the victim was found beheaded, horribly mutilated, *I'd never seen such a thing in my life*, the pathologist said, and the gendarme, a father of two, but as tough as they come, nevertheless puked up) – um, I almost found it touching, in fact – suddenly she feels cold, she gets to her feet and could ask him, ask him for example if the death of Sardanapalus was also the death of romanticism, though it's more usual to ask the time, Anne says men in Paris never stop trying to . . . He's going away, full of regret for impossible love. He stoops. Waits for his dog. If I had a dog we could talk dogs over the X of our crossed legs, while they sniff each other's butts – maybe the thing in the water's a dead dog, dogs recognize their dead, and why is it that they always blink when you stare at them? How do they know where your eyes are? They could look at our noses, for instance, our chins or our feet. The long stare of the dog, then fresh concentration on its search, is this smell of death from a colleague or a bird?

Tum te tum tum
There was a knight laid under a tree
Tum diddly tum tum
And he was as dead as dead could be . . .

47

A penguin, maybe. Sometimes they get washed up – a dog's psychology sketched out on the sand, tracks, zigzags, stops, hesitations, as it follows across the sands the varied traces of wind and smell, the dog sure of its rights, wrapped up in its cause, determined, absorbed in its task, dogs know what they're about, especially in pairs, with tacit decisions, unspoken agreement, trotting along in a straight line, then sudden diversions in unison, while humans are so slow, to follow, go on ahead, trot in front, trot behind . . . He's coming over. Stroke it. That's right. *Good boy. There's a good boy.* The dog so courteous, watchful not to disturb its master's thought processes, up there, hanging almost two metres above the earth. Maybe it's a little dolphin, a baby seal, a dead child spun about from sea to sea, the Gulf Stream washes up litter from Spain, islands of floating rubbish just offshore, the current picking up the scraps, Brillo, La Mayorquina, Carbonell, detergents and cooking oil, bleached packs of salt . . . *Nice dog you've got there*, the little bugger's sniffing at my, which only makes him laugh, *Charlie! What a clown* . . . Say something, speak when you're spoken to, they're calling to you from the back of the house, *I've seen you here a few times*, brilliant, he opens his mouth, *I'm staying at my brother's place at the moment, I'm hesitating about* . . . He points towards the house on the dune. A wave has taken the bundle away, the thing looks like the back of a porpoise in the swell . . .

(A spaceship lands on the beach, an initial study of earthly territory, *beep*, preliminary observations, *beep*: varied life forms. Twinned biotopes: limpets/rocks, clams/sand, fleas/dog, dog/human being. Human beings have dogs that have fleas, this particular one has four equidistant limbs and a torso and a sphere, piled on top of each other, how on earth does it remain upright, it must be a good six foot tall; a muscular effort from the feet, all standing on the earth, with a weak purchase on the sand, but a good acrobatic balancing act, don't chimps see us as tightrope walkers, circus attractions?)

48

She shifts from one foot to the other, between the sea and the dog's owner, soaking up the sun, soaking up the spray, with all this liquid salty presence, wondering what he's thinking, if he means to stay, whether she likes him or not, looking at her watch, will he ever make his mind up, ask for her phone number . . .

The Mother

I remember now that light on the open sheets . . . I was facing the sea, at the top of the hill where we always walked, John, the children and I. Everything was so clear, the cliff like a stack of plates, the blue crockery of the sea . . . When, in my dream, I asked, *Is this a dream?* I answered, *No.* There were three trawlers out there, it must have been about four o'clock, they were off sardine fishing, everything was coherent, the clock tower, the mountains, the little chapel, the arc of the town, the entrance to the port, the slightly bluer harbour channel, the breakers beyond the sea wall, and most of all that light, yes, an enamel tone, of places from my childhood, the sea breaking into white, more and more reflections laid out flat, like chunks from the cliff face in the breakers, curved glints, like from a pan or kitchen sink, light catches everything that shines here as if it was a magpie. I'm on the cliff, John and the girls have vanished, but I know exactly where I am, I have a better sense of sight and smell than in reality, the sea, the cliff, the wind and scent of seaweed, it's as if I understood them all, as if, for the first time, I knew precisely where I am, where I'm standing, between the four cardinal points, as if I could give my position like a ship signalling with semaphore. And then, maybe because the water's so clear and green, or because the cliff's so inviting in the wind, or because the sun's shining down obliquely and making everything glimmer, I can fly. I just have to open my arms and the air takes me up, softly, the air carries me, a slight pressure beneath my arms is sufficient, the sea glides past, to the right,

49

to the left, I swerve about, and the air density is real, less intense than water, more constant than the wind when out walking . . . The sea moves along in blue squares, the wakes of boats leave triangles and the trawls form circles. Through the water, I can see banks of yellow sand and strings of black seaweed gathered around the rocks. I'm not making this up, but the best part of all was the kick from the heel, the take-off. I'd landed near the semaphore, afraid I wasn't going to be able to take off again, but I could, all I had to do was launch myself into this palpable wind which was accompanying me. When you leave the ground, when you're free from gravity, you discover at once a different balance, another physical sureness, a different logic: turn to the right, then to the left, by twists you understand at once . . . The town, too, the bright red roofs, the streets, Rue Gambetta leading to Place Louis-XIV, Rue de la République and Boulevard Thiers, then Rue de l'Y and its bifurcation, leading to Rue Saint-Pierre and Rue Et-Miquelon, leading to the quay, and which are orange in the evening, where they face due west . . . The grid of streets, seen from above, I couldn't have made that up, and the market square, the rails, the roundabout, the packing house, the golf links, the suburbs . . . At the foot of the hills, the tiny patch of the town held in the folds of the earth . . . lean to the left, then to the right, swerve out over the sea. I cross a flock of gulls above a trawl, as many birds up here as fish down there, struggling furiously in the ropes of the net, and the gulls, with their yellow feet folded beneath their tails, wings perpendicular to their bodies, red bills, pink tongues . . . I'm gliding, I can do it, up and down . . . It's easy to spot the schools of sardines, and the dolphins, and I also saw a whale's forehead which I mistook for an island covered with limpets and mosses, but the black skin rolled back beneath the water and I glimpsed the bulk of this underwater cathedral . . . In the morning, there's still a sensation of your dreams that lingers, but I'm not sure what it is exactly . . . It grabbed me while I was making the beds, because the light on the sheets was the same as it had been on the cliffs. It's the kick of the heel which remains, a little too much power in the feet, the opposite of a nightmare . . . And then snatches, a fleeting image, the colour blue . . . Suddenly, the dream surged up again with its shapes and colours, you just have to unravel the ball, like the book title or name you have on the tip of your tongue and which bursts once more into your head with all that implies, a town, a family, the broadening world, reconstituting the gulls, the squares of the sea, the chunks of cliff shooting beneath me, everything back in place, an intact, former world . . .

Jeanne

If my sisters could see me at night, I'm ten years old. Bang in your head. Sleep has gone *soñando sus sueños. ¿Qué hora es?* The young *escracheros* are demonstrating in the street again. Five a.m. Rise and shine, BA. In Australia ten years ago, the call box beside the dried-up river and Granny silent on the phone, I could hear her breathing and I said, *wait for me.* Sand at the back of the throat. They said she'd had it, but her brain was still all there, and almost anything would have been enough then, when floating between noon and midnight, where her brows were cold, for me to see her open her eyes . . . She waited for me because she was sentimental. My return flight. Her life like a screenplay, wilful through to the very end. Airport scene on a hospital bed, *I love you too.* Undertakers of genius, brilliant cosmetics, she was smiling, you had to touch her cold forehead to believe it. Puffed-up bodies in the River Goumé, the cyclone with a girl's name, Flora, Lily or Magnolia. Just before dawn, before the parrots squawk, the night drunk to its lees, insomnia. Bang in your head. Grey matter centrifuged into mayonnaise stuck on your skull. The eye of the storm, the east–west wind tearing off the metal roofs, flattening the lyre trees, then silence, the stripped tree trunks, then the west–east wind throwing back up the roofs and lyre trees convulsing on the ground . . .

51

Just before dawn, the *escracheros*. That's what comes of living in an upmarket neighbourhood, no burglaries, no rapes, just the fear of being mistaken for one of your neighbours. The sirens breaking through the double glazing, through my sleep, from far away I can hear them. Every first Friday of the month (in France, the first Wednesday of the month, I remember now, the emergency drill, the alarm bells, Anne used to say that the Russians, Iraqis and Chinese would attack on a first Wednesday of the month at the stroke of noon). There, here, now, the terrible din of the children of those who disappeared. Below the windows of the admiral who's moved out, *hijo de puta*, in the penthouse I'd so liked to have lived in, with an even better view over the delta. My sisters who criticize me for travelling so much, being rich, happy, in love and living in an upmarket area of what they see as the Third World . . . all they can think of saying as soon as they cross a time zone, the inevitable speech they reel out, I played beneath the tables with Anne, Nore not there yet, Mum drowned in grief and now, thread by thread their crown of sorrows which they have woven against me, *la belle au bois dormant*, with my *bel hidalgo*, whose name they can't even remember, despite the fact Diego is as easy as pie, that motherfucker Admiral Biscocho, moving into the penthouse with his caged birds and assumed name – none of the other owners had any idea. Trumpets and yells before the budgerigars wake up. Scratching of washing boards, banging oil drums, tambourines, whistles and police sirens. The *escracheros* keep me jet-lagged. I used to get up – if only my sisters had seen me – yelling from the balcony along with the children of those who disappeared, not caring what the neighbours might say: *hijo de puta, dónde, dónde, ¡nunca olvidaremos!* But that wasn't my affair. Not my business. An admiral who's an *asesino* till you're fed up with it. In the eye of the storm. Diego said nothing until I caught on and closed the windows. The scene of the crime. In the murderer's house . . . Not my story . . .

Good little sisters. Make a mental note to mention that to

Dr Welldon. Like waking from a dream. Throat slit in my bags. At night, when stories take shape. In the grand bazaar, in the great well of darkness. I'll go to the house and scratch on the door. Tambourines and maracas. *Ma mère dites-moi pourquoi vous êtes triste*. Mothers in a circle around Plaza de Mayo. Father's turbines and darlings. Wanted us to call him Daddy and we called him John. Except for Nore. The earthquake. Bang in your head. The admiral in his penthouse swimming in blood. Diego's revolver. The idea occurred to me. *Ola amiral, buen día*. How could Diego have done that, every day in the lift? Good morning, Admiral. Everyone knew who he was. Pots of red paint thrown against the walls. My childhood in France. What innocence . . .

A woman giving birth in her cell, then biting her child's ear. Picture it. Getting shot in the head, then her marked child is stolen by a general, admiral, commandant. Just picture it, the gaping bloody wound at the back of the cell, placenta still in the belly and a bullet in the brains. All alone. Every day another story like that in the papers I read. When dawn really breaks, when they've gone, I'll go back to sleep. When the dawn chorus starts. Brains like mayonnaise. I read, leaning against the wall, not exactly peacefully, that's impossible, it was our childhood home, and I used to read in bed, leaning my back against the wall, a vacant afternoon, when I was fourteen or fifteen . . . then from the depths of the house comes the rustling of branches but with no wind. And then again from the depths of the house comes a crackling sound rising up from the floor to the unlit light bulbs, and the windows. Then again from the depths of the house comes the chinking of crockery. And furniture scratching and doors opening. Then it comes towards me. A wave. A drum roll from the depths of the house, of the earth, coming towards me. The vibration of a massive gong. Bang, bang behind my head. The wall of the house I'm reading in is moving. And from another room comes my mother's yell as she wakes up

53

from an endless nap. The bed tips up, the lamp slants, I recognize the floor, and the wall I'm leaning my hand on, bang, bang, while I cling on to my frantic bed frame ... Everything is shaking, becomes treacherous, autonomous, unknown, I'm now just a passenger in my own bedroom, and the relationship I have with the furniture, with the pictures in their frames and the garden, shatters under their indifference. Detached, possessed by a force that ignores us, they're plotting against us, altogether against the living. Then the lamp tumbles over, back to gravity again, back to the floor. And the noise stops. And my body recovers its controlling presence on my bed, back against the wall, at a right angle. And my mother appears. The floor is now fully present. She yells, *an earthquake!* Then we hear the wailing of Nore's seismic scale. A luxury hotel, sea views, where that friend of mother's called Maïder worked, the rooftop swimming pool spilling down the stairs, the scandalized guests were swept downstairs in their swimsuits and bathrobes by the flood. A window was ripped out, its frame on the floor, two lamps tipped over and a few smashed glasses, that's all we lost, but Mum had left her bed ...

They've gone now, recently there's only been about ten of them, the police and weariness are driving them away, the admiral was extremely well protected, our building too. How much of a saint must you be to wash away your sins? *Mira como soy y hazme como tu quieras que séa.* Twist and turn in the rumpled sheets, fold over fold, it's them that are sweating, and if you stopped moving, they'd attack, bite into your heels and buttocks, make bedsores out of gravity. Granny at the end of her life. John said, *if it happens again, then run out to the front, not the garden because of the trees.* But it never did. A slip-up, some anomaly in the ground. And if it has happened since, would they think to tell me? Mum's fortnightly letters: *the weather's fine, the crocuses are out, it's jam-making time, the plum tree's produced a good yield this year, your sister sends you a big kiss, so does Momo*. We didn't manage to kiss Momo for some time. When I was Nore's age now, I'd already been gone two years. Make your bed and lie on it. With Diego taking up all the space. Half past five. Come on, daytime. I'll never get back to sleep . . .

Wake up again and think you're back in the bedroom you had when you were little . . . The walls, the lamp on the left, the white daylight through the shutters . . . But the door's on the right and Diego's here and, beneath my elbows, when I turn over, there are my breasts, the hardness of my ribcage has gone, my bony hips have gone, a little body sunk into a large one. My brother in the bed next to mine, the wonder of Lego, with limbs, hair, supple little lumps you snapped together, Duplo, was it? He wanted to put wheels on everything. I woke up, he was already up. When I went to bed, he was still awake. Today, they'd slap a hyperactive ticket on him. He'd be what? Pushing thirty now. His hair would have got darker, less blond, more brown. You could, for example, read a bit. Use the 'do not disturb' lamp which Diego gave you. How to read without waking your neighbour. Open it at random and pick today's welcome sentence from the subconscious mind of books. Him or someone else. It could have been anywhere in the world. I've become a Patagony Aunt. Rooted here where no one has roots. The time Pierre was dreaming one hot and humid nap time, and he opened his mouth and started spouting Basque, like he'd blown a gasket, tropism, the climate, biotope, and no one would believe me, father pointing out that I didn't speak the language myself, but that's what it was, you could hear it, the mother tongue we maybe all spoke without realizing it . . .

I remember that attraction in the funfair in Blackpool. Mum stayed outside because of her claustrophobia. And the three of us, Pierre, John and me, what made me think of it and where was Anne? The three Johnsons stuck on a bench, waiting with three other customers in the middle of what was a normal-looking room, in fact, with a sideboard which had a teapot on it, a table, some pictures. I remember. We'd already been to the haunted house, with things brushing against you, sticky things at the bottoms of jars, fluffy things in your hair. Then, on the bench, nothing was happening. A fit of the giggles with Pierre. And John uneasily shifting around. Then something disturbing, with a hint of giddiness. First we'd been patient, then we were worried. Something had changed. Our neighbours' faces were a touch more pallid, more puzzled. Our hands were a touch more tense. There was more saliva in our throats, hard to swallow, horrible seasickness. Then we seemed to understand. The bench was fixed on an axis and we were swaying, my father, Pierre and me, plus our neighbours. Faster and faster. We clung on, laughing. We leaned further and further over, lost our balance. Shaking all over, we grabbed hold of one another, me on to Pierre, Pierre on to John, John politely on to his neighbour. Pierre was hurting my wrist, his hair in my mouth. Laughter and terror. We're going to fall! But something was up. Something was wrong. Something was missing. A sensation. Wind in your face . . . Real fear, real giddiness . . . Something in your body . . . Spinning through 360 degrees, we clung on to the bench. It was Pierre who realized you could stand up. My hair was hanging down, while everything was spinning around us. We were sitting in a rotating tub. That's when John passed out. From annoyance. From horror at this trick. He fell face forwards and rolled on to the solid floorboards under the bench. Cardboard furniture, fluttering cloth walls, spinning teapot, pictures filing past us, and John whiter than all the pictures put together, hunched at our feet. Later, *Diego querido*, years later, I played around with the idea of seeing Pierre again, not in the haunted houses of funfairs, but in an attraction like that one, sitting laughing on a bench, the room spinning around him, waiting, waiting for me to join him. *Diego querido*. It's almost daylight. October, the equivalent of March. Symmetrical equinoxes. Two sides of the planet . . .

I'm going to wake up and get up exhausted. Buy some fabric conditioner. I'll have to get used to the new maid, *Maria Pilar*, *hay que comprar*, how do you say 'fabric conditioner'? Suplín. And my lesson. *Bonjour, de quoi allons-nous parler aujourd'hui? Avez-vous passé une bonne semaine? Vous marierez-vous samedi? Divorcerez-vous dimanche?* Answer the questions. Who laughs on Friday will cry on Sunday. *Pleurra, pleurira. Llorará.* '*Il rêvait d'un pays en crue, débordant de ses frontières naturelles, quand je l'imaginais calme et paisible, une après-midi où nous serions assis sous les arbres à deviser dans la plus belle langue du monde.*' Or something like that. The French always think that theirs is the world's most beautiful language. Diego asking me if I'm the same in other tongues. I don't even know if I'm the same from one sentence to the next. The French wandering around in their language as if it was the most natural thing in the world. Small green meadows leading down to the river, beneath the bending willows. Yellow patches of wheat. Countless houses, tiles or slates, a turret, a dovecot, a clock tower on the horizon. Straight lines of poplars, forests of pines. A dash of yews, polished rocks. Half-timbered houses, benches beneath the plane and chestnut trees. The fresh crusty baguette and real croissants, jam, the hunger of being there is more poignant here than elsewhere. Here, in Buenos Aires, where you're in France more than anywhere else, where we're all in Italy, in Germany, in Spain, in the Basque country, in Sweden, in Europe. All exiles in a dream geography. In any case, we weren't really French. Maybe Nore is. Maybe Anne is. But I'm not, nor him . . .

Apparently, I spoke with an accent. Then I've always been fat. Another *millefeuille*. Finish the apple pie. Try the Basque cake, more cream cake, more cream buns. Tea time. The empty pampas, starved by the winds. So what are we going to talk about today? We ate grilled lamb and drank maté all together at Corrientes. We went to mass. Say it in the past, the present, the future. Are we the same in different tenses? Please discuss. Diego is almost certainly disappointed that I

57

don't yell out *oui* and *encore* and *mets-la-moi* in French. If I am different, then all I can say is that French is pronounced at the front of the palate: U, OU, OUI, CUL-DE-POULE. Spanish is pronounced in the middle of the mouth: A, O, QUERIDO, G and C emphasized, J rasped, the whole greedy mouth agape, MARIA PILAR COMPRAME SUPLÍN PARA LA ROPA. And English is a gutter language, with tongue waves sending the syllables back towards the throat: *the door was open, I was leaning against the door, my tailor is rich.* At the end of the seventies, in Stafford at Granny's place, a tailor meant a drug dealer, from the French verb *tailler* . . .

What's the time? Mayonnaise brains. Atoms fusing, molecules of grey matter rubbing together, burning out . . .

And just now, bang in your head. The nervous system. It's the brain that comes, with the vibrant cabled column from the sex to the head, bang bang, crackling as it goes. A guitar string vibrating, a knotted guitar string, like the knot of a boat rope, a capstan or a wall and crown, the knot of the clitoris at the top of the lips, like the skirts in *The Story of O* raised above the sex, held up by a buckle, pussy chops (architecture of ivy and hollyhocks hanging from rings in the Jardins de Bagatelle, with Anne chattering, chattering between two flights, I saw my sister, in Roissy-Charles de Gaulle, when the plane rose up between the clouds, those rapid ten seconds before seeing nothing but the atmospheric desert, pressurized curves, white-cum-blue turns when the plane took off, I tried to spot the place, the castle near Roissy, where O was imprisoned, in the plains, the woods, a tower, the one for *Anne, ma sœur Anne*), a guitar knot like on a box coat, tip of a tow rope, holding the tops of the lips together, closer and closer, more and more concentrated, the only organ, I read somewhere, which is solely designed for pleasure . . . And the vagina just the opposite, a clitoris turned inside out, the rear point receding backwards, outwards, spreading millions of fibres, connections, over a broader surface, the entire brain, when the vaginal surface and brain surface precisely coincide, then it's orgasm time, no doubt about it . . .

Membrane to membrane, fibre to fibre, nerve to nerve, two adjusted organs, brain/vagina, via a re-created body, there, right there, and dematerialized too, given over to gravity . . . difficult when masturbating, fingers never long enough, contortions, objects always too hard, too this that or the other thing, too object. Even though, right from the cradle, the clitoris is a toy to hand . . . Don't need anything or anyone to come. *Je n'ai besoin de personne en Harley-Davidson*, or *on Massey-Ferguson*, as John used to say. Women's magazines should deal with the matter in more detail, in more technical terms: with electrodes, stimulated bodies, piston engines, an exact study of different sizes, suckers, aspiration, rubbing, breast pumps and syringes; on the Johnson scale, this orgasm was 10 per cent clitoral and 90 per cent vaginal, calculate the contribution of the breasts, the skin, guts, this one was 50/50, but it's clear that . . .

Sleep, Diego my love . . .

That a third way exists, and a fourth, infinite possibilities . . .

Any old erotic dream which leaves you panting for breath, eyes wide open, woken by your orgasm: sex throbbing with blood, swollen feathers quivering violently, brains injected straight into your arteries, with no physical contact, not even the slightest brush . . . Orgasm in your brain. Bang bang. And the dream lasts only a second. Your hand goes down instinctively on waking, to see, to check. The architecture of the body in different time zones. The dry-cleaner's in Paris where I left my clothes between flights, what was the chain called again? Cinq à Sec, funny name. Me, or the person I am in my dreams, tied up, strapped, whipped, touched up, etc. Leather mask, two staring eyes and zipped mouth, like a funny face sketched by a child. Pleasure comes from details. Diego and Jeanne are on a boat. Jeanne goes overboard. *Don't cry for me, Argentina.* Sometimes fantasies fail. The phone rings, the milk boils over, pathetic banalities. Me, getting my foot caught in my skirt, in my dream. My father turning up. Diego, the masked avenger like Zorro. *De quoi allons-nous parler aujourd'hui?* Wily jabs of torture inflicted on my dolls. Skinning them, slowly burning them. At ten or at six, the entire psychology of murder, the same dreams since the beginning. Try the next exercise. *A tí te toca.* Your turn. Choose your work sheet. A little girl? Very good. Strap her up. Let's strap her up. Choose an instrument. We shall choose an instrument. *Une perceuse.* Or *un manche à balai. Un râteau*, yes, why ever not? *Perceuse* without a cedilla, *râteau* not spelt with an 'o'. *Un rato, un ratito*, a little rat, yes, excellent idea. *Une sangle. Un fouet*, naturally. *Un chat à neuf queues, un gatito. Une pelle?* What do you want a spade for? We're not going to bury her yet. *Un caméscope.* Plug *la perceuse* into *la prise électrique.* Use *un adaptateur. Une baignoire. Un couteau (cuchillo).* Wear *un casque antibruit.* Make the drill turn slowly. Camcorder on. *Un tibia. Une oreille.* Watch out for *le cerveau*, keep her alive. *Une tenaille, la langue. Les tétons*, classic move, there. *Un mégot de cigarette*, spelt *g-o-t.* St Eulalie of Barcelona, condemned at the age of thirteen to being raped to death, a Roman legion over her body. *Une cuillère* for the eyes. *Une lame de rasoir. Des épines d'acacia*, as used in Africa. Grab the clitoris between the thumb and index finger, then cut. Then careful, do a delicate job with the labia minora. The thorns used to close the labia majora or else *fil de pêche* will do if necessary. Leave a passage for urine and menstrual blood. Reopen with knife for deliveries, then close again. Your *bite* in her *bouche*, why not indeed? Mind out for the blood. Drill for the teeth, make her run, the holes will sing in the wind. Inject her with Koch's bacillus and watch. Oh, look, she's going to die . . .

Anne and me playing doctors and nurses, pissing, touching. She had her periods before me, when she was nine and a half, already nuts, from bad to worse. The house beneath the table, sheets thrown over, two pillows for beds, cardboard dinner table and us hiding there, silently. Then Mum calling for us, and us lifting up just slightly the sheet, tablecloth or curtain, waiting for her to go mad. When she found us, she could have murdered us with relief. She was what, thirty years old that summer, can't imagine myself in her shoes. Thirty-three and still childless. I'll have a papaya for breakfast. The idea of my morning papaya to put up with this insomnia. *How do you harvest papayas? With a pipitchfork.* Koalas in Australia sleep twenty-three hours a day, have no predators, stick their hands out to the eucalyptus leaves, chew, then go back to sleep. Where do koalas die? Do they fall from their trees? Or are they found with their long claws still sticking in the bark, dry, mummified, eyes closed as usual? Do guanacos miss their step and fall all arthritic into the ravine? What happens to dead fish that aren't eaten, do they dissolve? You never find the bodies, nature is self-cleaning. Do carrion fowl devour their fellows too?

Bang. The alarm clock. Diego's warm body, yes, *hombre*, another five minutes. If only you knew, *querido*, what the person who's not sleeping by your side has been thinking about . . . Twiddle a lock, then audit the sentences and synapses. With the sun . . . everything is better. When all of them, on the other side of the world, are asleep. When it's my turn to wake up and they leave me . . . I slide. Slowly. Head back, dark tumbling of the sun . . . a plane tree . . . A square surrounded by trees . . . The canal and the colour of the bend . . . Or the sea . . . With me, around me . . . Towards the yellow sun . . . *¿Quieres una papaya? ¿Una ppapaya? ¿Quququerida?*

Nore

In a previous existence, I had a violent death. That much is sure. It's the effect of the big waves, standing there, facing the sea, heart beating as they rise up . . . As though they were going to fall on me. My breast on adrenalin, air replaced as far as the depths of my bronchioles by a sea frost. He's at the far end of the beach now with his dog and striding legs. His

61

name's Nicolas, 05 59 33 31 19, scrap of paper in my pocket. We'll wake up under the duvet, his dog at the foot of the bed . . . Pre-programmed coffee-maker, breakfast in bed . . . We'll put on a record, I'll sink into his arms, he'll breathe into my hair . . . Sunshine . . . Then we'll read the newspapers . . . The first time, head back towards the trees, watching the moon up above the branches. I was sure it would hurt but it was like a knife through butter. Head back among the poplars. I may well phone him this evening. Rule number 1: accept their phone number, never give them yours. In a past existence, I had a violent death; I could swear to it. That photo of a charging elephant. If I had an elephant, I'd call it Sardanapalus, a good name full of 'a's for an elephant's great, open power. Nicolas's dog's called Charlie. Some people don't like people who give animals people's names. If I had a cat, I'd call it something nice like Caramel, for instance, or if it was white, something like Chamallow. 05 59 33 31 19, easy to remember. On the silver paper of his cigarette packet. We'll go to the house. I'll drop by to switch on the heating, it is cold, is it not? The end of October, the beginning of autumn. Even the dolls are still there. Anne and Jeanne's doll's house, which they let me play with, is still in there. Mum dropping by once a week or so to see if all's well and dusted. What on earth couldn't be well? Why doesn't she sell? I could buy a car. After all, it was Daddy who paid for the lessons. Jeanne says you're an adult when you no longer have it in for your parents. I don't see why I should have it in for them. Jeanne says Mum's still a little girl, dependent, that's what she told me. I wonder how I'd manage without the house. How on earth can anyone fuck in their parents' house? If I had to fuck in Momo and Mum's house, with them in the next room . . . Do they fuck, in fact, do they still fuck? Anne says that the vehicles in car parks in Paris bounce up and down at night, and that there are strands of hair and fingerprints on the densely steamed-up windows. Here, we have the beach till late in the season. And the grass of the golf course. Head back towards the trees, looking at the moon . . .

I'm sure that, in a past existence, my breast was crushed by a charging animal. An aurochs. Or a bear. A huntress. Or a martyr. A boar, maybe, surging out of the undergrowth as I bent my bow. A mammoth (its forehead, snout and ram). I was crushed, smothered. I can feel it here, below the sternum. My ribs shattered, heart crushed, lungs flattened. From the top of some waves, it's like falling from a building. The shock in the hollow of your chest, a charging animal, adrenalin within, the broadened star of the blow . . .

I'd like a man who'd ask me pensively what I was thinking: *à quoi pensez-vous?* While using the formal *vous*. Formal French in bed. Formal French when getting up. I'd like never to know what he's thinking about, to preserve the mystery. When we played Cluedo, even Jeanne joined in, playing the game, discovering the murderer, I was always a bit scared he was going to leap out in reality, a monster to whisk me away. They always let me win, a twelve- or fourteen-year age gap, I could have murdered them. Our brief shared life, a family life of five in a house where we don't live any more. Anne told me she'd seen a beached mermaid who'd had a botched operation, with three legs instead of two, but how can you walk with three legs? Daddy's golf clubs still in the house, or the flotsam, white with salt. *Un, deux, trois, nous irons au bois.* Anne having fun scaring me, and Jeanne comforting me. *Un, deux, trois, soleil.* Playing at statues and Anne cheating by pretending she hadn't moved. I could have murdered her. Dead, stretched out, still. A mermaid in a bundle, a bag of bones and scales, half fish, half flesh. Two legs in the same leg of a pair of tights, flapping around the house, clapping like a sea lion and Mum getting hysterics. The other leg of the tights trailing along like an unwound gut. Do they gut the mermaids they catch in trawler nets? Do they rape them? And by which hole? Questions Anne asked me. The skin of a squid when you take it out of the water is violet, pink, orange and golden.

Embroidered pigments. When you so much as touch them, they vanish, you think you're catching them under your fingertips like spangles, but they light up inside the squid itself, fading a little perhaps, a dynamo going wild, as the rudimentary life of the thingummy-pod winds down, with the round, black eyes of a human embryo. Because, on distribution day, they said, *these ones' eyes will do fine for those ones' eyes too.* 05 59 33 31 19 on the silver paper of the cigarette box. Where are the car keys? Sand in my shoes . . .

He and his dog have sat down at the end of the beach, as if they were talking. Maybe I'll call him this evening, his eyes, and the fact he's tall and thirty-something, oh yes. The key in my pocket. Doors unlocked automatically. I know the sea by heart. Coming down from some waves is like jumping off a building. The body half pushed out of the window by the wave, the building behind collapsing . . . It's like what Daddy says about wind generators . . . What was it again? . . . It's being scared that's dangerous . . . Rolling yourself up against the flow. Wanting to pull back. Anne when she was fifteen, crying with long driblets of green snot from her nostrils. I was the only one who could do it . . .

The idea of a rhinoceros, that's it, charging me, with its host birds holding on, feathers in the wind, crying, *Faster! Faster!* to encourage the rhino, then it hitting me in the solar plexus. Falling from the crest of the wave, holding on to Daddy. Host birds rid rhinos of their parasites. Discovery Channel. And baby giraffes falling two metres on birth, a crash landing on the world. And cats. Waking every morning and saying to themselves that there's something familiar about all this, about this place, this family, these smells, impressions buried in the mess of their neurones, just as we remember dreams or past existences in flashes. Maybe cats say to themselves, if they say anything at all, that they must already have been a cat here in one of their nine cat lives. Waking every morning from the dream they have left and saying, *well, well, well.* Then forgetting. Hence cats' blasé expressions, living in a world of constant *déjà vu*. Daddy says *déjà vu* in French, but in the English way, *deija vou*. It seems he doesn't like the arrival of the unexpected. An elephant charging, boom, into my solar plexus. My bones and guts turned to jam under its feet. A photo of a charging elephant, head on, viewfinder deceptive, final image, the photographer's last picture before death. The elephant's breath bursting into her face as she clicks the shutter. And that other photo, the Japanese tidal wave, *tsu* something or other, which Daddy had over his desk next to his darling Olympia – and still does have in Gibraltar – he admired the spirit of initiative, the speed and reactions of the Japanese man who sees the wave rising, who sees at once, *tsunami*, that it's huge, who realizes at once that it's monstrous, who immediately spots the point of salvation, a high military aerial, which he climbs up as, beneath him, the terrified people on the beach are scattering like crabs, and he takes a picture, hanging on with one hand. The tall dark wall of the black wave above Daddy's desk. Shaken, drenched, but alive, a survivor, the Japanese man hanging on to his mast. Dark water, what lives in it? A large waterfall, all the family in a minibus, my sole recollection of our holiday in Iceland, thank God I still have that much, that great fear, otherwise it's as though the entire family had gone without me. I was so scared by the dark water that I shat myself. That's why I remember. Black mud chased out by black water. A black purging froth. I know the sea by heart. But that column of falling water made any resistance useless, in a universe looking on agog: just that roar, the water, a frozen landscape, an event swallowing up its surroundings. Torn, chased out by the mud . . .

Anne

The news. Dr William Bass. And that other character, the paraplegic with electrodes in his brain connected to a computer. So as to move the arrow on the screen, he concentrates on the movements a healthy hand would make with the mouse. And soon, it's just by staring that he'll be able to group together the alphabet on the screen, the arrow will follow the short cut invented by his brain. His pupils are the joystick. He clicks A, B and C. He speaks. And then just the influx of neurones will make the arrow move, he no longer has to concentrate, not on his hand, nor on his eyes. To extrapolate: from the brain to the skin, to the muscles, or even to clothes, to make legs move via electrodes, the arms and the tongue, one foot in front of the other, walking. Various electronic levers and pumps will stimulate the hollow column of his penis, and his hard-on will jut out from his trousers as he stands up. My bionic lover. Electrodes planted in his limbic centre will, via stimulation, provide him with the usual sensations, the tactile quality of the other's body, the twisting pressure of ejaculation, and then the smell of the sea, the fluidity of oysters, wind in his hair, the speed of his car, the binary sluggishness of his walk, the tingling of the sand, the taste of pancakes at tea time, the sloping floorboards in a little hotel during a virtual dirty weekend. My bionic lover. Dressed in electrodes, undress him. Slowly, sweetly, reveal his body. Electronic striptease, robotic prick, just keep the levers. Unplug the rest. Only the bug eyes, what once were joysticks, will rotate in their sockets. Plug his electrodes into my body, an electronic barter . . .

Recruitment exercises. Put yourself in the shoes of . . . Know the levers of history, the ins and outs, explore consciousnesses. Total empathy, no interference from personality, anxiety, feelings . . . Near-death experience to the assistance of one and all. PURE EXPLORATION. OBJECTIVITY. Develop the brain's possibilities. Telepathy. Telekinesis. Teleportation. Long-distance love. The forecasting of earthquakes and tidal waves. The weather . . .

On the contrary: family psychology. This memory, for instance: John and Mum standing against a low-angled yellowish light breaking on to their figures. A doubled light, at night as in the day, where could I have seen such a dawn? Then separate, first and last memories, unless a photo comes between, superimposing itself on my memory: an overprint of a Nordic film about Mum and Dad . . . In the Johnson family, I want the mother, the father and the sisters. With my bionic prick. Anne. *Ma sœur Anne.* I'll take the brother, na-na-na-nerra, he'd have loved me so much that with just one word, just one look, we'd have . . .

Exercise: another newscutting. In 1937 Dr Shiro Ishii, head of Unit 731 of the Japanese army's vivisection and bacteriological experimentation department, operated without anaesthetic on Chinese brains, by opening a window in the forehead. Imagine being in that head at that moment . . .

A stretch of the world goes blind, a colour vanishes, half my body, the bit of my brain that says 'I' is snipped off, tipped over to the other side of WHAT IS ACTUALLY HAPPENING TO ME – while the person living without 'me', who will live through to the very end, is printing frenetically, pressing the NO button, ordering my hands to free themselves, my feet to run . . . A migraine drilling inside. Short circuit. High voltage lines severed. No more 'I', no more anything, thought fading, switch off, laboratory rat . . . Maybe pain continues without a subject, after all animals do suffer . . . Nerves getting direct torture commands, a frog's reflex movements – thanks to carefully placed electrodes, the lips frame a word, the wave of a hand, hello, Dr Ishii . . . Stop thinking. Stop thinking about it . . .

To be at the controls of the *mothership*. Turn the pages of the newspaper. Drink coffee. *What was Alzheimer's first name? You can't remember?* The cartoon page. A man with a moustache, spotted tie and square shoulders stopping in front of the Déjà Vu restaurant, from which a man with a moustache, spotted tie and square shoulders is staring out at him, glass in hand. (Such recognition phenomena. The reason why you were recruited.) Suddenly, awareness. Sense the shift, the disturbance, think round it. They came to the courtyard of the library. Here's my diagnosis. I was recruited a long time ago. Let's look at the testimony, the tale, the basic facts, and work them over. Memorize. Try the sentences out in your mouth, articulate them, practise them. Slowly and surely does it. Blacks have rhythm in their bones. Hitler's job was left unfinished. The meaning of conversation. Words at the tip of your tongue, stuck there like stamps. And knowing how to shift through space. On the courtyard of the library, or through crowds. They came for me on the esplanade. Recognized me in the crowd. Read my thoughts. My skills. They recognized me. They saw me. With the sun above the rooftops crushing everything. They recognized me. They stuck their needles in me to find the mark of the witch, across the entire surface of my body to find the insensible millimetre, belonging, allegiance, in a continuum of cries. Anne Boleyn. They took me from the wood, found me out in the forest. Inquisition. Tied hook, line and sinker to the flow of my neurones into everyone's thoughts. It is my secret, underground work to let you into myself. *Given that the surface of the vagina has very few nerve endings, most operations can be performed without anaesthetic.* With the flow of endorphins, the first spasm of the absence from self, nerves giving up at last, no longer feeling, a break . . . My mother giving birth four times, they say you forget, they give you drugs to make you amnesiac, but for the pain – nothing. Just hiccups. *J'ai le hoquet, Dieu me l'a fait. Je ne l'ai plus, vive Jésus.* Drink a glass of water backwards . . .

The Mother

Water noises. Splashes. Repeated trowel, slap of steel against powdered metal mixed with water. Smell of flour and iron. Momo's making concrete. Thick dust in the sunbeams, a white dance, house shifting with the flow, beneath the sun's spin. It must be three o'clock. Nore's still not back. Must clear the table downstairs. A fly is spluttering, in autumnal weak-

ness, frail tappings on the glass, microscopic words. A mildness pushing through even the hottest time of day. A pale,
dewy mildness. On the bedside table, a line of tiny bubbles
round the vase looks like aphids on stalks. Light rolls its
ensuing circles amid the roses, petals as fine as the backs of
your hands in woven translucency. The spiralling light is cut
clear at each side. A bee clings on, then dives. It dives and
engulfs itself head first in the first of the roses, cunningly luring it, unhesitatingly swamping it with pollen. A bouquet
placed on the meniscus. The upper thickness of water, peeling off as though beneath the feet of water boatmen rowing
downstream. Roses sliced finely into shavings, from a single
heart of roseate stucco, edges retaining the curve of the chis-
el. Winter rises up the stalk straws, the heads open. Momo
even thought of that, the company of roses at nap time, the
company of roses when half asleep, by the bed there, roses
through which time flows, in the silence of roses, in the waiting . . . The needle-eye centre gives way with its last petals . . .
Opening, mingling, withering, drifting . . . Releasing their
pollen into the sun-kissed dust . . . *flop*. When Nore comes
home, the house will unbend and new rooms will appear.
Follow the corridors, staircases and call. Unmade beds.
Nobody there. Roses punctuating absence. The tick tock tick
cluttering out in coloured time, coloured time cluttering out
its roses, in tea roses of autumn, as planned. The still-green
rose, head drinking in information with its water and becoming the rose it's expected to be, delicate, upright and solid.
The one you expect: not an orchid, not a dahlia, not a
cauliflower's ears, not a rabbit's or a human's hand, but a
rose, decidedly so, obediently slipping all up its flowering
ascension, curling around the spiral of its opening head. In its
rose silence, where time is displaced, there's nobody. The
hand that strokes it makes its water tremble slightly. The
meniscus looks as if it had been dropped on the water, water
looping up the sides of the vase, puckered and sucked up by
its own shape, neither oil nor milk, but water . . . wrinkles

beneath movements. The dust slowly unwinds, thus appearing in the sunbeams stretched from windows, and the house
breathes: a curtain's raised, a curtain's gently dropped. The
fly and its buzzing. Momo in full sunlight assembling his
planks. About to tip in the new patio's cement. In autumn's
garden, the tea rosebuds are still strong in the earth, waiting
to become roses, to break free, born in houses, naked elsewhere, belonging to vases, waiting for a life of vases and
houses, their cries . . .

Nore

The sea should be seen as fully as possible, filling the brain
like a sponge. Record the moment, like a seascape. Describe it
to myself, say it to myself, later. This sea. My heart swelling
with a feeling of endlessness. Big heart. Or else, a return every
day, back to the sea from a great distance, not to be afraid, not
believing all that's been said. Like a job. It's cooler in the car.
Make your mind up time, it's two thirty and you're still in a
dream. In a previous existence maybe I was a white shark and
a dolphin split open my chest with a single blow of its bill,
they always win, by bursting open their livers. Definitely a
violent death, something charging me. Describe the sea.
Heart swelling. To and fro, pompom. Turn on the ignition for
some heat. Key in. What's that in the rear-view mirror? A
surfer changing at the far end of the car park. Clumps of
gorse, sod it. Still dreaming. It's not so nice now the mountains have gone. My highlights got blonder this summer.
Only this spot on the edge of my nose, the sun's good for the
skin. How ever do ugly girls cope? Mum's going to nag at me
for moving the rear-view mirror again. The tips of the mountains there through the haze, a line separating them from the
sky. Describe the sea with a swelling heart. Ignition off.
Motor off. When you die, maybe it's as easy as that. Or maybe
we go out as slowly as we arrive, slipping into limbo, what
we were gradually dissolving . . . You're not going to tell me

eggs can think. So far as I know, Jeanne had an abortion when she was about my age. Through the bedroom door, I was five, supposed to be asleep, Jeanne crying with Anne and then talking about a child who wasn't me . . .

I've never seen anything in these waters. Never seen a caudal fin raised through the swell, an axe-shaped tail, a whale's spray, the schools of sperm whales passing Patagonia in Jeanne's tales. The sea's evaporating, the sky heating up. High tide at three o'clock . . . High tide . . . Pollution and drift nets. The bottles of Leche Pascual, Genio and Suplín we played with on the beach. The south–north currents circling around the Bay of Biscay. And just on the surface of the water, stick out your tongue, it's fresh, condensation above the salt, a fine layer of dissolved mist laid on the sea . . . From the corner of your eye, you can see that the mountains haven't completely gone . . . Look sideways at a star to see it better, or ghosts, a ghost seen straight on vanishes at once. Stare at a given point in space, just beside the place where you thought you saw them, and there they are again . . . On the other side of our pupils where we weren't looking, weren't thinking. A constellation. A stain on the roughcast. The line of mountains dissolving in the mist under a white sky, beside a white lighthouse. A violet line, barely a line. The sky swallowed by the sea. The sea that's so huge it makes us sad. *On m'appelle Éléonore Johnson.* Éléonore Johnson. Maybe Daddy left because we're all so sad. I could have been called Véronique, or Christelle, or Samantha. My name. My name . . .

05 59 33 31 19, maybe I'll wear my blue dress with crossed shoulder straps, unless it's too cold, in which case skin-tight jeans and the little white top . . .

Maybe I've got a few neurones missing since Anne made me sniff ether when I was little. Maybe that's why I have so few memories. Iceland, the waterfall and pooh-pooh. Memory and zigzags. What I carry around all the time above my head, an aura, a halo. A bubble over my head like a comic-strip character. When we were little with Anne, I mean when I was little, we played at emptying our heads, white, zero, nothing. Tilt. Ignition. Then you think you're thinking nothing. You think about what thinking nothing means and then you also remember not to think, you think about the effort. You think that not thinking is precisely that: a white, cottony vagueness spent remembering not to think. The day Daddy told me I was the most attractive woman he knew. At the Copacabana, with him in Gibraltar, the summer when I was fifteen. The turbines whistling and clacking, strong wind, light wind. The horizon ragged and hazy, like stars when slow and wheels when fast. Because we should have taken Daddy seriously when he talked about moving there, doing that job, he already used to make kites for the beach and Jeanne took him for a theme park Mickey Mouse. *The future's in the wind*, he made up the slogan . . .

The wind blew up
The wind blew down . . .

Surfers are tugging the swell along behind them. Parallel crests rolling forwards, in series of sevens, seven big waves, then seven small ones, you can count them, it never fails, Bluebeard's seven wives, turn your tongue seven times in your mouth, the exact seven seconds that a newborn baby wears an ancestor's face. And the seven prayers Granny repeated seven times on the seventh day of the month so she would go to heaven. Daddy listening to 'Stairway to Heaven' and also *Heaven is a place where nothing nothing ever happens* . . .

Of the three, I'm the one who speaks it the least well. Daddy left when I was three. Gibraltar where, when I was little, I saw monkeys scratching their arses. I should be a photographer. You can see, what? The shape of the coastland I know by heart, vanishing violet mountains, the lighthouse, holiday camp, beach, half-houses fallen from the cliffs and smashing into pieces, pink strata, blue strata, vertical cracks and horizontal cracks and slabs lined up on the beach. The film being rewound: one by one the blocks moving back into place, shifting back to where they came from, fluttering upwards with comic lightness – the jigsaw of the cliff and houses gradually being put back together. The bricks of the old castle on the floor and, crash! A baby's game, the square brick in the round hole, the triangle in the triangle, *what's done is done*, as Granny used to say . . .

It's impossible to watch the sea and remember it, recall its mobility – or else remember the sea like a face, in frozen images, like seeing ghosts in photos you move about. White lines rolling onwards, in the back-to-front film, at the beginning of time, rolled up again like a rug, perhaps we would see the sea recede, empty itself over the horizon, run down the back of the sky from where, what would happen? Lava, flowing back towards gases, fire – gone, the first dinosaur's wagging tail, after the arrival of the first fish, the first seaweed – the vaporized earth falling apart, flowing back to the primordial explosion, the big bang . . . Parallel lines advancing, unsticking the net from the foam . . . Thank God you can remember the sound of the sea; like you can remember voices in sequences. What's hard is to make it last, to remember the sea for a long time. You have to imagine the waves. Tell yourself that they're rising, dipping, rolling, then closing, there, you can see them, blue and green, grey and black, stretched in the coils on the preceding wave, below the froth as it drifts aside and vanishes . . . Describe the sea with a swelling heart, fit to burst, as though looking for air, there's so much more sea still to be described, endlessly . . .

I'll call this Nicolas character this evening, then we'll see. Maybe the cinema. The cinema to start with. In the brain fully like a sponge. Sod this carburettor. We're off . . .

Anne

Not much washing-up, she ate a spring roll – low in lipids, low in calories – which she bought at the takeaway on Rue

73

des Archives, and drank a Diet Coke, smoked two cigarettes, read the paper, a new data storage system has been invented, incredible capacity and new, ultra-efficient circuits with the concept of hazy logic: yes/no/maybe – a catalogue of doubt, a combinatorics of *I'm not sure. Hang on a moment*, says the modern computer, *I'm weighing things up, I'm on my way, watch out, anything is possible, I'm not sure about anything at all, I'm telling you what I think, but who knows?* She drops the paper to the floor, where it scatters, amazing how much space a scattered paper occupies, three times its normal surface area, page one, two, three, that's where we got to, I must think through this kind of idea, go to the lab, yes, no, maybe, is it possible, is it possible she didn't hear the phone ring, a fleeting weariness, mind wondering if Laurent called, to apologize of course, for this morning, standing this morning, stood up, but it was the right time and place, as arranged, she didn't get it wrong, then they just had to cross the Seine to go to work, between his woman's bed and place of work, yes, no, she didn't get it wrong, time and place . . . She picks up the paper or else . . . Is it possible that he waited somewhere else, cursing at her absence, because she was late, then he'd be furious and wouldn't phone, stood up there, circuits blocked, or – no, he could have called her on her mobile, he was the reason why she got one, he could have called, she drops the paper . . .

Phone number off by heart, at the tips of her fingers, she'll hang up if it's his secretary . . .

It rings in intergalactic space, not even an answering machine. Like he doesn't exist, that his place of work doesn't exist – in the MIR station, the Russian cosmonaut who's been orbiting for the past 107 years, drinking his lukewarm tea from his bubble pack, finding anything and everything a good laugh, he sticks his lips on to the kiss of the lukewarm water, on the swollen sides of the shrinking bubble, as it goes down his oesophagus because of the combined action of sucking and swallowing, thus creating a depressurization of the surface of the liquid. The tea-time cosmonaut glances at the blue planet, he could drink up its oceans, spinning on and on and righting himself, only the earth to look at, or the starry darkness, with neither top nor tail, the big black dragon spitting out flames for nobody . . . Meetings spread out too much, like Pyrenean bears, only seven of them left over a surface area as big as . . . chances of copulating becoming infinitesimal – the day when the inhabitants of the other end of the universe decide to broadcast a random message into the starry darkness it will be either too early or too late, and we'll pass each other in pathetic indifference, without feeling a thing – and the cosmonaut for the past 107 years, waiting for his time to be up, days lasting six hours, six sunsets per night, the earth spinning, boom-boom, boom-boom, the routine and measly moon at the end of the line . . . Do you get used to that? Stare listlessly through the porthole? Or else, do you watch the continents go by endlessly, without ever getting fed up with Australia's sheepish head, Europe's nose, Panama's bellybutton, Africa's skull, China's gut and the three genitalia, Tierra del Fuego, the Cape of Good Hope and Tasmania, then the oceans' blue-green eyes opening and closing, eyelids, head turning – do you get used to that? Another cigarette. It's the vacant hour, it gets to her, here, a shiver, she knows it only too well. Before the day starts again, babies arrive only at around five, with their mothers after playschool. Nothing to do but smoke, let the time pass. The early afternoon time, the clock stops in the hollow of her chest. If it could only stop for good, just for a second, if she could only breathe . . .

Most of the windows opposite are empty. Half-raised arms of a woman reading, the mass of her hair and white stain of the book; further up, a man's phoning, forehead against the pane, in that flat where the man, woman, child and nanny spend their lives on the phone, all in the same posture, looking down into the street, with their old-fashioned phone with its cord. They must be taking it in turns to relay information. A well-organized lookout flat, the air full of waves, appearing innocent, reading, living there right opposite her. Counter-surveillance. Surveillance of the counter-surveillance. Curtain. Sunrays filter in each side of it, exploding on to the wall, so white they look like a deposit of talc, three in the afternoon, in the buzzing half-light, Mum must be taking a nap, I wish I could. Lean a chair against the curtain to flatten it, that's better, no way they can see, if they can't see me, I can't see them. Report: *she has just drawn the curtain*. Infrared camera. Supersonic bug. Obey and continue. If need be, dwell in the dark. Live off spring rolls. One roll doesn't make a spring. A vocation. Don't believe what she deciphers, sort through what she hears. Be patient, wait in the right place. Wait for the recruiting agent. Decode the tiny but still detectable signs. Then start the experiments. Babies make an excellent cover. Hospitals are full of them, good recruitment centres. And so, you emerge from the coma, you've forgotten everything, and there you are, recruited. As for her, perhaps it's her particular sensitivity to waves. Panic attacks at three p.m. as a maternal heritage. Family modelled on a hail and farewell system. Perhaps, and it now seems clear, for several sources point that way, Pierre Johnson was recruited. An excellent element. Spotted when still very young. No doubt still active. She'll do what she can, but how can she contact him? Male elements presumably have more interesting missions than mere surveillance. Tom Cruise. Bruce Willis. Mum should be proud instead of being . . . proud of her son and daughter. But there's the official version. Stick to it. That pile of rotting mud tied up with seaweed and mucus is your son, your brother. Drowning is a truly classic scenario. On the beach, of course, an obvious place to recruit. You have to find, to nose out the points on the globe which are gateways, discover the bridges. Hold on to the hinge and wait. Sense the points on the globe that look like the sea: open view, fixed points in the sky or on the earth. Everything then appears clear . . .

In Paris, in the Jardin du Luxembourg, stand on the royal staircase, queens with crowns and pigeons on their heads, holding their skirts and marble children, *Si vous ne respectez pas une reine proscrite, respectez une mère malheureuse*. The esplanade beneath the statues, the octagonal pool with miniature ships, ducks, urban beach bums on green deckchairs, late tulips, early thoughts, where the lilac is wilting, the blue shade of the summer sun; further off, the Seine . . .

Position yourself in the direction of the current, choose a bridge, Pont Neuf, Pont des Arts, forget the crowd and stare at the water, the fishing lines, the clear wind, Notre-Dame, the masts, the moored boats, the gaping maw of the mouth, out to sea . . .

The Louvre courtyard for its beauty, as fitting as the sea, sit down on the coping by the pyramids, take photos for tourists with their cameras, *gracias, arigato, tak, thanks, merci*, smile, dream, welcome the world, eat an ice cream . . .

The effect of the sea, a high balcony, view over the rooftops, the mountains of Paris, grey zinc and grey slate, with clear waves on the horizon, stand still beneath the wings of the planes, keep the city horizontal . . .

The lighthouse of the Eiffel Tower, a beam sweeping over the city, a landing strip for night planes, electric circuit . . .

Orly, connections at the end of the runway, meetings on the jetty, emblematic recruitment points . . .

When you look at bridges, they should be seen not as points of departure or arrival, but rather as nerve centres in the web, incandescent meeting points, the ones that form constellations in the confused mass of stars, Whale, Dragon, Southern Cross; let yourself go, slide, hear the click at the moment of contact, then you're in the centre, one of the centres, one of the island universes . . .

Just a balcony, she thinks over what she knows about Paris, just a balcony, just have to close your eyes and waves break at the foot of the building, you can hear them . . .

Or else, the overhead metro, at night, the lit-up flats, a man smoking, the shifting geometry of electric cables, wire after wire, diamonds in a floating sky, between two hand-pylons, like a game with strings you cross over and over, figures of heaven and of hell, of the level-crossing . . .

For Jeanne in Buenos Aires, choose a bench near a tree, the giant tulip tree in front of the café where she likes to go, or else look up towards a *palo borracho*, a drunken tree, and fall into its branches . . .

For Nore, choose a seaboard and stand there, at this joining place, in its scattered, tangible centre, there, just there, at the point where sea and land meet, stand in the breach and watch the contact, the abolition of the vacuum in the midst of the wave . . .

Otherwise, in any old bar, the Hawaii, the Marly, the Yoyodine, with, if possible, a prow of bay windows . . .

Of course, you could prefer the Champs Élysées, or the Empire State Building or the Golden Pavilion, places people want to see, where they gather, see Venice and die or the Strait of Gibraltar and other ends of the world, Ushuaia, the Cape of Good Hope, Hobart. The best places for a view, the finest avenues, even if you do have to stand on one leg, on the edge of the edge of the world, where everyone leans . . .

Or a churchyard, a monument, even a small one, but still with an esplanade, with plays of light and a great open sky . . .

Or else, a field in Beauce, or the pampas of course, a field with nothing at the end, with a plain, empty horizon, and at the speed of a tractor stride onwards, eyes on the rim of the world . . .

In such places, you can breathe in the sea wind . . .

Sea-equivalents: the sea which stores, combines, mixes and remixes, calms down and starts up again, blue brains . . .

What matters is this feeling, being there at the appointed time, right at the centre, right where you should be, feet flat and back straight, you, the hollow human, arched above the small of your back and your brains balanced, dancing on its cervicals in its almost spherical skull . . .

At that moment in time, and at that point in space, you're on the wavelength, could be recruited . . .

Could plug yourself into the great worldwide brain . . .

Shifting the pages with her foot, she reads:

CAPRICORN
22 December–21 January

FEELINGS: Saturn is about to change the climate of the next three years, bringing with it passion and adventure. New romances will flourish, as demanding as ever, but sources of exaltation. In October, you will be bubbling over and in a charming frame of mind.

SOCIAL LIFE: Saturn will satisfy both your conservatism and your taste for adventure. These opposing trends will produce a creative conflict: you will surpass yourself.

She could go to the cinema, a museum, to the park, or work on her thesis, her conclusions about babies. But the snag is the sun. Money, the horoscope doesn't talk about money, she could call John, *Hi, Dad, I need money for my phone bill. – Oh, how nice to hear from you, how long has it been?* And he'd be quite right, but how to manage, on a student grant, and you can't call the rest of what she does exactly lucrative . . .

Maybe it would be easier to bear the sun outside – the Médicis fountain, maybe sit down by its edge, under the marble duo by the black basin, leaves building up as ducks slip by, *quack, quack, quack, I couldn't give a dying duck*, swift white triangles on the surface of the water, and her, Anne, sitting on the seat, sandals on the cast-iron spirals, vacantly reading, placed on the surface along with the leaves, Galatea's white breast in Acis's hand, and Polyphemus the Cyclops between the stalactites, hold on tight, and lichens on the granite . . . on the surface of the world, knowing you're there with no solution . . . The solution would be to go to the centre, that's where the link would be, the link with the rest, and not (the solution

79

Jeanne adopted) in constant travelling, nor – Nore's method – to stay at the centre of the mother-world (Mum, who's been centrifuged out to the edge of the world for ever), no, the solution, she thinks, is to concentrate, to rise . . .

This degree of intimate availability to the world, which is created by the state of being, which the state of being constitutes, wherever you are, in its centre . . . turns to atoms in the light, everywhere and nowhere, be a filter to the world, a sponge . . .

She makes the attempt, she tends towards it – like a dowser with a rod, with a pendulum, she needs something other than her brain to oscillate, that's it . . . Feel the weight, the attraction within . . . Spinal cord the prolongation of the meridian . . . Vacantly reading beside the fountain: *whatever the weather, I generally go for a walk at around five in the afternoon in the Palais Royal. I am the person who can be seen sitting alone, dreamily, on a bench. I conduct discussions with myself about politics, love, good taste or philosophy. I give myself over fully to this mental venery. I allow my mind to follow the first idea that crosses it, be it sane or insane, just as on Allée de Foy we can see the young and dissolute dogging a musty courtesan, with laughing face, sparkling eyes and retroussé nose, then leaving her for another, attacking them all and becoming attached to none. My thoughts are my trollops. If the weather is cold or too rainy, I take shelter in the Café de la Régence. I amuse myself by watching games of chess. Paris is the place in the world where this game is played best, at Rey's* . . .

Of course, there are always swimming pools, bodies in water, tiles shifting around like linen, and the waves, yells and bubbles, or else sitting on the edge, legs dangling, blue rectangle helping you breathe . . .

If it wasn't for the sun being there, that weight, the uncompromising outlines of walls, with no escape, the opposite of the sea – if it wasn't for the sun, she wouldn't have to traipse every day through this city looking for a bridge, for a watering place, the right connection – she would stay at home in a family mood . . .

One night, with Laurent, they jumped over the fence of an open-air swimming pool in the 13th arrondissement and went for a swim – an empty theatre, a forest, a park, just for them, in the gleam of the streetlights – like in the Louvre, where, for five minutes, they managed to get themselves locked in between two Etruscan centaurs, five minutes of night, hanging on the density of time, there, right there, in such stolen places, dumb with mutual amazement, in the silence, the lapping, the gleam . . .

So why didn't he marry her?

It's the awful hour of the day, before four, with the day in front of you, empty, dissolving into its minutes, getting lost between the two rooms . . .

Must concentrate . . .

J'ai fait la saison dans cette boîte crânienne
Tes pensées je les faisais miennes
T'accaparer seulement t'accaparer . . .

All songs lead to Laurent . . .

Which way to turn? The meeting place, the destination of the report, everything seemed clear just a second ago . . .

Make a report, quick, get back control of the *mothership*, joystick, goggles, dashboard, *This is Major Tom to ground control*, the runway is well lit, she goes downstairs, the street, outside, the people, she spots landmarks, a florist's sign, a bar sign, a pedestrian-crossing sign – the bright beacons of a tobacconist's, red traffic lights – turning green, it's the signal, off she goes – make a report before being disconnected, before the feeling fades, while she can still sequence it all, it seems like she can hear a language she once spoke – the ground is red and cold . . .

Keep walking, yes, streets as mnemonics and a search engine, activating cervical zones, she's been detected, she's sure, on their radar screens, they won't let her go now, she just needs to solve the transmission problems, how to organize the data and transfer them, she sometimes takes on board new sensations without being able to describe them at once – even her, the first person in the know, her ability to surf on the great worldwide brain, her exceptional empathy, her receptivity, all the things that led to her being recruited . . .

Maybe write postcards, Jeanne sends plenty – she, Anne, could click on a scene, like you keep a dream in your memory, and make mental postcards . . .

Or call her mother on her mobile . . .

Or else Laurent, no, not Laurent . . .

Or else go directly into Jeanne's brain, she just has to think of Jeanne to be able to get directly into her mind, what she's thinking about, how she's feeling, her irritating way of being sure she's doing the right thing, and it's clear that her, Anne's, contacts are distinctly determined by Jeanne's travels, plugging herself into the worldwide brain then becomes far easier, more immediate in the areas Jeanne has already opened up, because she's an intelligent researcher and a good, if unconscious, explorer, an excellent data provider. Dropping regularly into her brain, her tales, her albums, provides the basis: Jeanne in Oceania, Jeanne in the Philippines, Jeanne in the Land of the Soviets, Jeanne in Latin America, her memories act as a springboard, her postcards as refuges. It has to be said that it's easier for her to anchor herself in Jeanne's brain than in a newspaper article, and it's of course easier if the terrain's been opened up by her own travels, in which all her energy is devoted to this absolute openness of her mind as it surfs over global arcana: a particular smell, an image, a *déjà vu*, an unevenness in the surface of the ground, no matter slight they all are, Anne can absorb them, craquelure producing the slightest imbalance in a large cervical body which she's plugged into – Joan of Arc, Jeanne d'Arc, *arcanus* meaning 'secret', was quite simply another messenger, the agents have been active for a very, very, very long time . . .

And St Blandine and St Geneviève and the others whose names are forgotten, and Mary Stuart and Louise Labbé and Marie Curie and Frida Kahlo and Janet Jackson and many more, so why not Anne Johnson, working in obscurity, but the men are harder to single out . . .

Like Cherechevski, the Russian agent and memory man, who had the phenomenal memory of a circus freak – Laurent briefly had the same symptoms when he was young, after falling off his trike and on to his head he could remember all the number plates seen through the windows of the ambulance – Cherechevski pictured mental maps of his home town of Moscow in order to place, rank and organize the information he was absorbing: along the streets, along the numbered façades, under the shop signs, the crossroads, in the stores and wastelands, he built up his data bank. A neurobiologist called Luria carried out experiments on him – a little bit like she does with babies – he read to him long and illogical series of numbers (note that Cherechevski took just as long to memorize 1 2 3 4 5 6 as a random series), or else meaningless series of words (or else meaningful ones: *All happy families are alike but an unhappy family is unhappy in its own fashion*), endless lists, *rubber – flower – mirror*, for afternoons on end. And Cherechevski recited them, forwards, backwards, skipping every other word, or two words out of three, carrying out the gymnastics Luria asked of him. He could reel off a list from ten years back as easily as one learned the day before yesterday. Pleasant exercises, Anne supposes, which must have got them both laughing, unless the routine finally set in . . .

The best ways to *testify* are still to be invented. Prophecy, martyrdom and murder have shown their limitations. One day, when Cherechevski couldn't remember the word 'pencil', the Russian agent went back down his mental pathways and found it where he had left it, leaning against a fence. *They're doing building work on Gorki Street*, he explained to Luria, *and just as I was passing by the sun went in and I mistook a wooden stake for a pencil*. Anne also sees herself as working in obscurity. Keeping her ears and eyes open, using mnemonic techniques, going round town, spotting the cracks in space-time. Mental postcards to send by force of thought alone, the same energy which detects the entrance to the right network. Training, exercises, vigilance, which make a good agent of you . . .

To plug into the great worldwide brain, which rotates around the planet like a second atmosphere, everything having been planned from A to Z and open to decoding at some of the world's time-places, in certain conditions in which Anne excels, concentration and openness, aptitudes explaining why she was recruited . . .

The canyon of the street sliced exactly in half along a line level with the left pavement, with the sun in its axis: black to the left, white to the right. At an incredible height above the ground, the sky is blue, dotted with the zinc of rooftops. Above all, it's the angles which reveal, which signify a closing-off beyond the centre of the world . . .

Before, they used to use messenger pigeons, but it was hard for them to cross the oceans. The same problem with the post. How many engagements have been crassly broken off because of a late letter, a letter from Acis arriving in scraps to the shit-smeared hands of Galatea as she changes little Polyphemus's nappies? And few, so few telepaths, that's the problem – the advantage of no longer having to set down a text or organize an image – it's there in your brain and off they go, garnering the information . . .

J'ai fait la saison dans cette boîte crânienne
Tes pensées je les faisais miennes . . .

Can't get that tune out of her mind, a signal meant for her. A data sample. By force of will, the paralytic making the arrow move across the screen. And the blind man sees. Electrodes activating the optic nerve activating the cortex. Vision from

84

left to right. Vision from right to left. How does a Cyclops see? In the centre of its brain? A single optic nerve? And also, *if a person born blind has learned to distinguish by touch between a sphere and a cube, will he or she recognize them visually if sight is restored?* To this classic problem posed by Molineux, which is now known as Molineux's Question, the correct answer is: the question should never have been asked. In our present state of knowledge, that is to say, in the relatively advanced state (compared to Molineux's) of our knowledge, a person born blind will never really see anything. He will see colours, lines, a varied muddle of optical stimuli, but no relief, no way of organizing them. His brain will be incapable of decoding what his eyes are capturing and his nerves transmitting. To see, you must have already seen. Of the two case studies: 1) committed suicide; 2) committed suicide. Because the promised light was incomprehensible . . .

The human brain weighs in at 1.4 kilos, it is made up of 20,000 to 30,000 million neurones and about 10,000 times more synapses linking them together . . .

Milling data . . .

Gathering and organizing documents . . .

Specifications, estimations, inspections . . .

Sometimes, on a café terrace, a clear connection, a woman wearing a particular dress saying some particular thing to a particular man, and Anne recognizes them. They sit down at the appointed time in the appointed place. At the appointed instant, she turns to him and says the expected thing, which Anne already knew, Anne eavesdropping on them, as discreetly as she can. A perfectly paced gust of wind raises the bottom edge of the man's jacket, just as it was written. A lock of hair, lifted by the woman's swift finger, enters into the dance, as she slides it, as appointed, behind her ear and reveals what Anne already knew, a slightly gap-toothed smile . . . and he laughs, places two fingers on her hips and pulls her towards him, yes, it all happens just as Anne

remembers, a recollection which this scene is re-creating . . .
She could tell them what will happen next, the inevitable
words which will be pronounced. She hears and sees, there,
he's taken his fingers away, she holds them back for a second,
on her waist, in the small of her back, she plays at guiding
their kisses, only Anne knows that, they get up without fin-
ishing their drinks, quickly, laughing, the perfect sequencing
of *déjà vu* choreography . . .

That's all that's left, the sensation of memory, the activated
frontal cortex . . . A region in the brain, a lump weighing 1.4
kilos as if it was being squeezed . . . A caress . . . A contracting
muscle, palpitating, relaxing . . . Her brain's particularly
unusual, receptive, tactile and exhausting. She can spot the
repetitions, the games, scenes and signs. That's why they
recruited her, she can tell the difference between what's real
and what's false . . .

Nore

A bubble above your head like a comic-strip character.
Drinking a milk shake behind a bay window. Found a parking space just in front of Lopez's. A divine vanilla milk shake.
A few grannies with mauve hair. Far from the Houle with its
loud music and wearisome, good-looking surfers. So. All set
apparently. So . . .

If Sardanapalus is considered to be the paragon of romanticism
comma *his death would indeed have plunged a large number of his
admirers into affliction, metaphorically speaking, with reference to
the painting by Delacroix (1798–1863, 3.48 x 2.7m) whose bust,
borne up by his admirers, can be seen in the Jardin du Luxembourg
in Paris. Firstly, we will* (shall?) *attempt to show that* (that
what?) *that Delacroix painted this picture in order to declare to
the entire world that romanticism was not dead. Secondly, we shall*
(are going to?) *go about showing that it was only his detractors
who saw the death of romanticism in the work. Finally, we are*

going to examine what this nineteenth-century canvas has to say to us today . . .

Vanilla and milk? Éléonore Johnson, talented, a quick worker, but lacking in concentration, could do better. It will soon be time to . . . At Mum and Momo's place . . .

The Lopez tearooms look out across the waves, the lower town and the casino. A large bay window over the sea. Mirrors, gilding, pale green tablecloths covered with embossed paper, a chandelier of dull crystal. To the left, the Palais Hotel. To the right, the Bellevue Casino. In the middle, the municipal casino, known simply as the Casino. At a weekday tea time, it fills up slowly. She stretches her legs, pumps up the dregs of her milk shake through her straw without making a sound, or not much. To the left, to the right, to the centre. Hotel, casino, casino. And the sea viewed from above, large white oval bodies crossing the beach. Then giving up. And coming back. Changing, subtly altering their trajectories. Deforming the veil of white froth. Then giving up. And coming back. Their heads, their oval shoulders, the bulk of their white bodies stopping at their hips, where the human part of a mermaid ceases. Then changing their minds once more, deciding not to come out, to separate themselves. Reimmersing themselves under the foam. The sea viewed from above. A wave study. She releases the tension in her pelvis and leans back into the pale green upholstered chair. Sit back and relax, as Daddy used to say when imitating Mum, an air hostess's voice in a family minibus. This should be described: the sea viewed from above. To Jeanne perhaps, buy some postcards of here and of the region. Remind her where she's from. The Bellevue Casino, the Casino. A panoramic view. *Dear Jeanne, have you ever looked at the sea from Lopez's tearooms?* A supple electrocardiogram beneath the sand. The supple, beating heart of the sea. A raised, breathing ribcage. The Palais Hotel to the left, the Bellevue Casino to the right. The sea when viewed from above. The sparkling afternoon sun. Short-sightedness, perhaps. Can we know how others see? The curves of the sea's leash. If things work out with Nicolas. 05 59 33 31 19. She'll call him when she gets back . . .

She pulls out *Elle* from her bag. *Mention poésie, des robes comme des nœuds et des tenue façon millefeuille, Watanabe décline sa mode intelligente et romantique dans des couleurs de fards.* Mirrors, gilding, pale green tablecloths, a chandelier of dull crystal. A slight weariness around the temples, folded back like a wing. A woman in the bay window, leaning on the railings by the sea, her hairdo slipping away in the wind, a buggy beside her. The motionless gulls hover above, lying on the air, the baby can't be seen. She strokes the embossed paper covering the tablecloth, and watches herself as she does so: her hand, pretty nails, Granny's ring. She raises a finger, orders a *millefeuille* and some tea, then gets out her purse. She sees herself making these inevitable gestures, as inevitable as the bent neck of the woman outside, the precise undulation of the skirt in the wind, the bend, there, now, the gulls together, and the muffled impact of the plate placed on the green tablecloth, and the way she, Nore, sticks her spoon into her cake, which capsizes, the taste, the icing sugar, and the sunbeam, exploding in the middle of the bay window: dust, sparkles, stars of iodine and spray, exuding an entire theory of bodies in the tearoom with its pale green tablecloths and blotchy mirrors . . . While the waitress, in a green cotton apron, gives her the change, blinking at the outside world in atoms . . . A slight fatigue, definitely, hypnosis from the waves, which have made this moment inevitable for several seconds now: me, here in the tearoom, a little apart from the world, flicking through a magazine and eating a *millefeuille*, in the already cold sunshine of early autumn, not wanting to alter my time or place. These thoughts are inevitable, as inevitable as Nore's giggling as she watches herself laughing and thinking, and as inevitable as the rhythm at which the waitress placed the change on the tablecloth, *dix, cinq, deux* . . .

Then a sudden detachment. The world becomes new again,

unpremeditated gestures are made, an unrecognized cloud passes by. The sea unwinds, the sky stretches, the town opens up, the spell has been broken . . .

Time is flowing once more. The sort of time you don't think about. Time that beats in your veins, that you breathe in, that lifts up the sea, and not the gluons of recollection. She sips at her tea without saying to herself that she's already drunk it before, in a previous existence, or in the dream which left her with its taste in her mouth, which has left this hollow inside her ready to be filled by the taste, by the pale green table-cloths, by the Palais Hotel to the left and the Bellevue Casino to the right. She drinks without saying to herself that she's already lived out this scene, without building up a fantasy – walking out while counting her steps, soles flat on the floor so as to wake up time even more – that inevitably a high-speed truck coming down from the cliff will crush her breast. She drinks her tea without reading her destiny in it. She looks at the unique, renewed sea. The young woman with the buggy has gone. Everything's a-hum, the service is changing, green aprons pass from hand to hand, the till rings . . .

CAPRICORNE
22 décembre–21 janvier

SENTIMENTS: Saturne s'apprête à changer le climat des trois prochaines années. Dans ses bagages, passion et aventure. De nouvelles histoires romantiques fleuriront, exigeantes comme toujours, mais porteuses d'exaltation. En octobre vous pétillerez d'esprit, votre humeur sera charmante.

VIE SOCIALE: Saturne confortera à la fois votre conservatisme et votre goût du risque. Ces deux tendances opposées produiront un conflit créatif: vous vous dépasserez.

One of Daddy's stories, from the days when he used to surf. A conscript who was doing his national service relayed a curious weather forecast by semaphore: a cloud if it was fine, rain if it was sunny, a heat wave if it was mild; or else, a cloud if it was cloudy and rain if it was raining. But always illogically, without any obvious match with reality. And so – she mentally explains to the imaginary person sitting at the other side of the table – the difference between the weather as it really was and as it had been forecast became so immense that the town council ordered an inquiry. It revealed that, every day, the soldier was recycling the weather forecast of thirty years before, from the old war archives . . .

Her conversation partner has moved to behind the bay window. He's tall and patient. A bit like Arnold . . .

From here, she often expects to see what they've all seen. Watch it crumble, just once, as Anne, Jeanne, Mum and Daddy did, one Sunday afternoon in 1976, long before she was born, in the days that exist and yet don't exist. To see the cliff fall. You should have seen Anne's face, Jeanne's face, Mum's astonished stare. You should have heard the silence. And Chocolate (their dog), you should have seen his face. Apparently, she turns mentally towards her conversation partner, who's now leaning against the till, apparently everything freezes, like before a cyclone. Space builds up its strength. The wind falls. The sea contracts. The sun stands still. The shadow of the lighthouse stiffens. The Palais Hotel and Bellevue Casino each fold up along their sides. A cormorant hastens towards its rock, flap flap flapping with its diver's wings. The dog bounds after the stick, you have time to see the underside of its paws, it's as if it will never fall back to earth again, that the cormorant is engraved into the sky, while my mother's hair was stretching out strand by strand like a ghost. A drawing of a dog, my mother, a bird, my sisters and my father, whose face turns, brightly lit by the cliff, the white blotch of my father's face suspended in reflection on the block which has fallen, what remains of an old garden splits straight in half, a chalk line is drawn between the grass on one side and the grass on the other, the cliff releases its block. You can see the sand on the beach surge up, only then do you hear the crack, the whiplash, followed by a boom. A large white patch stands out new and apparently steaming on the cliff face and, lower down, already attacked by the waves, a piece of garden in three cubes, a tamarind fell down vertically amid a mess of hydrangeas . . .

Then time starts again, like a Super-8 film which has jumped a few seconds, the shuddering of an over-bright light, my mother grabbing my sisters' hands, my father yelling, the dog barking. Look – the person leans over – the patch is still there, it's darkened a bit since then, but you can still see the difference, and look, down on the beach, the three cubes, the big one, the medium one and the small one, *Un deux trois, nous irons au bois*, the tamarind died long ago, and now every equinox the sea takes away a little more rock from the three new outcrops. And there, higher up, towards the lighthouse, the wallpaper of a gutted villa – gutted isn't the word – sliced, more like, severed in half along the stairwell. When I was little, one of the windows was still intact. A blue bedroom, a green bedroom, a pink bedroom, a hanging wash-hand basin, a brown fireplace, a sink against a wall, white tiles, skirting boards with no floor. The bathtub must have been washed away. Jacob and Delafon out boating. The life of the villa with its coloured squares, westward ho across the waves, with a single wall still upright. I would certainly have been scared if I'd been there, the smallest one, just imagine it. Like in Iceland in front of that dark waterfall, when I shat myself. I have no memories of before I was two or two and a half. Arnold says that infants don't speak and so have no memories. That nothing exists apart from what is thought, in other words what is spoken. Jeanne's departure: the memory of an empty room. By the words 'she's gone' understand 'she's dead'? Violent terror, like dark water, the fear of falling into the cataract. Then we moved house. And Daddy left. Or was that before? Then we started living with Momo . . .

The Mother

ESTERENZUBI
50 years together

'Work is health', this is particularly true for Argixu née Laborde and Peyo Arditeïa, who were married on 4 October 1950 and have just celebrated their golden wedding anniversary. This couple of pensioners, who lived for many years on the Ur-Erreka farm, brought up a clutch of eleven children, one of whom tragically died young in an accident.

As exemplary workers, Argixu and Peyo set up a family business dealing in the door-to-door selling of heavy farming machinery, while working many hours both day and night, and now they can both make the most of their thirty-four grandchildren and six great-grandchildren in the villa Ongui-Etorri, which they built with the sweat of their brows and where they have lived since 1976. Their anniversary celebrations began with a blessing, given by Father Urnxixa, and were enlivened by the local vocal group Bat Bi Iru, with Maïder Aramburu on the music, then three of the honoured couple's great-grandchildren gave readings and made speeches. After the aperitif, the children, grandchildren and great-grandchildren gathered around father and mother, aïtaxi and amaxi, for a slap-up meal – what a delicious day for the entire family!

We should like to address our warmest congratulations to Argixu and Peyo with our hopes that they will remain as spruce and healthy for many years to come.

You can see Maïder in the party photo. Looking suitably posh. The idea of having to dress up and going there, all that way in the heat (it was still so hot last Sunday). But it was nice of them to invite us, especially Momo. For people who don't know him (especially the children) it's true, he can look a bit . . . I must call Maïder. She has her mother, father and all her children. It was her little brother who died, I remember. On the way home from school, we were laughing on the road, beneath the trees, and whistling. Maïder could whistle extremely well. On the road that led to the farm, in the broad avenue of plane trees, with summer leaves as big as three hands. A neighbour came up to us and said, 'Take that expression off your face, Maïder. Misfortune has struck your home.' The little boy had drowned in a barrel. What was his name again? And the two old people. Fifty years of marriage. You see, it is possible. But all the same, eleven children. And what about desire?

It was nice of Momo to bring me the paper. Shall I ask for some coffee? Ten past five. We must leave in half an hour . . .

BASSUSSARRY
The anti-golf-course committee
attracts support

I mean, are my daughters all right? In that respect? You can't ask them . . .

Jeanne Anne Éléonore . . .

Walking on three legs like a limping dog . . .

Clip clop clip, clip clop clip, clip clop clip . . .

A big beast with three heads and a single cloven sex . . .

Argixu and Peyo, Maïder's parents, him with his beret, her with her hands crossed on her lap. Eleven children. One hell of a womb . . .

Or else, just desire, that kind of irritation, the need to rub, to fight . . .

Or imbalance, the feeling of being off-centre, looking for a leaning post . . .

93

Or electricity in your legs, prickling, no, the socket there, grasp it, laughter in your throat . . .

Or else a languor, softening, the bed, half asleep . . .

Or just a localized burning, like tongs between your legs . . .

Or a need, a craving crying out to be filled, so empty, so void, available, crying out . . .

La maman des poissons elle est bien gentille
Elle a l'œil tout rond
Et moi je l'aime bien avec du citron . . .

Or else awful, a full house, audience besotted, the desire to refuse yourself . . .

Or simply rest, to be reassured, comforted, nothing to do with it . . .

Or just desire for skin . . .

I was beautiful, could have done anything, beautiful like Nore is beautiful . . .

Si la photo est bonne qu'on m'amène ce jeune ho-o-mme . . .

You feel better when the light starts to fade . . .

When you've got something to do, six o'clock, the tango lesson . . .

Another fifteen minutes under the duvet, time's flying now, for sure, off like an old temperamental machine, I'll never understand it, what to do, with the sludge of early afternoons?

Si la photo est bo-o-nne . . .

When John left, when I left John, six months without touching a man, I didn't recognize myself, I could have pounced on the plumber, the postman . . .

And the one in that seedy rum bar, the Cargo, on a night of panic . . .

Desire or panic . . .

So alone, at the bottom of an oubliette, the ground falling from beneath me . . .

Une femme de pierre, une ombre, une statue mortuaire . . .

Telling me I had beautiful eyes, that's what they tell ugly women, as for me . . .

I remember a film, a man on an island . . .

(Eleven deliveries, she must have done Pyrenean perineum exercises . . .)

A man on an island . . .

In love with a shadow, an image, dancing with it . . .

The woman was a machine, a hologram set off by the waves . . .

She was dancing alone, her arms open . . .

Years back, on that island, white evening gown and tuxedo . . .

All that was left was her image . . .

Some people playing tennis, you could hear the bouncing balls . . .

Cameras coming on, silently recording . . .

And the inimitable images of the hologram weighing more heavily than vanished bodies . . .

On the island . . .

Like Marienbad, my God, how long ago . . .

At the Bellevue Casino in the days when it was a cinema . . .

When bus loads of Spaniards used to come to see *The Last Tango in Paris* . . .

Total solitude among the shadows and people were dying of some terrible skin disease, it was falling away in strips, life being filmed through their pores, till they turned into holograms . . .

ARNAGA
The Rostand house auctioned off

I can hear the swell . . .

CAN YOU HEAR THE SEA?

He must be on the patio, can't hear me . . .

You always have to yell in this house, it's so big, his pride and joy . . .

Time redistributed by turning back strong tides, under the effect of the currents, undersea machinery . . .

Thank God the light's fading, the day is leaving the black pit of afternoons and it will last as long as life does. Waterlot couldn't do anything about it. What could he have done . . .?

The sea must be strong, we could go by and look at it from the sea wall . . .

Get up, get dressed . . .

Above all, avoid flashbacks, backlashes, relay batons . . .

Jeanne

The right place to live. The balcony, potted lemon trees and the *Boca* on the horizon. The mouth of the *riachuelo* biting into the Rio, wanting to be as big as it is. A balcony, a huge airy flat, and the sea not far away. A country house just an hour and a half's drive, traffic jams included. Stretch out in the sun, the marvel of having a body. Fissured muscles beneath your skin, sun, sleep gradually slipping away, out of your body, dreams and paradoxes, nocturnal cramps sloughed on to the floor like dead skin. Shoulders crack. Shiver down the back, chest out, stretch till the vertebrae separate – a past as a dancer that comes back to her, lost among shared memories floating over the city, evaporating at once . . . She's so looking forward to this evening, at the Tigre. When she was little, she didn't imagine a country house would be like that. In fields of cinnamon, between the marshy arms of the river, picking her own mangoes. And the incredible birds of this landscape without meadows, or cows, or hedges, or hares. As though barely sketched in. Barely allowed to exist by the green waters, barely emerging from between the canals full of eels big enough to devour hens . . . It's already extremely hot on the balcony. The city steams in the sunlight. This pawpaw is good – when you know how to choose them, very fresh, they don't have that smack of vomit which pawpaws have once they've been carted over to France. The heat haze rises over the Boca. The din of traffic is dissolving the noises of the night. Everything is real, full of morning, luminous and moving. Droplets of sperm are dripping sporadically between her thighs – stand up, put on some panties – sit down again on the balcony with your pawpaw, tea and *tostadas*, sit down again and think:

1) all this hasn't been stolen (the balcony, view, lovely flat)

2) this time, maybe she's pregnant

3) she should describe her dream, or dreams, to Dr Welldon

4) this pawpaw is good, it doesn't have that smack of vomit which pawpaws have once they've been carted over to France

5) once and for all, she should remember not to get distracted, to recover her dream in its entirety, with all its details, no matter how irrelevant they may seem, something more than the sirens and the *donde donde estan nuestros padres*.

A large sunlit square . . .

After the session this evening, she'll join Diego at the quay for the seven o'clock boat, can't wait . . .

Those domes . . .

A large sunlit square . . .

The right place to live: a) a European capital with Europe at the other side of the world; b) water, a river, canals, the sea; c) the countryside just an hour and a half's drive away, traffic jams included, an easy decision to make . . .

The shape of her dreams. If it's true that the cinema has altered how we dream, their structure and plot lines – she often dreams she's in front of a screen showing a film which she can get inside, like *Last Action Hero*, did people have dreams like that in the old days? In moving pictures, you show yourself to yourself without even thinking . . .

Especially the recurrent dream she had when she was young. A terrifying film: she can't close her eyes, it's a pursuit through the night, but then she suddenly notices that the killer is sitting beside her, she slowly gets up, slowly, in the half-light stippled by flashes from the film, she goes to the back of the cinema and up a dark staircase, which leads to an identical room with the same screen on which you can see the killer, now alone, suddenly waking up as if with a start, getting to his feet, going up the stairs . . .

She's in the film, the film has become real, she runs, terrified, now part of the horror.

That wanker Waterlot . . .

Just after Pierre's death, she fell down the stairs. *My knee hurts*, she said. *Genou*, he replied. *Mal au je-nous*.

Just as in films later on, art-house gangster movies, *The Killing of a Chinese Bookie*, to lose people tailing you take:
– a bus
– then a cab
– then another cab (jump from one to the other)
– go into a cinema
– leave three minutes later
– walk through a grocery store
– go into another cinema, sit down panting and mop your brow.

The wanker who treated the family, he must have kept Mum on his books for a good fifteen years . . .

And you didn't need to be a genius, or psychic . . .

The cinema, of course, if she'd gone into films, then that might have been the right place to live: the cinema, films, the absence of self, the black hole of the projection, John was already a buff before he went to Gibraltar, with his trips to London and Paris to see the films of the seventies . . .

Vanessa Redgrave . . .

See Redgrave and die . . .

A delicious pawpaw, scrape out the fibre from the bottom of its boat-shaped rind . . .

Then, in the street, you walk like Julia Roberts, swaying your endless acrobatic legs, with four joints in each at the very least, ten minutes of sequels before shrinking back to your 1.5 metres and eighty kilos, an instant of lightness, of forgetfulness, of an American accent . . .

I should have done it, gone to that film school, instead of dumping everything in Africa and God knows where . . .

Oh, she has no regrets . . .

It was nobody's fault . . .

When Diego comes home, I must . . .

No, we're meeting at the quay . . .

What's left of dreams on waking?

The coat of the tree's seed stroking your cheek, the trampled floor beneath your feet, embrace and inhale time's flow, its tempo, the passage between places . . .

The tree's seed blown against your cheek, the trampled floor shooting beneath your feet, faster, slower, and breaks in time in that body you have in your dreams . . .

(Domes, height, sunny esplanade, something like density in the sunlight, like a single broad oblique beam, particles on a Pompeii-like town, dust after the disaster, the fall-out – or a compact, milky springtime full of seed . . .)

Memories of her first books, when they read *Noddy and the Bunkey*, *Five Go to Demon Rocks* or *The Caravan Family*. And they read them to Pierre – the little yellow car, the bell on his hat, and what was his fat friend called in French? *Potiron* . . . And little Nore, the late arrival, a sunny period at last . . . When she was two (or three?), they visited Iceland, one of those stupid trips in the Volkswagen . . . and she looked like him, enough to strike the whole family dumb with amazement: Pierre's reincarnation sitting quietly at the back of the minibus. *Flashback Attack on the Caravan Family* . . .

Books of twenty years back, the dream of last night . . .

Ah, the postman, I'll have to go down, or they'll steal the mail – isn't it hot for the time of year, a second Rio of steam above the river . . . yesterday, you could almost see Uruguay and Montevideo, Buenos Aires's outdated little sister, a blast from the seventies . . . Nostalgia, what an obsession. Books of twenty years back and the dream of last night, suspended images, but above all this feeling, or sensation, the acupuncture of memory, something jabbing into you . . .

I must water the plants . . .

Some new graffiti from last night:

ASESINO

Red on the white wall of the building . . .

At our last address, it was an escaped Nazi, it's as if we attract them . . .

A smell like honeysuckle in the air, or like sperm, yes, it smells like sperm . . .

When mum had her flashbacks, her mental repeaters, like from an over-full gut, she used to just sit there, but you could see it, bang in her head, features deformed, the photo of the Vietcong getting shot . . .

Or else it was like a projector in her eyes, a wave over her face, a terrible variation in the light, you had to know her to see it, the hand of the ghost grabbing her face, cheeks, nose, eyes, mouth . . .

As though something had grabbed the room by its middle, the room where she stayed most of the time in bed, something pulling it like a blanket, and her face went with it, yanked by the ghost towards its world of disaster, the room and my mother swept through the eye of the needle of a parallel world – her eyes were the point of departure, the space around my mother's eyes became distorted – like a piece of fabric, a skirt or a curtain being pulled through a ring, the bedroom puckered up around my mother's face – then she swallowed the surrounding space through her pupils, her mouth, she digested the window, the rug, the bed, the TV screen and all her collection of newspapers and piles of pillowcases, everything crinkled up to be swallowed by my possessed mother, what my mother could see, and you had to know her to see it, her son in the current, the whirlpool under the sea that sends children to another world, a piece of flotsam spinning around the Bay of Biscay – a network of oh so natural currents, high tide, low tide, with no malice aforethought – the little pool by the beach where the babies paddled and whoosh! out to sea, what to say, what to think, her son in the current, her child, my little Pierre, my little brother, lost sight of him for an instant and then for ever, him standing there in his red trunks, holding his bucket, wanting to fetch some water . . .

The sun . . .

A dazzling view around my brother, the only one born in August in a family of Capricorns, he was just three, he was a Virgo, I remember the flash of sunlight dissolving his contour, the flow of light throbbing around him, as he stood against it, he had such dark eyes, a mask-like mouth and hair aflame . . .

Thou little boy . . .

Stifling water in his lungs . . .

Alone . . .

So small . . .

Amazed . . .

Amazed he'd been left so alone . . .

In Stephen King books there's a clown, *How you'll float!* The amazement at having been fooled . . .

HOW YOU'LL FLOAT!

101

What a pain, stop it, get it out of your head, those gunshots in your head, bang, bang, coming back like a song, a saw, a dentist's drill . . .

Seven years old, old enough to look after him . . .

The tulips are drooping, how hot it is already, half past eight and someone's taken our parking space, even though it's marked *privado*. I'll have to call the cops again. And the pansies I bought because they were blue, now they're mauve, and the roses, twenty buds blossoming, at least these plants weren't a rip-off, swollen fit to bust, sap rising . . .

All alone, so small, Anne and me holding our breath as long as possible to find out if it hurt. Did he see the clown under the water? We were thirsty and hungry and the joke wasn't funny any more. With the police we searched the entire beach. Twenty times, up and down, calling for him, John slapped me because I wanted to pee. It was at the onset of winter, in autumn, that the body came back. I wasn't allowed to see him, supposing it was really him, we wondered if the fish had eaten his eyes, which seems obvious now, the rest too . . .

Anne

Testing. Testing. One two three. Just a second. I'm at the end of the tape. OK. Testing, testing. Anne Johnson, 24 October, baby number 4, name Philibert. One month, three weeks old. Mother tongue: monolingual French. Preliminary observations: the subject as presented is calm, well fed and alert. When offered, the rattle was taken at once. So, into the cubicle . . .

Give him to me. Give him to me, I said. Here we go, then.

The subject reacts well to isolation in the cubicle. Have you plugged his pacifier in? Electrodes. The subject is struggling. Pacifier in. Current on. Just a second, this isn't NASA you know, come on, leave him his rattle. The subject is calming down. No, no, numbers two and three kept their rattles too. You OK, madam? Not too off-putting, is it? You can tap on the glass a bit if you want, so he can see his mum's here. Wave your hands. He can't hear you, but he can see you. Fine. The subject is looking at its mother, and loses interest in its pacifier. Jesus, this is going to take for ever again. What? No, I told you, the rattle doesn't make any difference at all. It's the mouth we want, suck suck suck. Hang on, I'll show him, otherwise this will take for ever . . . There we go, he's spliffing away nicely . . .

He's calm . . . Where are we at now? Sixty per minute? Thirty . . . forty-five . . . that's fine. OK, I'll hit him with the tape.

Parkamarazanatalbarna? Matay? Madaraasantanplataka-mal? Kalrazanaalanatardamaladanataladachasarsanambrpla-takanatr, danlanfanatadakalalnaapapladarazandachazarlank alatrraananatanplakalatr?

Sorry? It's Pascal's Pensées in A. Entirely in A. We replaced all the vowels. By computer. Further observations: hearing the French text raised suction to ninety, no 100 per minute. OK, now I'll hit him with the Finnish. Finnish, madam, the language of Finland. But Chinese would be just as good.

Avasanjaakaapamjahaakaansanvalassamaastana. Saallaa-lakaksatamaataajapalagrayaraanaastasaasapastakastakaan. Kammaahanapalaasa, raakaadattaasahantavalmaaska *what?* jakastanhamaasan *hang, on, turn it down!* Waamaanan-panaanansada *TURN IT DOWN!*

Oh, I don't know. We've got some Turkish as well. But it's all much of a muchness. One moment. On playing the Finnish text, we obtain a suction of . . . sixty-two per minute. Nothing, all that proves is he doesn't care much for Finnish. He recognizes the phonemes of his mother tongue. Well, yes, that's all. It's the subject of my thesis. And this is my thirty-second baby. Just 100 or so left now. I love babies.

Nore

When you think about it, a cow's just as weird as a duck-billed platypus. Hard to get out of this parking space in front of Mendez's. On the Mendibure dairy truck is a dozy cow, seen from behind, with a bulging udder. *A nice bit of the udder*, as they say. For the tenth time in five minutes, Mademoiselle Éléonore Johnson checks out the effect of her new glasses in the rear-view mirror: perfect. The double-parked truck means she has to inch her way out. The car doesn't have power-assisted steering. God is it heavy. But then, she did park in the delivery space. Where the cow should be. Because if you think about cows, a cow, if you saw one for the first time, what would you make of it? A being that can move, which is, apparently, alive – extraterrestrials might start out by approaching a cow, or else a car, depending on which looked most like them, with a terrible risk of making fools of themselves – or if they landed in the middle of the Sahara, they might think the planet's empty, or in the ocean that plankton rule the world . . .

While the grey, blue-streaked sea goes by, under the blue, grey-streaked sky, and a final glance at her glasses assures her of her loveliness – *chicks with glasses have hot arses* – so back to the cow, how to see a cow as if for the first time, she should try to describe that, a head shaped like a, like a what? On the way home, she'll find a cow, before it slips her mind. Like a big box, for example, designed for chewing, shaped like an iron, *une vache qui mâche c'est beau*, chewing its cud in the mud, shaped like a hat, a cap, like a fez, yes, that's it, placed on a neck, which is itself screwed into two solid props that finish up in hooves down on the ground, ground, ground. All of which has been positioned in front of a body which extends back and 1) downwards to an udder, equipped with four nozzles, and 2) upwards to a whip-like tail, able to reach halfway along its flank and, if the neck is twisted round, its head and its eyes as a fly-swatter. The base of the tail and the top of the udder are linked by a thigh placed on a shin. When sliced in half lengthwise, the cow reveals its splendid stomach, which is divided into four: the rumen, the omasum, the abomasum and the . . . Always one missing, like Pondicherry,

Karikal, Mahé and Yanoan, except there are five of them, or like the tributaries of the Seine. Mum's education. Back to the cow. The cow *moos*. It stands tall on its withers, a bit like her, Nore (she measures herself mentally). Why four teats, feet, stomachs rather than two? And why that size rather than another? And why its slow, placid brain? Four feet, melancholically on the earth. On the road to the slaughterhouse. Ruminating away. Enough to put you off being born, coming out of a cow's vagina. To say to yourself, for the last time when you see the ground just below, a metre and a half away (how much nearer than for a baby giraffe), to say, *Oh, well, looks like I'm a calf, then*. The time needed to get that into a head of such pathetic grey matter. Judge a tree by its fruit . . . Amber at last. What's this guy waiting for, Christmas?

Like the man who had completely and utterly lost his memory. Wandering around limbo without a properly defined body, with no ancestors or descendants. Forgetting why he was there. The first time he saw a dog after coming out of hospital. A leaping ball of fur, his own dog, with pointed gleaming teeth snapping at the air and yelping – how to imagine there's a brain, a system of recognition, in such wildness? The man hid behind the person claiming to be his partner. On the road to misery. Out into the wild blue yonder as dumbly as a calf coming out of a cow. Not even remembering there was a sun. One sun, and not three, one sun rather than nothing. A sun, and the moon at night. Waking up with his head bandaged, the invisible man in a white hospital . . .

The best view. The sea breaking on to the cliffs. Six o'clock. The news, or else pop songs on the radio . . .

Everywhere I go every smile I see I know you are there . . .

While the endless sea passes beneath the endless blue grey-streaked sky and that shadow passing, as though across a face, swift sadness before evening – light from the west, the waves dark already . . .

Makes me wanna dance . . .

Local elections in Paris and phantom voters, the libido of the panda and another case of mad cow disease . . .

Bovine spongiform encephalopathy, which mankind catches as Creutzfeld-Jakob's Disease . . .

A referendum about the constitution . . .

Was the Death of Sardanapalus the Death of Romanticism? Yes, 50 per cent; no, 50 per cent.

Having to change down to second on this bend, what a drag this car . . .

Light from the west while, at the North Pole, the sun rotates like an eye around the ice, light so white that a polar bear looks yellow as it glides off to hunt seals, and while Jeanne, in her car probably, what's the time over there, is going to work, through the traffic of Buenos Aires, in the heat and plain springtime, one day I'll go over there, Jeanne really does my head in, she says, *What I miss most of all are the changing seasons . . .*

Makes me wanna dance . . .

Waking up with his head bandaged, the invisible man in a white hospital . . .

A milk shake and a *millefeuille* and Rice Krispies this morning, and still two kilos to lose . . .

Rediscovering the taste of courgettes, he didn't like courgettes and so his partner, or the person claiming to be his partner, brandishing photos of lost time as proof (is that my face, give me the mirror, these features, this nose, why these ones rather than other ones, and let me see my father, and my mother, and my grandfathers and my grandmothers – and maybe in his coma of the memory he saw ghosts around him, dead or alive, maybe the shock to his brain took away his past but replaced it with the gift of scrying, maybe he could enter into other minds and eavesdrop on their secrets), *he never used to like courgettes*, his partner declared on Discovery Channel, and so she tried them out. What was physically left of his dislikes? Those little seeds in watery green flesh, as soon as he tasted this utterly new food, he spat it out . . .

Still without words. Waking up in the world younger than a newborn baby, without even their memories of heart beats, uterine rumblings, and a voice with its first words . . .

A brand-new him in a thirty-year-old body, he didn't even miss missing himself – he didn't feel the need to smoke, even though he'd been a heavy smoker – but when it came to courgettes, no way, the ability to savour a NO!

Whoops, the right of way . . .

For instance, I'd forget to bite my nails, to snack for no reason, to have wild mood swings, or to forget important things, important for Mum, that is, who's otherwise indifference made flesh . . .

With no neuroses, a white brain, a white whale instead of a brain, when he sees the whiteness of the hospital, his first unspoken idea is that everything's white, he thinks he's going to stop thinking for good, then his vision broadens, with squares and cubes, rectangles, light, space, all organizing themselves . . . something is hurting his eyes, making him blink, turn away . . . he now has a gold ring on his retina . . . Later, he learns that it's the sun. Creatures come in and start making sounds. A word is repeated just beside his face. They are naming him. And her there, discovering that he doesn't recognize her . . .

On the road to misery. Amazement at such misery . . .

Like the duck-billed platypus described by Jeanne, when she sent me a postcard from Australia of course, I was nine or ten. *Is it a duck?* the right lobe of Jeanne's brain asked. *No*, replied the left lobe. *Is it a fish?* the left lobe asked. *No*, replied the right lobe. *Is it a beaver? An otter? No and no.* Jeanne was trying to pin down the platypus, it was there, right in front of her, there are loads of them in the rivers of Tasmania, like carp around here, or coypus, geese and lizards. But no, not one of those animals fitted what was flopping around in the stream. *God created Australia on the eighth day.* The creature in Jeanne's eyes had names she knew in two languages, but she was incapable of freeze-framing its image or of deciding if it belonged to the known world. Pulped brains. Then, a box opened, with the typical 'pop' of bubble-wrap when pinched between two fingers: two neurones linked up, a synapse along which the platypus, *l'ornithorynque*, slid, duly labelled bilingually, recognized, opening out on to no other reality than what was there, vibrantly there, before her eyes. A new branch on the tree of animals in Jeanne's forest of representations. She clearly felt a bump forming on her brain, then sinking inside, assimilated at once. Thus do boxes in brains open, those of the man who forgot everything, and sometimes my ones too (the brain reaches maturity at the age of eighteen or nineteen), for example, when Arnold took apart 'nightmare' to make a nocturnal female horse when talking about Shakespeare, or else showed how 'cinema' comes from *kine*, meaning 'motion' and 'infant' from *infans*, meaning 'not speaking'. Then, I can hear a 'pop'. A draught of air opening boxes, and sometimes just a single idea leads to an entire spring-clean (Mum every April in our childhood home. Shutters open. Windows open. A shaking of sheets and rugs. The house awash with dust, you can almost hear her cough). Arnold says: *when the idea is clear, the sentence is clear*. And yet . . .

There are images with different densities, night dreams and day dreams, memories and flashbacks, and sometimes I see places and people from way back, even from before I was born, but Arnold doesn't believe me. Showers of barely glimpsed, wordless images. They must mean something. And sometimes a complete sentence, with a visible image of itself, a sequence of mostly black letters, plus some other colours: *a* is green, *e* brown, *è* beige and *ê* ochre, *i* is yellow, *o* red and *u* blue. But Arnold doesn't believe me. Éléonore Johnson is a bit of a sad name – beige red black, red black, black red. An eighties name. And the Princess of Clèves is as blonde and as pale as her beige and yellow name. What remains of books you've read? A form, and colours, sometimes a few words, and a certain density of images, different from what you get from films, and closer to personal memories. I remember an eye operation in a book Anne lent me, a writer on his bike with a handicapped child. One eye in its socket, the other dangling at the tip of the nerve. Can a dangling eye still see? The round blob, white sphere in the surgeon's hand? The globe with its coloured patch, containing the soul, or so some say. Or can't it see without its lid? I must describe that. Or else see the world as flies, spiders, cows and platypuses do. See the world like Spiderman – *Can a normal college student cope with SUPER POWER and a SECRET IDENTITY, or must DISASTER follow?* – to climb up the cliff face, the lighthouse, through the doors and windows, stick on the glass with my suckered hands, take the baddies by surprise, spin invisible webs . . .

Makes me wanna dance, that tune stuck in my mind . . .

Or memory like a sponge, a memory superhero out to keep it all, like water, names, figures and everything on the TV. The problem then is to sort through it all . . .

The Smurfs, for example, he thought the Smurfs really existed and so he started smurfing, his wife, or his partner, had to sit up with him for hours in front of the telly, handing out truth, that yes, this no, but soon she had to give up, UFOs, fiction, God and existence all too difficult. He asked childish questions with cascades of 'why's . . .

She must have loved him terribly . . .

And their first night of love, his virginity, does that come back like riding a bike? And teaching him about money, the difference between three and 3,000 francs . . .

One, two, three, four . . . five, six, no five, and six and seven and him, what was his name? The Spaniard in that nightclub, that makes eight, but does just a blow job count? Call it seven and a half, then, and if we add the other half of Michael and the one I said no to just at the very moment when, but it does still count given the fact that we were both naked and he had a hard-on, and of course nine with Lucas, that makes nine in all, even though I thought I'd got to ten, maybe this evening with Nicolas . . .

I didn't like the way Lucas exploded, balling in my ear like a caveman, and Thomas was even worse, yelping like a skinned rabbit . . .

What can he remember now? Can he remember the first days in hospital, given that he couldn't speak? Put out a hand and touch, gauge distances, organize shapes and associate them with contact, touch and smell, taste and colour, the great messy world. As for me, I can remember an image, black lines on a white background, impossible to work out if you were supposed to look at it from the inside or the outside, which side of the contour was right, which side was the inside and which the outside of the things . . . as when you recognize words individually but the sentence makes no overall sense . . . Only at the end of the book was I able to read both the words and the pictures. It was Noddy in his car, with the Bunkey perched on the boot, in a simplified landscape of a road edged with trees. Inside and out, curves and angles: a puzzle, a seal placed on the page, which seemed so coherent to me, who was then on the outside, in the incomprehensible world . . . And my sisters, who had read it before me . . . I was more stupid and ignorant than them . . . And the colouring book, with empty spaces to fill in by number, then little by little the picture became clear, filled in here, still empty there . . . blue, orange, yellow, and you can see a giraffe . . . Then turn over – sick at the back of the minibus, that horrible taste in my mouth, Iceland, it was cold, I had blistered feet in damp trainers, I've never trusted sports shoes since. Turquoise hills . . .

shall I go back via the woods or the hills? From the top you can see the mountain, so clear this evening, maybe rain tomorrow . . . but I like the woods too, they smell so good, pines like freshly sharpened pencils . . . When it's hot, you forget how tall mountains are, the haze conceals them and mingles them in with the clouds. Like lighthouses, barely glimpsed from the sea, you forget . . .

Anne

Recover command of the *mothership*. Baby talk filling my mind. *Ja sa parla caraman la baba*. I can speak fluent baby. A quarter to eight. I could maybe catch a film, wrap myself up in the dark. Credits, then away we go. Brain on stand-by. Twenty-four images per second. At the cytological rhythm of impressions on the retina. A flow of sensations, an undetectable emptiness . . .

Retina samples in cultures, salamander retinae, with electrodes connected to amplifiers. The cells give off their potential for action in bursts, whoosh, whoosh, the sound of waves breaking on the beach. The same rhythm can be imagined in mammals. Fresh baby retinae. In profile, a nice fat brain looks like a nice fat baby asleep on its heels. Head hunched, knees bent, stomach on the floor. In Houston, between the museums and oil wells, during my course at the Texas Medical Institute . . .

They at least make no bones. *Storage of declarative memory. Epilepsy of the temporal lobes. Section of the corpus callosum.* Still so mild for an October. Mild enough to make you weep. If I was beside the sea. Red sky. Round wind and the swifts still not gone. An orgy of bugs above the rooftops. On the verge of being on the verge of relocating a memory, like a patient with an attached electrode. That sensation of being on the very edge. They stop stimulating the temporal lobe and the sensation fades. But if they start again, then that awful feeling comes back. *I'm at the corner of the street*, says the patient, *in*

South Bend, in Indiana, on the corner of Jacob Street and Washington Street. A childhood memory, from thirty years back. And that other epileptic swearing she could hear a mother calling for her little boy, *it all happened a long time ago,* and in another place in the brain, *yes, I can hear voices, it's late, it's dark, there's a party going on some place . . . some sort of itinerant circus, I've just seen huge trucks carrying animals . . .* Penfield's seminar: *Does this mean that memories are stored in the neocortex of the temporal lobe?* You can feel thoughts going on up there, not in the heart, as Aristotle thought. And then there was Cherechevski, the man who had to make an effort, not to remember, but to forget. He probably had to concentrate hard on a particular region of his hat-box of a memory and remember to forget, remember to eliminate every trace with precision. *Eraserhead.* You can perform a lobotomy quite easily with the tip of a pencil, in the kitchen or living room. You glide it behind the eye, a slight pressure, the bone is brittle at the back of the socket, you twist it a couple of times, and there you are . . . no blood, no trace, no visible scar, no more anxiety, no more mood swings, no more crises or blues, no more projects, no more concentration: a complete, pleasant, carefree distraction. A lunar person, not a lunatic. In 1949 the Nobel Prize for Medicine went to Dr Edgar Moniz, for developing the frontal lobotomy. You can feel thoughts going on up there. You can feel the cloud, the halo which says 'I' and the circulation of ideas. The internal clock which goes tick tock. Deprive female hamsters of light and they keep a perfect circadian rhythm of twenty-four hours, no more, no less. Mimosa leaves reach for the light, then fall back at night. But in a dark room our cycles go down to twenty-two hours. You walk past the terraces and see the hats, big hats on big heads, the bubbly, the frothing champagne of the parties in the heads. It mixes with them, runs and agglutinates. That's how the oblivious talk . . .

A simple experiment to test your capacities. You're alone in a street, facing some café terraces, with music, conversation, cars creeping along, shouts, laughter and pigeons. And you're able to home in on and listen to any particular conversation. Even better, in a room full of people, Laurent's thesis party for instance, you can home in on a particular person's voice and detach it from the surrounding din so as to listen to what is being said to you. And if someone, Laurent for example, calls to you at that moment, you'll hear your name ringing out alone through the noise, you'll hear it through a mere murmur . . .

That huge hat wobbling around the head, not the heart, you can feel its extensions, its branches, a bubble escapes from it, it's a bubble hat, two hats conversing around a scintillation like saliva around two copulating snails (you raised them in shoeboxes with holes punched in them, you made them run, so to speak, waddling nonchalant shells behind two horn eyes, waddling across Nore's horrified body, then they all died of boredom back in their box, making a mush of dead snails) . . .

J'ai fait la saison dans cette boîte crânienne . . .

What do you call a woman who can balance pint glasses on her head and still beat you at pool?

Luckily, you can still lose yourself in the crowd, you can even go home . . .

Beatrix Potter. Beer tricks potter . . .

L'accès de l'ascenseur est interdit à tout enfant de moins de douze ans non accompagné. En cas d'arrêt inopiné entre deux étages appuyez sur le bouton alarme. Ascenseurs Heurtebise cabine n° 75 B 489 my keys . . .

Who can I phone apart from Laurent? Alice I haven't seen for ages, or Edith Anderson, left without a forwarding address, Valérie Blin married Damien, so finished for me, Pascal Zalk, that guy at the lab, but I'm hardly going to, and Stéphanie bores me . . . anyway, I don't feel like seeing anyone, I'd have to expend so much energy again just to stay afloat . . .

What's in the fridge, on the telly, draw the curtains . . .

When I sniffed ether with Jeanne and everything went oblong, we were about ten or twelve, in the living room, Mum and John were out, we couldn't feel the floor any more, and the music, instead of chugging along with the rush of time, stagnated and yet remained dynamic, on the beat, but no longer emptying itself out, the first phrase above the second phrase above the third . . . hanging there, the track was over but its phrases were floating till the end in a harmonious canon, I still have the blue taste of ether in my mouth, and the chill in my lungs, while the music froze solid . . .

The smell of ether in the hospital reminds me every day . . .

You could see the music, its phrases piled up, an iceberg in the living room, rigid . . .

Standing on a beach with a gun in my hand
Staring at the sea, staring at the sun . . .

The entire song could be memorized at once in one single phrase in our ears . . .

And the amazement at such prodigious clarity . . .

Brains unleashed, limits obliterated, with ether everything went solid and limpid all at once, my eyes were opened, my ears dropped, for the first time, I could see . . .

Walls aren't right angles, roofs aren't placed on houses, the angles sharpen, the fullness eases itself further, the sky bends down to touch the trees and the street rises with me. Afterwards, no more need for the ether . . .

In the big seascape over the mantelpiece in the living room, the hub in the midst of the sea formed a ha ha, a hole collapsing in on itself, a line drawn in the middle of the canvas, space spiralling and emptying itself. Coriolis came through the wall, through the whirlpool of that moment of ether, and I can still see, I can still go there whenever I want, in the living room of our childhood, in front of the large painting in the house of phenomena . . .

I think about it in the evening . . .

The year the street rose up to the windows, as high as the frieze, here, below the balcony, a flood and everything became clear, as clear as before: what matter is up to, its strengths, its colours, I could trace out the lines with my finger and immobilize its products, mark them out as you record a child's growth, centimetre by centimetre on a doorpost, mark with a line the water's highest point . . .

Its invisible ascent . . .

Photos, clothes, the tomb, they remembered to efface everything – but are the marks in the living room still there? And Nore, the innocent fool, in her world where people never die, may she cry at last, may all four of us, all five of us, cry, the witnesses, the survivors . . .

Mum will have had them painted over. Momo probably lent a hand . . .

And him there, playing between us in his little red trunks, babbling out his stories, he smelt of the sea, one side of his head was a huge mollusc, his own flesh transformed by the sea into a shell of himself . . .

An incrusted red tumour, black stripes, exactly like the limpets which you know have soft pink skins beneath the shells, clinging on to the rock, burnt in the sun . . .

He smiled with half of his mouth, and we handed him his little sand moulds, the frog, the boat, the star, and he used them to build wobbly towers on the living-room carpet . . .

For Jeanne saw him too; coming out of the ether, less than a quarter of an hour had gone by and I felt like I'd been through an infinite night, impossible to fit into the course of time, everything was thinning out, yet remaining accessible in superimposed regions, you just had to find the bridges, break the codes, until the sluice gates swung shut, leaving us there, Jeanne and me, then only me, in the house, on the beach.

The Mother

One, twoa, three, foura, it is a walk, in a line, picture it, straight, one, twoa, three, foura, we're in the salida normale, Madame Johnson, look, take your time, there's a little bajida there, the musica, the musica, listen to it . . .

MENTIRA, MENTIRA, YO QUISE DECIRLE, LAS HORAS QUE PASAN YA NO VUELVEN MÀS, Y MI CARIÑO, AL TUYO ENLAZADO, ES SÓLO UN FANTASMA DES VIEJO PASADO, QUE YA NO PUEDE RESUCITAR . . .

Take your time, listen to the musica, the floor, the floor, follow me, let yourself go, floor, floor, floor, make a square without losing the line . . .

CALLÉ MI AMARGURA Y TUVE PIEDAD, SUS OJOS AZULES MUY GRANDES SE ABRIERON, MI PENA INÁUDITA PRONTO COMPRENDRIERON, Y CON UNA MUECA DE MUJER VENCIDA ME DIJO ES LA VIDA. Y NO LA VI MÁS . . .

Your back. Give me your back. You're too much in control. Give me your back. Follow me, follow me. Don't think about your feet. The musica . . . the musica . . . Y no la vì más. That's right. That's it. There. There. On the floor. The floor. Look for the floor and the sky at the same time. Straight. Si, close your eyes if that helps you. There . . .

VOLVIÓ UNA NOCHE, NUNCA LA OLVIDÓ, CON LA MIRADA TRISTE Y SIN LUZ, Y TUVE MIEDO DE AQUEL ESPECTRO QUE FUE LOCURA EN MI JUVENTUD . . .

Lighten, lighten your toes, and don't pivot on your heel, always think you're standing up straight. In the tango, the woman follows, she's totally available, but this is an active abandon, her head is still there. She's a sad thought dancing, you can feel it . . .

TEN CUIDADO, MARIPOSA, DE LOS SENTIDOS AMORES,

*NO TE CIEGUEN LOS FULGORES DE ALGUNA FALSA
PASIÓN . . .*

If I think about my feet, I get completely stuck, but if I don't,
I float around in his arms, how I like having him explain
while Momo's watching, it's the best moment in the lesson.
His hand on my back, give him my back. My hand, a little
higher up his biceps. Listen to the music, yes, pompom, pompom, the square . . .

TEN CUIDADO MARIPOSA . . .

Victor and Rafaela must be sleeping together, if they're not
then I'm the queen of England, just look at the way they're
staring into each other's eyes, and dancing together, it's as
though space was spinning around them . . .

Y TUVE MIEDO DE AQUEL ESPECTRO . . .

Of course, with Momo I don't dance so well, but you can't
blame him, it was already very brave of him to come here,
what with all these mirrors, it must be hard for him, even
after all this time, but he'd never admit it, pompom, pompom. These lace-up shoes Jeanne sent me are lovely. They
make a good contrast, like Olympia's neck, and the skirt tumbles down nicely, a great waistline for a woman my age, four
pregnancies and not a trace. I could have had all the men that
I . . . Pompom, pompom. Concentrate. Momo will bawl you
out again. The rows we have at tango lessons. You can see the
new arrivals wondering, the old ones too. It's always the
same thing. The efforts they make to speak to him, to be nice
and normal. And that characteristic fluttering of the eyelashes, as though they're in pain in exactly the same place as . . .
people, spectators contracting the very part of their faces that
Momo has missing. You can see them wondering: disease,
burns, AIDS? There are dog bites too, when you get bitten
young, the scar's already horrible, but when you grow, it
grows too, white lips separating, a spider's web beneath the

skin, a larger face pushing from below . . .

TE VI PASAR TANGUEANDO ALTANERA, CON UN COMPÁS TAN HONDO Y SENSUAL QUE NO FUE MÁS QUE VERTE Y PERDER LA FE . . .

What a magnificent couple Victor y Rafaela are, they're obviously sleeping together, you don't dance like that if you're not at it, how people dress these days, even Nore doesn't dare, Rafaela with her tiny skirt laid on his incredibly tight, tight trousers and his little navel-revealing tops, and the nape of his finely chiselled neck . . .

Momo's paces are too short, we won't have room for the *saccada*, all the couples having whispered rows beneath the music . . .

AYER DE MIEDO A MATAR EN VEZ DE PELEAR ME PUSE A CORRER . . .

There, how to do it? The feet, one, twoa, three, foura . . .

PENSÉ EN NO VERTE Y TEMBLÉ . . . DECÍ, POR DIOS, QUÉ ME HAS DAO QUE ESTOY TAN CAMBIAO . . . NO SÉ MÁS QUIÉN SOY!

It makes my head spin, and yesterday I couldn't hear in this ear properly, plus all those nasty turns, it's mad cow disease, a brain tumour, in the scanner they'll find white particles all full of sponge, holes in my brain, and I'll throw myself, like a madrepore, into the sea . . .

The worst of the lot are the Jehovah's Witnesses, or salesmen who ring on the door, ding dong, see Momo's face and their hands instinctively go to protect themselves, to ward off a punch, dodge a blow, or else about to cross themselves, those silences in conversations and the inevitable slips of the tongue, all they can think about is Momo's scar: a bomb, cancer, mutation, fungus, his mother rubbed herself while thinking about you know, post-nuclear rashes, roses maybe growing on his face geologically, he brought one back from the wild blue yonder, and when children start to cry, that's probably the worst part . . .

ACASO TE LLAMABA SOLAMENTE MARIÁ, NO SÉ SI ERAS EL ECO DE UNA VIEJA CANSIÓN, SÓLO SÉ QUE UNA NOCHE FUISTE HONDAMENTE MÍA . . .

Let's stop to watch them dance, he can lean on my arm, he'll never mention it again, just that rainy night when everything was soaking, the sheets damp, as far as the insides of the cupboards, which go mouldy and are so hard to clean, and outside, the entire night was stippled with rain, me always to his left, just as he wants, in the morning he has the profile of a handsome man, he is a handsome man, in fact the gun blast only took off the right side – as though along a central dotted line which runs between his eyes, down his nose to the hollow of his lips – when he hears a motorbike start up with a din, he jumps, or with certain films on TV, or even with the rain when it crashes down too loudly, and the worst bit, he says, was that Kabyle crucified with a white-hot chain across his belly, then suddenly with all his intestines on the ground, the first thing he thought was that maybe they could put them all back, a moment of innocence before understanding the irreparable . . .

An unrolling impossible to wind back, metres and metres of tubes inside the belly, that's what he thought at that moment, impossible to repair . . .

And Sharon Tate, whose baby was ripped out of her belly when she was nine months pregnant, how horrible, I remember that in *Match* . . .

When Momo cries, only his left eye sheds tears, the right one has been boiled dry by the gunshots, a dead, fish eye . . .

I just had to see him, the others didn't understand, but I had to be sure, two months spent waiting is something no one can understand, you can't explain it, and I thought all I'd have to

119

do was to take one look at the beautifully drawn tips of his lovely little fingernails, what a fool I was, he didn't have any nails any more, nor even any fingers . . .

His red trunks were still intact, just a bit torn, the fish hadn't wanted them, they were synthetic . . .

But all the little boys at the time had the same trunks, they were on sale at the new Carrefour hypermarkets that had just opened . . .

A coral body, fauna growing all over it, and most of all I remember those *opernes*, with their pincers and antennae, a Spanish delicacy, but I don't think it was really him, it can't have been . . .

Momo is elegance made flesh when he dances with Rafaela . . .

Be the man, be the woman, *a real dancer can play all the roles, picture your partner's space* . . .

Floor, floor, floor . . .

When Victor and Rafaela dance, everything becomes clear, time stops and rolls itself up around them, with the music, one two three four, with me there suspended as habanera time sways, these people do me good . . .

EN LAS SOMBRAS DE MI PIEZA, ES TU PASO EL QUE REGRESA, Y ES TU VOZ PEQUEÑA Y TRISTE . . .

And sometimes when I dance it's miraculous too, when we dance, sometimes, the steps arrive without me and with me, the clearness of this body, this rhythm, on the open floor, the ease of the walk . . .

Like those distant days when I forgot Momo's face, when I no longer saw it, the missing half of his face was no longer there . . .

Ten to eight, I must concentrate, it's crazy, the lesson's almost over . . .

Nore, who used to cry when she saw him and then apparently she forgot all of a sudden, she was about three, what a change of father . . .

And Jeanne, who didn't beat about the bush, *do whatever you want, I'm pleased he makes you happy, but it's him or me* . . .

And Anne, I never could handle her properly, she was the only one who was willing to talk to him, ask him questions, with him telling her that a secret agent had thrown acid in his face in a phone box, that a dog had bitten him aboard a Greenpeace zodiac, that he'd been recruited by an undercover team of potholers and that his lamp had exploded in his face, he liked joking with Anne . . .

And Nore, I hope she'll be back home this evening, she thinks she's living in a hotel, Momo's good to her, sending her to Gibraltar again this year, living with her paternal, maternal languages . . .

What a bore . . .

I can't wait for it to be over . . .

And I'm sure that Mademoiselle is going to take us for idiots . . . with her student airs and graces . . .

Sometimes you feel like dumping them by the motorway or catch yourself regretting not having done it . . .

Jeanne

Having to listen *toda la semana* to French being recited, you end up not knowing what's right and what's wrong any more, you feel like you're on an island in the Rio or in the middle of the sea, diluting me like the sea digs out shafts in atolls, collapsing from the centre towards the edges, you stand on one foot, on the toes of one foot, you sink . . . The coffee machine, thank God there's an eleven o'clock break, the only thing they do well in this country is their coffee, beef too, what a gift from the gods mad cow disease was for them, I'll check my email, I may have a message from Nore.

Teaching is like performing, not a moment's respite, unplug-ging, completely unplug your head, severed like a what do you call it? Pollard. How many office clerks would accept such a minute by minute occupation of their brains – I must drop into the supermarket on Calle de Montijo – what's this . . . *¡mierda!* The coffee's dripping all over the place – *¡Maquina de mierda!* – and no more *cambio*, I'll go and ask *dime, me das un peso, que no queda cambio* . . . Secretary, what a crap job, apparently sleeping with the . . . Like in the super-market on Calle de Montijo, that woman weighing fruit and veg all day, not even time for a hello, goodbye, thank you, next customer, next bag, remove the ticket and stick it on, all that carry-on just to avoid a few grams being shoplifted, I ask you, is it really worth it? . . . And when you stop and think about it, it's a task for a machine, you'd just need a basic pro-gram, but this country's so . . . With a camera equipped, for instance, with an optical detector, *beep*, apricots, *beep*, papayas, next customer. Why do they keep on with jobs like that? It's like with languages, in fact soon I'll no longer know what's an apricot, papaya, avocado, tomato. Associating a coloured shape with a name day in day out is child's play. Anne would say that the worst jobs should be the best paid, but when I think of Diego, for example, aren't his responsi-bilities hard, doesn't he earn his salary? I could stop work-ing, but I want to stay independent, that's what I told him last time on the phone, that really shut him up, there are loads of jobs which let you daydream in peace, even though they might look horrible to outsiders . . .

No email. I hope Mum knows what she's doing with Nore. I don't want to play at being a substitute mother, what time is it over there? Seven or eight in the evening. Where is she? She can't have gone out already, I feel like I've got three daughters in France and a son in Gibraltar. Nore is a bit fancy free, at her age you're at the mercy of . . . And I know Mum lends her the house, because her Momo won't have any boyfriends under his roof, the house is so isolated, I said

122

to her, *all we've got are bad memories there, let's not add another one*. And she just pretended not to hear, spends most of her time in bed, but I'm exaggerating, there are good memories too, when a couple splits up, the good ones end up resurfacing, the iceberg tilts over and you discover the seaweed sticking on the bottom of the submerged 90 per cent, and there they are, all those lovely memories defrosting in the sunlight, they can even turn into regrets, so I said to Mum, *buy her a tear-gas spray*. Diego bought me one, I'm pleased to say, and Mum goes, *it isn't exactly the Bronx round here*. Sometimes I even wonder if she knows where BA is. Nore's beautiful, everyone says that, and so trusting! I said to Mum, *your luck can run out so suddenly*. Mum's still got a good twenty, thirty, even forty years in front of her. She's in good shape, except for her nerves, who will get the house? That's something which will have to be settled. Anne already thinks it's outrageous that Nore has the keys. But in Paris, what would she do with it? Definitely not take boys back there, like Nore. Anne's life. What a mystery. As I've always said, I definitely would not like to spend the night in the house on my own. All those trees in the wind – but I used to like it in the summer, the damp green hiding places in the garden, breathing in the fragrance of the trees, then, in the evening, going for a dip, the sea suddenly changing colour, blue and then red, anyway, I hope Mum knows what she's doing, how can anyone wake up every morning next to Pizza Face, Baboon Arse? – At the zoo when that ape tried to grab Nore's hair, who saved her? Who knocked, *bang*, on the reinforced glass? Chimps are dangerous, with the same hand practising auto-fist-fucking he was ferreting out his own shit and gobbling it in a closed circuit, and the little chimp, just Nore's size, staring at her and staring at her, its little dick erect and pressed against the glass, and its podgy lips, you could see each salivating wrinkle, and its hands, life line, heart line, flattened in front of Nore's face, giving her bunny ears, bunkey ears, what a carry-on, that day at the zoo, she was still a toddler, a packet of nappies on legs, little white bonnet over her chestnut ringlets, we stopped being blonde so early, but Pierre was till the end – and who was looking at who, we wondered, with its pathetic human eyes, its human hands, and it could sit up better than Nore, take objects between thumb and index finger better than Nore, you might even think that at triangles and triangular holes Nore would have been . . . Who had more brainpower? . . . To lose a second one, in the ape pit, Nore, lost in a game, Mum (a second late) grabbing her hand. Maybe she feared for her virtue. And we were yelling and stamping our feet, when the big ape stuck his fingers back up his arse to select the most succulent pieces of its shit, with all the attention of a gourmet, while the little one was gawping at Nore, with her whingeing on and hopping from foot to foot, hand on her parcel of nappies, I'll never forget Reykjavik zoo. All those creatures in glass cages, the protective atmosphere heated by volcanic water, it stank of wild beasts and sulphur, and the orange-and-black-jigsaw giraffe had a sort of porthole, its telescope head popping up above its cube of glass, with everything getting steamed up . . .

Standing up all the time makes my legs hurt, how hot it is already, they could at least put some benches in this yard . . .

At the end of the trip, a cascade of geysers, an ape hung like a donkey, and Mum's hand obviously glued on to hers, on to Nore's, our little troll, in the land of the proscribed you keep hold of each other, the gyrating giraffe watching over us in Reykjavik. And John and Mum always checking we were still alive. I was right to leave. Eighteen and already in Africa. My diary, today I'm seeing Jimena, when I stop to think she's due to deliver in January, how she's going to suffer from the heat. Maybe last night it worked? That makes 1, 2, 3 + 7, that means it's 25, no 24 October, so it's the thirteenth day, exactly one day too early, I had it on the 11th, but at two days' interval maybe it could still work, after all, we aren't machines . . .

Nore

I like it when the house is empty. You can walk around naked, I don't like being naked in front of Momo. They must be at their tango class, pompom pompom, diddly-dum di dada. I like the time when the sun goes down. Anne says it's the hour when everything closes, when the sun comes down over the earth like a shop's shutter. But I think it's the opposite. The light on the floor tiles, whose colour has been well chosen for once, flaming red, even though Mum didn't agree, the earthenware pot calling the iron pot black. There's nothing in this fridge, she always buys margarine instead of butter, how many times have we told her that so far as calories are concerned it comes down to the same thing, and some own-brand taramasalata, just imagine what it tastes like, I think I'll have something else. At this time of the day, there's less dust floating in the air. I wonder why. These empty, limpid sunbeams are weird. A little haze, maybe, over the woods. The wood's alive in the evening, at night too. Night as it spreads up from the sea. I like it when it's quiet. I like being alone, just before going out, it's nice to be alone before a date. I must wax myself before going, what's the time? . . . Mum keeps her nail varnish in the fridge. She must have read that in *Modes et Travaux*, carmine for your toes . . . very nice. And it goes especially well with the red floor tiles, sod it, where's the sponge? And for your fingernails, let's see . . .

That cat scares me. Always hiding in cupboards. Nine lives of a cat of which one is spent hidden in a cupboard. I can't stroke you, my varnish is drying. They'll be back in half an hour's time, you can wait, can't you? What goes on inside a cat's head, I wonder? *Qu'est-ce qu'il y a, dans une noix, qu'est-ce qu'on y voit?* The weirdest thing of all is that they dream. Their eyelids flicker, and if you touch them you can feel their eyeballs rolling, left and right, after a mouse or whatever, hard to imagine, and their paddy paws stiffen, claws out and whiskers bristling. After all, pink and grey look good as well. I could wear a hair band. Go for the grey one. Or else the blue one with pearls will go well with my eyes. Where have I put . . . my hairpins . . . if I put my hair up, it'll set off my face. But if I let it down . . . Let down, it looks sensual. But can also look slatternly. Take the opportunity of playing some music before they get back. No, this silence is lovely, without Momo's concrete mixer, chainsaw, fretsaw and lawnmower. The silence of dusk. Like passing through cotton. The birds have shut up. A thickness, a red density . . . I wonder . . . A pin . . . How would this suit me? . . . Is that a spot there? . . . Some blusher . . . Need more light in this bathroom . . . Mum must have . . . Would it suit me if I . . . There, can't see it any more . . . Or just one immaculately negligent lock . . . In Lord Johnson's castle, there lived his three daughters. The oldest one was dark, tanned by the sun and experience. The second one was only slightly younger, blonde, thin and pallid because of her work. The youngest one, who was as sweet and as good as can be, took after her father, the best man in the world. Their mother had left him to live with a man with a ravaged face, which was a cause of constant amazement for the older daughters . . . Big fat cat aged seven times eleven makes seventy-seven years old. Do you have to follow me everywhere? Big fat castrated cat. But you still get hard-ons, don't you? . . . Make some room on the bed. I wake up a cat. All I have to do is go downstairs and beg for food, after dreaming out my human existence . . . The blue current out to sea, above the green one . . . What would he see? A shadowless, hostile world. The soft sand beneath his feet. The seaweed stinking of fish. God, did they go on at me about currents when I was little. Those welcoming tidal pockets, like the ones we weed in, apparently they snap shut like a trap when the tide turns, flip flop, like folding pieces of paper into games shaped like boxes which you hold in your fingers, one side open, one side closed, to read the future. The pockets excavated in the sand empty out when the tide turns and there's nothing you can do, you're swept away helplessly . . . In that helicopter . . . I was with my sisters and John was there too, perhaps a group of girls, that's right . . . And below us was the sea . . . only a part of the town emerging, skyscrapers like sugarloaves and big empty parks in the hills, plus sometimes villas or casinos . . . From the helicopter, we could also see the old, submerged town, with its foundations and Roman mosaics beneath the turquoise water . . . The broad blue sky around the helicopter and the town in two halves, water as transparent as air, just more golden, marked out by the sun into grids and placed like a thin film over the ancient world . . .

What's the time? What am I going to wear? If you feel your way forwards through the transparency of the air . . . If you go blind through the transparency of the air, putting out your hands towards the slight fluttering motion you can sense . . . Towards the chair which has just gone *crack* all on its own . . . Then you meet . . . Daddy's favourite book, *The Invisible Man*. This dress . . . or that one . . . It's cold now. Night is falling. I'll get out my thick jacket for this evening. Mum must have tidied all that stuff away in boxes. All the same, cats are weird, with their little, clawed bodies. *Tu m'accompagnes à la cave?* Come into my arms and down to the cellar. Or the storeroom. I don't know what it's called. What with Momo constantly building and excavating new rooms beside, above and under the house. I can hardly remember my way round this place. How cold it is outside. The temperature fell as fast as the darkness. This evening, with Nicolas, we can always talk about the weather . . .

I look wicked in high heels. The switch is on the left, isn't it, hang on a minute, don't wriggle like that. Over there, at the back, there's yet another cellar, between the foundations, which he dug out of the earth. Why? To lay down wine or air? Large cubes of black air below the house. Boxes behind the bikes. I'll have to pull the lamp over here, they're so hard to open . . . Well wrapped up in plastic sheets, Mum's speciality . . . I wouldn't like it if Momo suddenly put in an appearance. It's not that I . . . But it's as if it keeps moving. It's red and puffy with bristles which keep growing all over the place . . . I can understand why he doesn't want to be in any of our photos. But think about our family album later on, if he dies – and he will die, sooner or later – what are we going to tell people if there's no trace of him? I can't find anything in this mess. What was I looking for? The big, blue jacket with a detachable plush collar I had last year. Not here. What's this? Some old clothes. I wonder why Mum keeps all this stuff. And here? There's nothing underneath. Just earth as fine as soot. What is this thing? The cold and the soot are getting into my lungs. This cellar stinks something rotten. The air's stuffy, cramped, cemented into blocks. It crumbles between your fingers like . . . Like some . . . Or some . . . Imagine if the door swings shut. And they didn't find you. It'd take them ages before they thought of going down to the cellar. Wait! The little bugger's scampered off. *Attends-moi!* Too bad. I'll just have to wear my denim jacket. Anyway, it isn't that cold. How silly. My heart's beating like hell. Like when Momo decided to harden me up by sending me down here to fetch some wine. Éléonore Johnson, aged nineteen, disappeared on 25, no, 24 October. At first, they'll assume I've been murdered, or run away from home, but I'll be under the house, between the foundations, trapped in the solid air. Such things happen. Mum would never recover. Like the film Jeanne told me about, with the woman locked inside an empty house. My date will be accused. Dead in high heels and a nice hairdo. Maybe Nicolas will feel sorry he never got to know me. They'll end up laying my ghost in an empty grave. And I'll have discovered a secret passage and will re-emerge reborn into the fresh air and change my identity. Then I'll peek in through their windows to see if they're crying and through Anne's window to see how she makes love, if she moans. I don't reckon Jeanne makes love that often. Or Mum. I'll find a secret passage and I'll come to see them at night, see Mum crying or gazing paralysed into space, incapable of ever uttering a single word. Momo behind his pizza face not knowing what to do. I'll go to see Daddy in Gibraltar, he alone in on the secret. I'll just have to snap my fingers and I'll see them all in despair. The gift of ubiquity. Then I'll be able to write all the books I want. That story I used to read when I was little . . . It was only at the end that you understood that it was a monster speaking, chained up in a cellar with a bowl in front of it . . . The son of the house, born like that, who was secretly and implacably building up his strength, a monster aged three, four, five . . . It's warmer outside, what have I done with my car keys? Night fallen in the streets, in the hollows beneath the trees. Roses almost all gone. Buds like little propellers, spinning at night, and the garden hums, a massive insect lying under the trees . . . All those books must be in the cellar, in the cellar of our house. And the one about the cosmonauts, their spaceship exploding, each of them with a little reserve of oxygen shooting off in a big bang of humans through the void . . . In radio contact towards certain death . . . I'd have switched the thing off. One hour to die while speeding straight through space, boom . . .

Anne

Quelle chaleur . . . The sound of her voice in the empty room startles her. *On se croirait un soir de juin* . . . It resonates like metal in the air. She can hear bellows, a blade, *juin* . . . The room is vibrating. She could go through her old address books and maybe look up some old friends . . . Or go to the late-night swimming pool, like she used to with Laurent . . . How hot it is. Like a June evening. Last summer at the same period. She plugs her ears and now it's inside her that her words are vibrating, the sound of what she's saying, like the swifts above the rooftops, *shriek shriek*, they'll be gone tomorrow. A countdown in that small, pointed body glutted on bugs . . . fattened up for migration. Time's hormone . . . melatonin, an hourglass, drop by drop filling up its two-tone head until it sets off due south, the pan of a scale, a swerving wing . . . There are twenty-five or thirty of them chiselling at the sky. Through the window frames opposite, three little girls in smocks are reading or daydreaming on oriental rugs, in the last light of the west. The two poplars through the distorting pane. A bubble in the glass cuts one of them in half, doubling its trunk with its green arms, you just have to shift slightly for the tree to come back together again. The pane undulates in streaks, the poplar leaps across, image by image. A swallows' mirror in which nothing happens: poplar, poplar, poplar. John Johnson and his Johnson Daughters crossing the moors in their motor vehicle . . . A fan you can fold and unfold. Punctuating the interminable journey, each row of pines, open, shut, a row of pines revealing yet another row of pines. Time passing through the windows like rotating repetitive stage sets, behind cars in old movies, the same pine tree, same cornfield, same occasional cow . . . And those long-necked watering machines, fossil diplodocuses amid the furrows . . . A rotating, picturesque time, nothing's changed . . . Laurent's got married and the babies she handles are only two or three months old . . . At the centre of that pool of centrifugal time, around which the two bare poplar trees are turning, budding, greening, yellowing, browning, then bare. All you need is a November gust. The trees' municipal workers will come and pick up the leaves, then in spring they'll be back, after a discreet night, to stick on the leaves newly grown in the city's greenhouses . . . Especially the leaf of the chestnut tree, the hardest one to obtain, which reproduces the tree's shape fractally. The sun is moving to the other side of the roofs, which undulate sonically. It's like a June evening. The café terraces are packed . . . She switches on the light, then turns it off, then back on again. Is it time to go out yet? Outside, people are talking. The weather's not what it used to be. At the end of October, in Paris, when she arrived ten years back, you needed a coat. The southern climate is rising northwards. The planet's heating up. Now that the sun's slid down, they need to light the lamps. What an incredible difference. The tips of the poplars are still being lit by yellow flames . . . Something is clambering up towards the top, a wave of darkness, raising its hand . . . a dead zone . . . Rising from the ground with the chill of October . . . The Dead Zone really exists, at an altitude of 8,000 metres above the planet, there are just fourteen summits which emerge from the slick of mental water, all of them in the Himalayas. In oxygen-free white and cold, you do stupid things, like taking off your gloves, running down slopes and singing, absolutely dying to make a snowman . . . Your brains frozen with euphoria, or knowing you can fly . . . In the tower at Parma, at most only 200 metres above sea level, you couldn't blame the air, the oxygen or the cold . . . Not even the effort, all of you lying there in deckchairs, under blankets, in mid-August . . . In the park . . . Under the open hands of the trees, which were waving at them, goodbye, goodbye, stay on the quay when the boat moves off . . . *Maintenant, c'est moi qui pense pour toi*, as Waterlot said, and having someone thinking for her did her good. It's a real holiday when someone else takes charge of your interior. Nothing more of what she thought could possibly be serious or true, the machine was spinning away on its own and what it produced was streaming out through the sluices straight into Dr Waterlot . . . As high and as tall as a lightning conductor, who took care of all the family, barring Nore of course. Then, when you left, you took back command of the *mothership*, you just had to. It must have been at the tower in Parma that she was recruited. They do a lot of recruiting in those parts, the doctors are either blind or in cahoots . . . She was there, one of the people lying on deckchairs . . . So, for two months she took the tests. Successfully. They made her conscious of the worldwide consciousness circling the planet. It was at that moment. Unless it was before. That ability to plug herself in . . . The circles of the secret . . . The deckchairs, when you knew how to pick the right ones, were often equipped for the tests . . . And most of the hospital furniture too . . . Directly into the spinal cord and from there into the cortex . . . Yes, she can see that, she can clearly see how, in her deckchair . . . Via the earthed plug . . . Or by airwaves . . . Directly from the spinal cord into the clump of neurones at the bottom of the brain. Umbilically. The tests consisted of seeing a maximum number of . . . Of answering as quickly as possible to . . . Child's play . . . How to face any given situation at any given moment . . . If you had to tango in Buenos Aires or hunt polar bears in D'Urville, she'd know how . . . To climb 8,000 metres or give birth to sextuplets . . . She is perfectly prepared for any mission . . . All that she experienced in the tower at Parma that summer, before coming back to Paris . . .

The curtain hanging opposite looks like a hanged man. A face looking at her. The last gleam of evening. Plus the training to stay motionless for hours on end in a deckchair . . . Come what may, being gang-raped, red ants, torture, she'll be able to stay motionless if she wants . . . Play dead. Trained for it. No one will suspect. Take that lamp, for instance. The wooden stand she repainted the other day. She can see it now. She sees that you can still see traces of the old colour beneath the fresh coat. Like when you varnish your nails. At the beginning, you can't see the places that need touching up or possible spillage. But then, a few hours later, holding the bar in a metro carriage or pushing open a door, or checking the tape recorder while the babies listen, then you discover that familiar thing – your hand. Or when she was twenty, finding in a trunk the glasses she'd had when she was fifteen. Did she really use to look like that? It is not possible – unless you totally metamorphose it – to see the lamp which has followed you from bedroom to bedroom since your adolescence, nor is it possible to see your own nails, especially on the side of the palm, fingers folded, without immediately seeing a family: the father, the mother and three children, a double smile from all of them, white edge and a half-moon. So it is with everything. It's either too familiar or too new. Hence the problems with her reports. In the same way, is it possible to perceive people without their names, floating, spelt out all around them – L.A.U.R.E.N.T. – better than a face, and to remember them this way? (After all, Nore says she sees letters in colours, but maybe she's being pretentious and taking herself for Rimbaud.) Take John, for example. What she can see of him is his name and fields of wind turbines in Gibraltar. And it's obvious what she can see of Momo. *What's yellow, sings and weighs fifty kilos? A canary. A really BIG canary.* Stupid jokes sparkling around a huge body. Something crackling and a bit painful, like sparklers held too close to your face . . .

The bulb is dangling from the ceiling. The tap's dripping. The table's stretching its legs and baring its nails. All of the frozen hostility of the world rushes in via a chemical reaction to the various objects scattered around her. You're not welcome here. Interference from the universe. Otherwise, she could perceive everything, receive everything, she, Anne, all the data, all the visits. She's perfectly capable . . .

Lying on her bed in the darkness of the fallen night. She, Anne, holding on, surfing over the network of the worldwide brain by empathy, connecting to consciousnesses, rather like a guardian angel, except that telepathic agents must remain passive. Everything comes out in the report in – to be precise – the act of transmission. In the secret of the deckchair or the halo of a lamp which is neither new nor familiar . . .

The phone hasn't rung once. As hostile as the rest of it all. Something positioned. A shellfish on a rock. She, Anne, in her deckchair or on her bed, receptive to the world. Bigger fleas have smaller fleas. Listening. You know the tune. *Avoir fait la saison dans cette boîte crânienne.* A season in that cranium. Signs meant for her. Or those tall white birds, egrets maybe, standing on the backs of rhinoceroses – *rhinoferocious*, as Pierre used to say, and Nore too – digging out louse by louse the folds of those massive hides, bug by bug, tick by tick, well-ordered parasites interfering with . . . Start with yourself . . .

She, Anne, walking in suspension above the street, keeping parallel to the shifts in its surface, she senses in her heels when it goes up or down, a twitch along her back, shoulders back, straddling balconies is like dancing, on the raised terraces, the fresh air fiends are floating too, clinking their glasses, drinking the warm air, to their loves, in the evening, the seats sink down a little, and beneath us fewer and fewer cars are being driven, a scent of honeysuckle rises to our level of hanging terraces and gardens . . . Or is it my neighbour's perfume? She's getting married tomorrow, a Tinkerbell head on a shot-putter's shoulders, October lilies-of-the-valley. Around their bodies, their skin is misty, perspiring directly into the air . . .

On the inner side of her arm, the skin is fine and veined with blue. From an unexpected opening, she'll spill out as a sack of innards . . . Her skin isn't white, it's off-white, with a hint of ivory, slightly darker at the bend of the elbow, violet veins and pink arteries, light brown beauty spots, freckles more brown than red, a bruise is turning green on the side of the cubitus; the outer side of the elbow is red and rugged with blotches; when she extends her hand, her nails have orangey traces on them, and two phalanges are underlined with satin white, Avi 3000, from having repainted the lamp yesterday. Dermatology and neurobiology, the skin is organized in strips, in dermatomes, each region of the skin being associated with a piece of the spinal cord . . .

You could be born crossbred like a zebra, with a strip of Irish freckles, then a matt southern strip, ring by ring, in epidermal ribbons instead of being melted in a pot. Shingles following the circles. A mummy's bandages, or those of the Invisible Man. If the circles of skin hardened, then there would be no more need for vertebrae. A shell would cover the body like with insects. The egret's bill on the rhinoceros would make the sound of a drum . . .

When she used to sleepwalk, the year she started her periods, aged nine and a half, in the morning, they found the photo albums had been taken down from their shelves, and the photos rearranged in an order that neither she nor anyone else could understand. In the same way, some books had been opened, pages read, thumbed, she must have invented what they said, dreamed the books which vanished when she woke up. And the empty bottle of Coke, the fridge left open and dripping, drop after drop, on to the floor tiles . . . And Chocolate with his lead on, muddy fur, eyes a little wild, what could he have told them? She got dressed. She opened doors. She knew where was what and who was who. And the dog recognized her and agreed to follow her. The person she was in her sleep liked Coca-Cola, didn't bother to close doors and went for walks in the moonlight, and these three trivial characteristics seemed more real to her, more *Anne*, than everything her waking self pretended to be. But the dog kept their secrets. They'd have had to dissect its brain, unfold its cortex and project it on to a screen. But that wasn't possible. A dog's cranium is a safe, a tomb. So what about her own sleeping memory? Under hypnosis, maybe. Things would drift up, like dead miners after a firedamp explosion. In strong rain, you see a finger emerge. Then a hand. An arm. A shoulder. Finally a helmet and a black face. Indian cemeteries, throwing up their dead in office workers' swimming pools. She, dressed in white, alone and free in the moonlight. It made her wonder. Who was she at night? During the day, it was having to bear gym classes with a wodge of cotton wool between her legs, doing the splits, cartwheels, warming up, the beam, with a coagulating sanitary towel, itching, dripping, leaking . . . sluices open. The body from before, as closed and as safe as a seed, suddenly germinating and betraying her . . . It was out walking with the dog at night that she lost her virginity, she's sure of it. That feeling of *déjà vu* the first time . . . and no blood, even though Jeanne told her that she hadn't bled either, and it was because of all that sport. The sessions Mum insisted on. A healthy body in a healthy mind, unless it's the other way round. Or genes, maybe. Born with no hymen. Just a piece of skin, like you have under your tongue, as a brake. They should clean out babies as soon as they are born, with a quick jab of the finger in the vagina, along with all the other peeling skin and mucus . . . As clean as a peeled apple. Isn't it better to be a man? Another cigarette. Obsessionally running through comparative tests. Now they don't even have to do national service . . .

In diaphanous white in the moonlight. Discovering there are two holes where she thought there was one. Not the same one for peeing and for . . . It didn't just happen in front, with the electric button of the clitoris. It also happened around and inside. Cucumbers and courgettes. Watch out for the aubergine's barbed tip. At the start, she would always say: fingers will be enough. But once you've begun. A desire for more. Inside. Developing her own method: warm up all around it, push inside, then, with a single motion, click, like switches with chrome studs, make the link with the clitoris, internal explosion, diffusion, disintegration . . .

Her mother had found her out walking white and diaphanous, she still talks about her horror, a good story for family mealtimes: paralysed with fear, thinking she'd seen a ghost walking straight in front of her, down the corridor of the house . . . Then recognizing her daughter, putting on the light, recognizing her, Anne, and taking her by the hand. The right instinct, to take her back to bed, a reflex, or else something she'd read somewhere, in *Femme Pratique* or *Modes et Travaux*. Information being built up, scraps of an encyclopedia accumulating day in day out, the radio, magazines, TV, conversations: you store it all, it's a psychological reflex, just as you forget about the yellowing, now almost invisible postcards under their magnets on the fridge door (just as their father had told them all, *because it might come in handy, you never know*, that grinding your teeth disturbs encephalograms – *where did he pick that up?* – or that emperor penguins have just one chick, while regular ones have two, and that you just have to put vinegar on monkfish to stop its flesh from going crumbly), so where had her mother learned all about somnambulism? How did she know that if a sleepwalker wakes up with a start, it's like falling from the top of a high building, and that you should lead them gently by the hand? On discovering Anne walking, her eyes wide open, as though at the bottom of the sea . . . having overcome her initial terror, she took her back to bed. *How strange it was to find out that I seemed always to have known what to do in such circumstances,* she told her friends (and not, which is revelatory: *To discover my daughter sleepwalking,* or, *That the little girl I bore, fed, etc., well, I don't know who she is, in this world where she walks down corridors dressed in white*), *in the same way* (she, her mother, went on), *we must have a reflex that makes us press a burst artery in a thigh, or breath into the lungs of someone who's been electrocuted, or makes us instinctively lie on our back and play dead when attacked by a bear, or else kick our legs in front of a shark to imitate the giant squid, and so every evening I took Anne back to bed until she grew out of it.* That's what her mother had to say about this particular case of motherhood, and the whole table laughed about Anne sleepwalking, what a surprise, what an upset in family life, ha ha ha. What's yellow, lives in a cage and weighs fifty kilos?

In the same way, there was the Great Family Discussion, cool-headed and common-sensical, because John was leaving, Momo was arriving, so the whole family sat round the table, Nore on Mum's lap, Jeanne furious, her bags already packed, and her, Anne, waiting for what? . . . Mum stiff, her eyes red, John dishevelled and grandiloquent, self-denying, when everything had been said, *You're gonna stay with your mother and we'll see about it later,* sorted, while Mum kept crying and claiming that she wasn't leaving him for another man, that the problem was just them, him and her, and John said that everything had already been said and that THEY WERE NOT GOING TO DISCUSS THAT IN FRONT OF THE CHILDREN, and he stood up, and it was all over.

Daddy John the Pelican, tearing his chest out, and so dignified. Dishevelled and numb, a pelican, wings open, tearing open its chest, rather abandon his place than see his daughters with no *nucleus*, with his impossible accent, he was going, he had accepted a contract in Gibraltar, to develop *énewgies de substitioution*, he was off to set up wind turbines, which would provide electricity for entire stretches of Europe, that's what Daddy John the Pelican was saying – after all, they'd been brought up, how to put it? Another cigarette. After all, they'd been taken all over the place, the Caravan Family, for years on end in their Volkswagen van, with a *Nucléaire Non Merci* sticker on its rear, she can still see it, and so it was *plutôt un stepfather que les pawents qui ne s'aiment plous* – the night has fallen, leaf by leaf, on to the poplars, cuplets of shadow wavering under the sparkling sky of glitters, diffuse neon and pollution – how to put it? It's a real puzzle, what these parents thought they believed in: balance, peace, children and a dog, and precisely why John said he was going, *plutôt des éoliennes que de l'uwanium* . . .

Uwanium Non Merci . . .

And the dog yapping between the two of them, without Pierre on one side, and Nore on the other, −1 towards the past +1 towards the future, *hitting the road again* in their green Volkswagen, all Nore ever saw was Iceland, just before they split up, just before John commandeered the van for his own use and drove down to Gibraltar, in exchange for the house which (breast torn) he left for his little family. Luckily, Momo had a R16 and a brand-new house. They (she and Jeanne), who had always thought that despite what had happened, despite everything, the summer on the beach, that forgiveness had finally descended on the family, that they were going to lead a *normal life*, despite everything, Daddy, Mummy, the dog and us, and that, with Nore, *hope would be reborn*, until Daddy started his pelican act and talking about turbines and Mum fell in love with a man with a pizza face. Then Jeanne vanished into humanitarian work. And she,

Anne, stayed there, stupidly playing the fool with baby Nore, until the episode in the tower at Parma. Maybe that was exactly what John was on about with his turbines, he too was like a teenager hanging about in the street, a scout, a procurer for modelling agencies, he was waiting for them too, his alternative energies, the chance of a lifetime to escape from home . . .

She just can't help it – when their dark blue eyes (a common colour at that age) suddenly stop for a second, stare fixedly, when their fingers stop fiddling with their rattles, and their mouths stop sucking for a second, then you can see a wordless idea forming, a wide-open idea, which seizes them, shakes them to the bone, unfolding at once, *I RECOGNIZE THIS, I'VE ALREADY HEARD IT SOMEWHERE, BUT WHERE?* when they hear, taratara, their mother tongue . . .

So what do you think? John asked them, while Mum was fuming, *he's taking the minibus.* Those two adults, summoning them all for the first time, each speaking in turn, finally chairing a meeting with all the recommended psychological techniques of the time. And Jeanne as closed as an oyster, in the hatred of their silence. For once we were talking, and it was *à toute à l'heure, alligator.* It was seeing them fumbling about, seeing them being so clueless, turning towards their daughters for the first time, their faces as open as their hands, their pathetic stares, waiting, for once, for their opinion, Mum and Dad the Pelicans, a couple of haggard seabirds, and *The-Last-Time-They-Made-Love* sitting dribbling and babbling on Mum's lap, perfectly sealing the silence – at least she'll be spared, they were probably telling each other, let's be done with it once and for all – so what do you think? they asked, talking about their separation. And watching them fumbling around like that, feeling like them, feeling like us, so uncertain, so clumsy, incapable of answering the questions they were asking, then, suddenly, in a flash, like the throwing of a switch, she, Anne, became an adult . . .

Jeanne

Sitting on the terrace of the Biela, waiting for Jimena, who's always late, a quarter past one, the tangled leads of the dogs being walked ten at a time by students, in packs, for a few pesos, she's always wondered how you convince the dogs to get on with one another, by affinity, character, all those people who've had children because they can't have dogs, leads tangled over ten different trajectories, meeting at the student's wrist, an approximate walk, the weaving of geometry in motion, triangles, lozenges, straight lines, moving through the air like anarchic electricity grids below the motorway viaduct, in those semi-shanty towns you have to cross to get to the airport, the sea, Paris, at the end of the night flight . . . Dogs pissing on each other's paws, they don't have enough room between the leads to reach the trunk of the *palo borracho* leaning all its roots on the shattered square, BA's oldest, finest, loveliest tree, *it would take more than twelve children hand in hand to encircle it.* It's no longer just one tree, but an assembly, creepers falling under their own weight and getting glued into the slime of vegetation. You can play hide-and-seek between the sheets of bark, among the folds and ridges, the hangings rolling out from the tree – apparently, it's a sort of grass, or is classified among the grasses, some can live 1,000 years, several storeys high, their bark as resistant as a building (whatever can Jimena be doing?) like that petrified object, 30 million years old, which was dug out of the Paris valley, a stone, of course, but which looked like, which could be taken for . . . A big log, a displaced stump at the Jardin des Plantes in Paris in the days when she strolled there between flights, and that bear swaying from one foot to the other in its medieval pit; its snout and muzzle worn down by all the time it spent snuffling at the bars which enclosed the females, flayed from all that ferreting . . . Between two humanitarian missions, passing by Roissy . . . Hotels . . . Waiting for a fax for a new assignment . . . Getting peckish. Twenty past one. All the languages she speaks badly, from Kinyarwanda to English and Spanish. And now, with French, more and more words on the tip of her tongue. She'll end up not speaking at all. Going back to France was especially about the trees. Normal trees. Elms and poplars, rich and not rubbery. No lianas, no varnished hides, no bottle-shaped trunks, or thorns and fruit as big as three heads together, or dead stumps as the desert advances. The smell of the trees in Roissy. Head back in the trees, behind the house, when they were little, those huge raised plants, the earth spinning beneath them . . . flat on their backs, in the sky . . . the light breaking up in a breeze of confetti . . . The Paris valley 30 million years ago was a mangrove. *Les pa les pa les palétuviers* and the crocodiles of the Paris valley . . .

That huge stag looming up in her headlights, the tarmac thundering, it leapt up when it saw the car, feet forward, bucking like a circus horse, and with one flick of its powerful hind legs, hard hooves on the hard road, it vanished . . .

Half past one. I mean, what the hell is she doing?

What's in the paper?

CAPRICORNIO
22 de diciembre al 21 de enero
AMOR: Saturno se dispone a cambiar el clima de los próximos tres años. En su equipaje, pasión y aventura. Florecerán nuevas historias romanticas, exigentes como siempre, pero repletas de exaltación. En octubre tendras un ingenio chispeante y tu estado de ánimo será encantador.
VIDA SOCIAL: Saturno confrontará a la vez tu conservadismo et tu gusto por el riesgo. Esas dos tendencias opuestas producirán un conflicto creativo: vas realamente a sobresalir.

Will this be her creativity? . . . A child to be born . . . He'll

141

see her bending down over him like a tree. Branches spread out, trunk upright, swaying and solid . . . Above the cot, the weeping willow of her hair, her smiles, hands dipping down . . . That must be one of her memories. Mum when she was maternal. She'll buy a test tomorrow, no, you have to wait till you're late. You should feel it at once. And she feels nothing. Face facts. She feels nothing. Sitting on the terrace of the Biela, waiting for Jimena. Before, this used to be what? A cycle shop. Buenos Aires' first bikes. How was it? Penny-farthings. Prehistoric pushbikes. Women in puffed-out trousers and fluffy hairdos. Boneshakers. Coca-Cola was a tonic sold at the pharmacy. Look, no hands. Look, no teeth. Half an hour late. Anyway, abortion's illegal here. Jimena had one two years ago in a private clinic. It cost even more than liposuction . . . And to end up like she is now. How to know at what age it starts thinking? Bang, conception, contact between two conducting bodies, a time bomb . . . First connection, it was black and then . . . Even if it's just the sensation of being here, of being here rather than nowhere, warmth, presence, and the din of a train, a beating heart, no ears yet, just the vibrations of the mother's heart, and skin not yet skin, something growing and beating in turn. She'll go. Have a bite to eat, then go. *Oye . . . una tortilla con ensalada . . . mixta, si . . . y agua con gaz, y la cuenta, rápido.* I must phone Mum, before she goes to bed. It's been at least three days . . .

0033 for France, 5 for the south (Mum and Nore), 1 for Paris (Anne), 0034 for España and John, beep bop bap, the little melody associated with each sequence of buttons, Mum a monochord, John a nursery rhyme, mi re do, *three blind mice* . . .

Start out this evening straight after the session if her psychiatrist isn't too late, she'll be with Diego on the quay at about ten past seven. Let's hope the shutters haven't suffered too much. With all this rain, they're getting impossible to open. I must phone Mum before she . . . What's in the paper? A photo . . . The anniversary of the death of . . . In '75 presumably. Suddenly the grown-ups started yelling. Cries in the village and an influx of friends to the house. We were what, seven or eight, and didn't know if this was a happy or sad event. Pierre had died when? In '74. And laughter in the house. A stone being raised briefly from over us. Fresh air. I've never told Jimena about that. But it would interest her. It must have been in '75. And, suddenly, joy in the village. Dad and Mum laughing and raising their glasses with their friends, we didn't have the telly yet, the news must have come on the radio. The entire country heading southwards, wide open for the first time. The sensation of being Europe. The next day, a family trip to Spain after the years of boycott, sick as usual in the back of the Volkswagen. Mum's cousin, Otxoa, or what was her name Ortzadar, tortured in Bilbao. Yells in the village at seven o'clock, the newsflash, what they'd been waiting for, the death of the Caudillo . . .

It's weird. But you don't visualize time, the calendar, in the same way when it goes back as when it goes forwards. When backwards, there are dates, numbers, perhaps a colour for each decade. When forwards, empty space after empty space, month after month, and day after day even in the weeks near at hand . . . With a red ribbon for my future periods, and also season after season, blue for January / February, pale pink for March / April, green turning to yellow for May, June orange, July / August caramel red, September gold, then brown for autumn . . . Her projections are better organized than her recollections. Vertical strips with the names of the months like rainbow wallpaper, October, November . . . Maybe she'll be pregnant. If so, right now . . . Then it'll be for . . . June. Born at the beginning of winter. A little Gemini. Or a little Cancer. Franco was definitely a Scorpio. Should check with Jimé. Whatever could have happened to her, an accident, in her state? Oddly enough, the imaginary colours of the seasons haven't changed. Yet January is stifling here, bright red sky, orange pollution, thank God they've got a house on the Tigre. But the calendar dates from her childhood, '74 or '75, as soon as she became aware of . . . As soon as she distinguished one

day from another, a successions of befores and afters . . . Cries
of joy in the village, parents popping open the champagne,
friends dropping by and them, Anne and Jeanne, spinning
round with their arms stretched out, laughing without knowing why, jumping, screaming and wriggling . . . Anne had a
nervous fit, huge sobs like she had lumps of bone stuck in her
throat . . . Their parents didn't care. Franco was dead. The
next day, heading due south, to Spain, as if the country suddenly existed again . . . As if the entire south had suddenly
been rebalanced, rediscovered, the ballast of a wobblyman
who was now standing straight up again. Before, all there
had been was the sea to the west and the forest to the north.
And they almost never went east, towards the continental
stretches reaching as far as the Urals in her school atlas.
Definitely in '75. The following summer, '76, was the great
drought, you can't have it all at the same time, a hot summer
and Franco's death. Whatever is Jimena doing? *A man who
dies is like a library on fire*, the sort of thing John came out with.
The drought of '76, Mum bare-chested, playing with the
hosepipe . . . All those adults who weren't as we thought, as
they said they were, what we understood . . .

The Mother

His favourite meal, omelette and chilli peppers, sure to
please. But only once in a while, of course, because of the
cholesterol. She scratches out the bottom of the pan to check
that all the eggs have been . . . Not runny at all. He's already
sitting at the table. Tangoing is exhausting. She'd like to sit
down too, and what about Nore, missed her again, hardly
seen her all day, barely a good morning, the flower beds need
watering as well. It hasn't rained, despite the clouds, with
everything still left to do, bed's a long way off, with puffy
ankles, dancing's all very well but – it annoys him when she
scratches at the pan, but she must, discreetly. The living room
needs tidying too, the morning's cups are still hanging

around, a real battlefield, and it would never occur to little miss Nore to . . . The sun's setting earlier and earlier . . .

And Nore out on the road, with her A for *apprentis* stuck on the rear of her car. She doesn't like that. Damp towels in a heap and mascara left open, her trademark. Just popped in to change. And dirty cotton buds beside the bin. What about her bedroom? I daren't even look. Three daughters. Like raising pigs. Tangoing sharpens Momo's appetite. Sometimes she wants to peel him, grab hold of the scar at the top, like a flap, then rip it off all in one go, like the reds strips on those portions of cheese, or new beauty masks, a thick film you peel off. And beneath, to find what? Pale, whole flesh. And he'd even have an eye. A real eye in the right place, rolling in its socket in time with the other one . . . *Non, ça va, je n'ai pas faim. Je suis fatiguée, tu sais bien.* Last night, that documentary about the Bengalis, he changed channels at once, the trace of the acid spray, melting the eyelash, the eye, creating a landslide, the cheek where the chin should be, and the cheekbone on the neck, a devastated face, burnt to the bone, because the mouth had said no, or the hands made a gesture of refusal – *splash*, no more nails, or fingers, instant leprosy. And that book Maïder had me read about Chernobyl, the liquidators who made the concrete for the reactor's coffin, its sarcophagus, who had been exposed to the *fourteen-day sickness*, how horrible, just fourteen days for the mutation to be complete, the nose sliding over the ear, the eyes tripling in size, squeezed out of their sockets, not fitting any more, the nose bone no longer going into the skull, nor the eye in its socket, the tongue in the mouth, the ear in the ear, or the hand in the hand, everything running, dripping, going all over the place and dying . . . The grass looked green and friendly that morning in Chernobyl. But walking on it for three seconds in the dew made cancer rise up their legs, tiny holes widening where the droplets fell . . . How strange to be born in a town whose name is now synonymous with disaster. Even Momo's voice is a bit, a bit ... As though something had gnawed at his vocal cords, and he has problems closing what remains of the right side of his lips, you can see the yellow of the omelette and green of the chillies, a grimace of soup ... She kisses him, his eye smiles at her ... But his story about the machine-gun doesn't wash. The scar's too widely spread, the face is too swamped ...

The last red of the sun in through the fanlight. It's getting decidedly cooler all of a sudden ... From one day to the next, every year's the same, but you still don't get used to it. It's the same way with nausea, you can't believe it when it's happening, and you can't believe it when it stops, with your guts all raw ... And the sickness gone. Each food item recovering its odour. Apples smelling of apples, fish of fish. And the trees too, smelling of trees and not corpses. And John smelling of John. Everything in its place. Jeanne and Anne in their places. And the child in its place, well rooted, alive. I must tidy upstairs, otherwise who else is going to do it? Let's hope she's taking precautions, I haven't seen any Tampax hanging round recently, and then there's AIDS. And there's the load, soon time to turn off the machine and take down yesterday's wash ... Waterlot always wanting her to suffer, to be angry, to speak out, taking her to the trough and forcing her to drink ... The grass is green and tall for the month of October, damp and chill, we're lucky, lucky to be able to ... How to put it? Trust nature. Walk in the grass and eat our own fruit. The vine along the bottom of the patio has given a good yield, and Nore's in excellent health, and the water's drinkable, cold and hot from the taps, and light from the switch ... Even though it's nuclear power ... Sometimes she doesn't know what to think. Nore on the road, with A for *apprentis* stuck on her rear, the roads are slippery at this time of day. We hardly see her any more since she passed her test. But statistically less dangerous than scooters – Anne's old scooter down in the cellar with the bikes, she still hasn't bothered to take it off our hands – how cold the washing is, the seasons descend on to the clothes as they hang, the background temperature sinking into them like sponges, a winding cloth soaked with what is to come – winter, frost . . . Then, at the end of March, a hint of mildness in the weave. She must start putting on her cream again, otherwise she'll get dry skin, when she thinks of the sores her mother used to get, it's a good job we don't hand-wash any more, the boiling pot, stirring that disgusting soup, soot and the entire family's secretions . . . And the towels, the linen, as they used to say, the undergarments you washed on your own, the stink of the half-dried blood at the bottom of the basket . . . Enough to make you disgusted by your own body. She hopes her daughters . . . That she's been a good . . . Anne, so early, at nine and a half, cause and effect, no doubt. But with a boy, she'd have been incapable. She just couldn't have. In the big sheets, heavy with water . . . The red sun when her mother . . . This conditioner smells nice. Odd, the cellar door's open. It's cold in here, as cold as the . . . What's this . . . The winter coats. Nore. We must take them up. Get a box and take them out. Big shoes. And snow boots. From the time when we used to go skiing. Little dungarees. Little mittens. Why has she kept all this stuff? Out and water the flower beds . . .

The large sun, white as a blind eye, an eye which has once seen, sun . . . A frozen atomic bomb up in the sky, a mushroom of hours and seconds building up below your skin . . . Irradiated, second by second, and sick . . . The veins in your neck beating two months to see the suspended sun, screwed tight there, nailed there in the middle of the sky, a cross, a reminder, a white stone, as if she could ever think of anything else, August, September, October, to think of something else for just a second, to forget for one beat of her heart, the valves and ventricles battling on, announcing the assault, remember, remember, each beat with its adrenalin and collapse, you could never fall further, rise higher, taut as a bowstring and silent as a carp, August, September, October, the spring tides gave him back, except that it wasn't his body, impossible . . .

Water the flowers. Stretching and closing . . . Relaxing into the air, after the staring eye of the sun. Beneath the can, it smells of earth, liquorice, a whiff of violets and incense, a syrup of decomposition, damp humus . . . The rabbit's thigh cut by the knife, the mother-of-pearl layer peeling off, the scent of pink, cold flesh, peonies . . . A microclimate's descended on to the garden since they planted the peonies. A migratory mood, big heads, big clusters of flowers, sea anemones and peonies, of course. And this evening, Nore, in that house, her sisters were less footloose. Or more distrustful of the place. Or of boys . . .

Nore

Here's what really happened. There were two bombs. The first one worked by collision. Imagine two large spheres (he mimes, his hands cupped) *which smash into each other inside the shell. When they collide, they set off a chain reaction and there's an explosion. The second worked by collapsing. A single sphere* (he mimes, his hands joined) *which folds in on itself* (he mimes on) *like a crushed meringue. But they were small bombs, of course* (he touches her hand)*, with only about thirty kilos of uranium. To give you an idea, Chernobyl weighed in at two tons. But without an explosion. In some ways, that's worse. Very few people die straight off, but they will die sometime between several hours and thirty years later, not to mention their children* (he mimes: wonky face, dangling tongue, shaky fingers)*. So, basically, if they dropped the second bomb, it's because they wanted to test both sorts, collision* (mime) *and collapse* (mime)*. As for the famous theory about a malfunctioning camera which meant a second bomb was necessary (although your teacher was right on one point – the only existing photos are indeed of Nagasaki), well, I'd just say it was the sort of thing that creates paranoia, and that paranoia thrives in lazy minds.*

This time, he doesn't mime, he lights a cigarette and throws himself back into his chair. He's an extremely expressive lad. She loves listening to his explanations – like with Arnold, who has made a career of it. She did right to phone him, to accept a date, she could listen to him for hours. Something is rising along her skull, between her skin and her bone, like this morning with the ophthalmologist. The roots of her hair stick up, or retract, her skin tightens, becomes too tight for her skull, which is slowly expanding as he talks on . . . She follows the movements of his mouth, his fingers, slowly, so slowly, it's rising, like a laying on of hands, and her thoughts become detached, start floating, she likes that, her fingers and lips grow heavy . . . Just don't stop talking, her languid eyelids fall, her neck relaxes, shoulders recede below her heavy yet airy head. They always have to do their explaining . . . Which suits her, the waves are rising up below her skin, he has a good voice, a steady, deep, appropriate tone . . . Regular, unchanging, enveloping . . . Perfect for wallowing in . . . A precise, central point, which she is approaching, sliding along his voice . . . Nearly there . . .

Did you know that Truman, he is now addressing her directly, *had the National Gallery opened for him every morning? That really doesn't fit with the image we have of him, does it? He used to meditate in front of one or two paintings before going off to decide the fate of the planet. Real art lovers only ever go to look at one or two paintings at a time. Be they modern or classical, they let themselves get hypnotized. Do you like art? I was sure you did. There's a concert this evening at the Chat Rouge, how does that sound?*

Yes, she did right to call him up. He's perfect. She can quite easily imagine spending her entire life with him. He would explain all sorts of things in all sorts of fields. That feeling is there with Arnold too, sometimes, but only if he speaks directly to her. If she grabs him in the corridor, that's what counts, it's the individual attention that matters . . .

To earn a living, he's done umpteen different jobs, from diving to dishwashing, *de la plonge à la plongée,* as he puts it, laughing, she drifts back to him and laughs. His car smells of sand. From now on, this will be the car that comes to pick her up, he'll say hello to Mum and Momo and, as always, her heart will skip a beat when she recognizes the sound of the engine, of this engine, this will be the car that she will later remember, just as she now remembers the metal-grey AX and the old Diane, the Peugeot 406, the little white Fiat, the huge Audi (which only lasted a weekend), the Kangoo, which was always breaking down, and the nice Smart, which was used for more things than its designers had planned. And, of course, the good old R20, with porno mags lying on the seat, *they're my father's*, Lucas used to say, the windows rattling in the wind, ratatatat, in the bends, a spluttering of colour images . . .

For instance, he's done pharmaceutical tests, *Wanted, men aged between eighteen and fifty-three, non-smokers, or smoking under ten a day, for hospital tests*, yes, he's done that, ten days spent watching TV and playing cards, *you weren't allowed out, but the pay was good, because of the neuroleptics, the risk of remaining a bit* . . . (he releases the wheel to mime), *which may well explain certain things about me* (he laughs, she laughs). The sea is night blue, the Chat Rouge is red, *danse* in a neon tube on the cornice, a welcoming hat and a cane. The play of light when the cat leaps into the air, brandishing its hat, is caught synchronously by a beam, which projects the scene. The road looks narrow between the black sky and dark sea, he's driving a bit fast, he wants to impress her, and she's certainly not going to tell him she's scared, *it's like Clint Eastwood*, he gives her a questioning stare, *the actor with two expressions – with or without a hat*. She laughs alone, he hasn't got it, she was referring to the cat, the reflection of the cat in the water, jigging across the waves. The park beneath the tamarisks with the sky flashing, red and white . . . She can hear street music, circus music, a barrel organ in the tide . . . Her hair, wet with the sea wind, keeps getting in her face, it smells of shampoo and seaweed, she holds it back with one hand. Gravel crunches under their feet. She's cold in her light jacket, but that's OK, to make summer linger on a little, they'll play crazy golf and drink some daiquiris, score some coke from the DJ at the Belle Etoile, but it's October and the Belle Etoile is closed and there's a nip in the air. Her heart beats faster, life is passing away at such a speed, she knows that already, she's had a few drinks (she hopes he can hold his drink and his course). A sudden nostalgia grips her. She could almost weep for her nineteen years that have flown. How hopeless it is to be mortal. Thank God the bar's open. The bouncer and Nicolas are waiting for her, the curtain raised. The cat, with its cane and hat, is playing golf with their heads. To the right, there's the coast, dotted with its grid of lights, streetlamps, cars, the yellow interiors of houses, a sparkling ribbon running up as far as the mountains. To the left, there's the sea and deep night, a line of boats separates her from the darkness, with a dotted line of sleepy lights . . .

Black water beneath a black sky, the weather's texture changes, it lingers over them in a sluggish, thick mist. The cat's neon lights dim, cutting out a halo against which the bouncer is smoking, leaning against the red steam: a cold forge, they used to call it the Grotte and, more recently, the Rhumerie. A slow bass line, thump, thump, thump, can only just be heard, as though rising from the depths of the cliffs. The group's set has already started, thump, thump, thump, a poster is flapping slightly against a planked wall, she remembers its name when she was little: the Cargo. She turns round. Now the sea's started smoking, the bouncer and Nicolas look round as well, or else look at her, she doesn't know, a huge white mass, thick and fluid, is advancing towards them on the crest of a wave, moving into their eyes, into their noses, through their clothes, she can feel the chill of the wind on her belly. Another second, and they can't see each other any more. The air is talcum powder swollen with water, tasting of iron and chalk. Then the fog recedes, the white tide runs down the cliff side and rolls back with the undertow. The air's clear once more. A transparent blackness around a red cat. Nicolas's eyelashes and hair are sparkling with droplets. She hangs on his arm, the white wall is advancing towards them again, another wave. The timer has tipped over, the cat raises its hat and the bouncer pulls back the curtain. They go into the nightclub.

Anne

She slips on her jacket, and switches on her answering machine, *Vous êtes bien chez Anne Johnson, s'il vous plaît laissez-moi un message et je vous rappellerai dès mon retour,* how pathetic, her lonely electronic voice in the empty flat. The poplars are spluttering in the courtyard. On the side overlooking the street, the windows are flickering in TV blue, blue break, blue-grey variations, a sudden red background as the montage progresses. She opens her window, flicks her cigarette. A white, creamy silence of lampposts and moonlight, the air above joining the air below. She feels the earth bending, distancing itself inch by inch from the sun, and when the machine beeps to announce that it's ready to receive any unlikely messages, it's the signal for her to melt into this autumnal night . . .

She's in the street. Pink traces at the foot of the canyon, the night has not yet occupied the entire sky. Outside and in – she could forget her address, access codes, place and object of work, position on the planet and purpose of her mission – absolutely anything could make her tip down the slope, with everything going topsy-turvy, and so lose the very idea that a home can be yours, and that tomorrow may bring you something specific, something just for you . . .

She stops for a moment, looks at her feet, at the sky. She might start falling, either upwards or downwards. But, she reassures herself, there are no cracks. *Anne Johnson,* she whispers, *Anne Johnson,* out for a walk . . .

Take sentinels, for instance, that's something she couldn't stand – may the brains at HQ spare her that ordeal – having to stare at the city as if it was a glove turned inside out, with the streets as the interior and the buildings – their walls – as an impenetrable exterior, gates as exits, but blocked ones, the tarmac as floorboards, porches as narrow bedrooms, squares as halls, façades as ramparts and, through the windows, dinner parties, capons, sweets, little match girls and inaccessible heat . . . Hansel and Gretel in their gingerbread house, the witch fattening up the children – it's always the same question: where to live? It's not so much what to do, it's more, where to place her body, where to tidy it away, where to get rid of it. She always knows *what to do*, even without her body she would . . .

Without her body, there would be only the anxiety and euphoria about her next mission, and the desire to take off into the air . . .

For instance, that painting in the museum in Houston, blue sky going turquoise over white arches in limpid air, clear-cut dream architecture, an equestrian statue in the middle of a square edged on one side by the arches, the ground extremely yellow, on the far side (perhaps) by a red-roofed building and always that evolving blue sky. The painting was so blue, so yellow, red and white that it vibrated. Noon time for ever, frozen on that canvas: exactly how the sun is when it's unbearable, beating straight down on the snare of the walls, vertically cutting out the uninhabitable zone which our habitats describe . . .

Maybe it was there, who knows, in front of that picture, code name Chirico, that the man in the dark suit who was standing behind her whispered the next appointment to her. They must have spotted her there. She has a talent for being in the right place at the right time, a first-class sentinel, a mind sensitive to variations just as plankton changes its course according to shifts in the planet's magnetic field, as open to the seasons as migratory birds, listening far away in the south, as though a spring in a clock had relaxed in their brains – working up speed, taking wing unthinkingly in V directionals, supra-sensitive, recruited for that very reason. She perceives the slightest mood swing, the slightest signal, the slightest accident interfering with the world's encephalic field, spinning like a Cantonese puzzle ball around the network of consciousnesses . . .

Like the plant, aptly named *sensitive*, which (deprived of any possibility of flight) shivers, folds and rolls itself up when touched discreetly . . .

Of course, at night, she's off duty, her shift's over, at night, she can relax, questions are less urgent, white walls cut out by the sun are so blatant . . .

The Chirico Mission on the Zarathustra Programme . . . she'll be ready when she has to infiltrate the minds of clones, she's already visited so many sites, so many heads, homed in on so many voices, recorded so many whispers, eavesdropped on so many mental bubbles, when the clone thinks, she'll know . . .

When the clone walks beneath the empty arches, she'll hear him . . .

All these people, still on terraces . . .

Gelatine between her and the world . . .

The moon dissolves its threads in the echoing night . . .

Her favourite exercise, all alone in the isolation box, sensitive only to interior noises, no interference, when she manages that, what a success . . .

She could have a quiet drink here, the music's so loud, the bass is thumping, the systolic rhythm, bar stool quivering up to the whites of your eyes . . .

She was fifteen when she used to listen to that, *NIGHT TIME GONNA WAKE YOU UP*, a vodka, *UNE VODKA, GLACE*, the barman's not bad . . .

154

Unless she was recruited extremely young, when Pierre . . .
As a replacement, so to speak. Unless Pierre's somewhere in
town. Death is the ideal cover, everyone's looking for a hiding place, Jeanne too is probably hiding what she's up to . . .
And John, in Gibraltar, perched on his rock, he must be doing
it too, it's obvious with such a strategic position, not one, not
two, with his vanes controlling the weather – having a father
in the network isn't impossible, as for Momo, I wouldn't dare
imagine what he's done, from father to stepfather, from
Charybdis to Scylla . . .

UNE VODKA UNE AUTRE LA MÊME CHOSE . . .

When we were little, the hermit crab out of his shell looking
for a new one. The first shell (a font as resonant as a church)
was as heavy as a stone and so huge that its rear legs couldn't
get a purchase on it, nor its front legs drag it across the sand.
The second one (a winkle in which nothing could be heard)
was so narrow that, once inside, it couldn't move its feelers
and its feet, a real corset. The third one (a lovely shine, as
spotted as a sea leopard) was the right size for both its front
and its back feet. Inside, you hear the sea . . .

There were wanderings between these three shells, whose
names varied according to Mum's conchological vocabulary
. . . The struggle with the crab, the storm, man overboard, the
equinoctial tide and the little naked foot . . . Which belonged,
according to the maternal mood, to Jeanne, to Anne and later
to Nore . . . Nonore . . . Ronron . . . Momo . . . And her unbearable tickles and her fits of euphoria as hard to put up with as
her fits of rage, or her silence . . .

The three shells, Goldilocks and the three bears and, of
course, the three bells, the small one, the middle-sized one
and the big one, which you could see in the clock tower from
the upstairs bedroom window and which chimed the hours:
dong went the big bell, *dang* went the middle-sized bell, *ding*
went the little bell, the hours, the minutes and the angelus,

the big one chiming for Jeanne, the middle-sized one for Anne and the little one for Nore, and then there was another one, even smaller, above the stained-glass window, the fourth bell which chimed only at funerals, with Nore always asking what it was for . . .

UNE AUTRE LA MÊME CHOSE.

The Father

This is exactly how he felt . . .

It is exactly this house which he has dreamed of all his life.
Exactly that scatter of mountains in the distance.
Exactly that line of trees sweeping towards him.
Exactly that neighbour's wife coughing on the balcony.

He puts the book on his chest. Frank Kuppner. This is exactly what he's dreamed of all his life: a large balcony over the sea, a deckchair and poetry, a flock of engines working for him on top of the hill. Africa in the distance. That scatter of mountains, purple and black, hazy. Sometimes the haze is so thick it reminds you of Ireland. If you forget the constant warmth. When he saw the house, he knew that it was his house: he recognized it. He just had to put some flowers on the balcony and to buy a deckchair. Details into place, fitting into a pre-existing frame, something he's already planned or seen: and it's there. A sudden gust of wind. The nearest 50/750 gives a crack, in an effort to rise, to fly, but the earth clings to it – electricity. The 30/250s are harvesting the wind at full speed. Their fluffing reaches a peak, a brief shriek, like a flock of birds of prey . . .

He almost missed the phone ringing . . .
  JEANNE . . .
He presses a finger in his ear; the forty 18/80s are clapping their epoxy blades in excitement, hissing *wiiind wiiind*, while the medium ones, twenty-four of them, the 30/250s, buzz in

156

the upper field, turbines on maximum, the ground will burst out and take off . . .

Elle va partir pour le delta du Tigre, ils ont a pretty house there, he's never seen it, they sent a photo once . . .

El Tigre, he's always fancied that land striped gold and black, long lashes of bee-like vegetation under a bee-like gold and brown sky, tiger hiding in the bushes, his eyes like humming bees hovering over Jeanne, something gold, dark and dangerous, in that faraway land – his oldest one, his beloved Jeanne, his Daddy's girl . . .

He wishes they would have a kid . . .

A son so he could be a grandfather . . .

He'd know how to do it, to be it . . .

Nice guy, Diego . . .

He screams over the turbines, a fool in an empty house, *I'D LIKE TO SEE YOU BOTH WHEN WILL YOU COME TO SEE ME? – When will YOU come to see us, Dad?*

Hija mia, *what's up, what's the scoop, what's the dirt, how are your sisters, do you get news sometimes? – You could ring them, Dad, I live an ocean away while you live just a country away, how are you, I was thinking of you . . .*

I'M FINE, he screams over the wind . . .

The deep bass sound of the 50/750, the big one. Good machine, that. He likes the sound of it. Flapping and flapping as the mill goes round and round, heavy, patent, palpable. A huge helicopter over Gibraltar, over the war of Gibraltar. The boats from Africa, loaded with Arabs, crossing the channel through the haze and the dark. From what distance do they start hearing the big shuffling noise, the sound of this land? Or does the sea muffle it?

THERE'S A STORM COMING IN BUT I'VE JUST ORGA-NIZED IT ALL I'VE JUST MOUNTED A NEW DEVICE OVER THE VOLTAGE PROTECTIONS, IF THERE'S A POWER SURGE AND THE GRID GETS DISCONNECTED – YOU'VE

GOT TO ACT AT THE SPEED OF LIGHT, YOU KNOW – THE MUTATORS WILL BE PROTECTED BY THESE EXTREMELY FAST-ACTING NEW FUSES I'VE JUST RECEIVED . . .

How interesting, he hears . . .

I know what you're thinking. I know what you're thinking and I'd have known it at the speed of light, I've always known it, my only limit is the speed of sound, the speed of the fucking telephone, *I COULD COME AND KICK YOUR ARSE RIGHT NOW*, mentally, I mean, *HOW'S YOUR MUM? AND HOW'S HER MONKEY? HOW'S MAURICE THE MONKEY?*

Well, how are your own monkeys, Dad, how's the rock, still standing, still British?

I THINK WE SHOULD HANG UP, COS OF THE STORM. CAN BE DANGEROUS. As in *Tintin and the Seven Crystal Balls. I'LL CALL YOU BACK. TAKE CARE.* Love you. Love you.

The 18/80, eighteen metres in diameter, 80kW maximum . . .

The 30/250, thirty metres, 250kW . . .

And the 50/750 . . .

Advanced Wind Technologies . . .

The sky is blood red over the sea, tiny little boats approaching, bellies full of immigrants like eggs in fish-pouches. Sometimes they are found dead on the morning beaches. Bloated, drowned, betrayed. The wind is blowing harder now, sweeping away the haze. A big, big rotor sound is saturating the air. Crashed helicopters planted on the hill and still turning, like animal flowers flapping and breathing hard. Or big, dangerous flies working all night, and the sound of the swarm makes him feel good. Engines working while we sleep. Watching over us. Taking care of us. That very special noise. That's the magic of the big 50/750. When they decided to abandon the gearbox: that was the magic. You can hardly hear the electric system when the wind blows so hard. When they abandoned that conventional roto-gearbox-generator drive-train. Directly connecting the three-blade rotor system to the generator: that was the genius of it. No more extensive, expensive gearbox maintenance, and the noise: you basically hear the big, deep voice of the wind. But he likes the 18/80 too. A thin, long stem, like a sunflower. That's his girl. Elegant. Solid. Reliable. Turning *every day*, in the lightest breeze. So swift, like a sparrow. You never see the blades, you see a little silver sun, shining. And the sound, the mere sound of it, like those little Japanese bells, that little tinkling, it refreshes you. That's also the way the sound of the 50/750 helps him sleep at night. Humming big in the night. Crooning him to sleep . . .

Is there wind on the Tigre? Is it a windy place? Surely not. Swamps, lianas, vegetal wicks . . . How did it go? *Tyger tyger, burning bright, in the forests of the night,* he learned that at school in Dublin. He can see huge dragonflies setting fire to the canopy like sparkles, and the roaring of the fire like a huge tiger-lily set to life – but the forest where she lives – only for the weekends – that rainforest north of Buenos Aires, couldn't burn, too wet; a wild country but she's safe there, *El Tigre con el acento,* why worry?

In three notes the closest 50/750 slows down, mi re do, *three blind mice,* and then stops, period, click, trigger still. The wind gets its breath back. Everything calms down, everything is fine. The twenty-four 50/750s are all slowing down together on the hill, the wind flows back, mi re do – *three blind mice, three blind mice, see how they run, see how they run, they all ran after the farmer's wife, who cut off their tails with a carving knife, did you ever see such a thing in your life as three blind mice?*

Jeanne

I'm pleased to see you, doctor, I've got several things on my mind, not to mention my friend Jimena, who's just stood me up . . . No vinio a nuestra cita, *I hope she hasn't had an accident . . . and then*

there's my father, I've just phoned him, he's still stuck in Gibraltar
looking after the wind, he's quite simply going round in circles, he
ought to make a fresh start, Diego and I had a row yesterday, I
intend to spend my next holidays in Europe, while he wants to take
me to his parents' place in Corrientes, and he criticized me because
apparently I'm incapable of saying anything bad about my country,
as if he, and you, you Argentinians thought you'd all floated down
from the skies and crash-landed in your lifeboat of a country, in any
case, my father's Anglo-Irish, my mother's Basque and France is
just a bridge between us, I'm far from being patriotic . . .

Anyway, I was thinking about all that on the way here, cars are
good places for thinking things out like that, your hands and feet are
occupied, but as for your head, your mind, there's a song in France
that goes Alouette, gentille alouette, so anyway, I was associat-
ing away in my car and what crossed my mind – I don't know why,
it's a bit silly really – was a film or a TV show I saw with Anne
when I was about eleven or twelve, maybe I've already told you
about it . . . the whispering house . . .

It's like a dream, it was a long time ago now, pieces of it are missing,
and maybe I've reinvented it, but it goes something like this: there's
a young woman, married but without children, who, for some rea-
son that escapes me, is extremely attracted to a house – I can still
picture the building – but the house is evil. She herself knows that
and tries to resist, and yet at the same time she knows that this
house is her home. *Her husband and her brother help her to resist*
this attraction. When the house is empty, whispers can be heard.
Hundreds of tiny, rustling female voices, chchchchchch, the mut-
tering of voices which are plotting, weaving their trap to take this
young woman back to where she belongs *. . . When the two men*
go inside to clean the place up, so to speak, to open the shutters and
air it, as soon as they go inside, the voices fall silent and materialize
as hundreds of little spiders which scamper off behind the cast-iron
frames of the broken fireplaces, where there are huge woolly nests,
unravelling, shifting about in all directions . . .

The two men talk the woman into moving far, far away from the influence of the house. So she asks just to go round it once. They stand on either side of her, holding her hands. They walk from room to room. Their footsteps echo. It looks almost like they're house-hunting – the young woman has no recollection of any of the rooms, nothing inside it rings a bell – except that, the further they go, the more terrified she is by the attraction she feels for it, by the obvious connection she has with these walls, despite the love she has for her husband and brother, despite the normal, comfortable, pleasant, even desirable existence she leads outside. She wants to make this place her own, to curl up inside its walls, to chain herself to its furnishings, to shut herself up in its fireplaces . . . I remember the way her eyes roll back as she advances one foot, then another, and the two men are dressed in black . . . the double doors in front of them open with a sigh, in slow motion . . . the visit comes to an end, the three of them leave . . .

– And?

And the young woman follows the two men, her head drooping, maybe she's crying and doesn't want them to see. The gravel crunches beneath their feet, an old rose bush, which climbs up the grey façade, stretches out towards her . . . When they get to the car, she turns back to the house . . . an expression crosses her face, her eyes . . . then suddenly she starts running, she leaps up the steps, opens the heavy door . . . its two halves slam shut as if they've swallowed her, as if . . . And then you hear the voices, like one terrible, excitedly merry voice, laughing, and, happiest of all, the voice of the young woman above the rest . . .

– That reminds me of another film you told me about, a silent movie with Lilian Gish . . .

What, The Wind? We saw it together in Paris, my father, my sister and me. Dad was a film buff and Paris is the only real city for buffs. With her little hands, she rubs the dishes with sand . . . In that waterless town, in the American dustbowl, while her shack is being shaken by the wind . . . Her cowboy husband has gone away to catch wild horses far off on the prairie, and now the charmer she met in the train comes back to seduce her, to promise her a dandy life in the big

*city. He's crazy with desire for her, but she kills him with the bread
knife because she's a good girl, that's why. Then she tries to bury
him in the sand with her little hands, but the wind keeps uncover-
ing the body. There's a huge sandstorm, and she thinks her husband's been killed . . . Then, when he at last comes back, she realizes
that she loves him so much . . . and he buries the body in a deep
grave, with his masculine tools, if you see what I mean . . .*

– And?

*I was thinking about that plane crash . . . you remember, on
Manaus. I heard on the radio that only one family survived. The
father picks himself out of the wreckage. He supposes that he's the
only survivor, everything's on fire all around him, and then he sees
a woman, his wife, and then they find their children, who are alive
. . . the sole survivors of an entire Boeing . . .*

*– If I remember correctly, there was also another survivor, a little
boy whom they decided to adopt.*

*That's right, it's a recomposed family in fact, ha ha ha . . . I mean,
how can anyone possibly come through such a tragedy? Apparently, the father's turned mystic and the mother's been struck dumb . . .
They're suffering from, not Stockholm Syndrome, that's for
hostages . . . Survivors of the camps say the same thing, that sur-
vival is just luck, courage and greatness of spirit have nothing to do
with it, not even cunning or prudence. You quite simply owe your
life to good luck . . . Refuse to see any meaning in it. Here, in Buenos
Aires, people say that heroes can't easily be defined in terms of who
talked and who didn't . . . that, under torture, you never know
whether a person will talk or not . . .*

– That will be all for today.

The Mother

The frogs are chanting in the undergrowth, it's so damp that
it goes all marshy as soon as autumn arrives. The green
aquatic songbirds chant and coo. The cane toads where
Jeanne lives which eat hares. Jeanne's Africa and America are

162

there, below the window, in the night of the south-west of France. Mi re do, frogs and toads. Bubbles in the liquid night, voiced bubbles popping, a spluttering of running water, ech-o, ech-o, I am the Toad, bubbles explode. The black night falls and spreads like a slick, dripping, from the window to the bed, while he covers her, *cover me* . . . The comfy depths in the hollows of the swamp, ech-o, ech-o, he's patient, constant, she can count on him, slow and heavy, that's why she chose him, knowing straight away that she could count on him . . .

Not like John, who was so handsome, so crazy, as fickle as a butterfly, toads eat butterflies, scrunched wings, mangled antennae and legs, a body of colours crumpled in a magnifi-cent pile-up . . .

He shakes his head, he doesn't like her to touch him there . . .

Chiselled, humped, hammered flat, red copper . . .

Concentrate . . .

Slow, patient efforts, so familiar, so soft, crabs asleep beneath the rocks, finding their echo in what's still asleep . . .

Make up your mind, get moving, something's beating, it's simple, just think, deep down, about the red depth he's mov-ing, like the bed of a lake throwing up humus, it's a question of habit, she knows him by heart, he knows her by heart, a question of slowness, he's off and away, that's certain, the frogs crow or croak, rooks crouched in the depths of the swamp, a leap, suckers open . . . Sucking the depths, breath-ing in, letting go . . . you have to think about it a bit, you just have to think, don't lose track . . . then it comes naturally . . . keep yourself within, stay there, inside . . . the rough skin of his shoulders, dog's head, seal's head on a minotaur's body, a house builder, one room, two rooms, a corridor and more rooms, a labyrinth you know by heart as far as its centre, its red centre . . . he's there, it's him, touching what she herself can't reach, the unattainable red centre . . . the whole body up front, a big body face with two legs sticking out, and the cake of the stomach . . . unclosing before, behind, the back, the

163

underside, the fold, what can't be seen . . . what becomes full
. . . concentrate . . . she's that flat thing, crushed beneath him
and dug at by a real space, getting bigger and bigger . . .
enveloping her . . . and digging deeper, staying there, there it
is, in this room draped with red, softened velvet, which
widens, shrinks, a tunnel, a beating artery, containing her, in
the middle, exactly in the middle . . . now there's no escape
for them, the wheel's been set spinning, straight forwards,
bounding into the enclosure, they're both entirely wrapped
in red . . .

Nore

She looks at him. They can't hear each other. How annoying.
They didn't come here to listen to music, that guy on stage
chucking his voice at them as though he's about to collapse at
the end of each song, as though only his ribcage was keeping
him upright. It's tedious, and everyone's smoking, she needs
some air, she's probably gone red – she puts down her glass,
puts on her jacket with grandiose gestures, and leaves – he
catches up with her. The air is mild. The moon's red through
the cat's hat, he kisses her, made it, she closes her eyes . . .

Her great desire is ubiquity. She looks at him to see if he
understands the word: to be here and also there, at once. *Yes
indeed*, he ups the ante, *and the only way to be ubique is to change
the course of time, project yourself into the past, or else into the
future, even just for a moment, and then witness your own presence*
. . . You could even, she starts getting carried away, sleep with
your father and kill your mother, throw everything off
course, you could make yourself vanish from the surface of
the planet, *phut!* in a thousandth of a second, to have never
existed, almost anything would do, it's the butterfly effect,
you prevent your own birth – *But*, he remarks, *you could sleep
with your father and kill your mother now*. She pauses to think . . .

How can I put it, it's a form of suicide, you look for the cause of your arrival in order to suppress it, to commit suicide is to vanish from your own memory (Paul Valéry's 'Monsieur Teste', Arnold's class about anti-romanticism). She looks at him to see if he knows that. He looks at her. He looks at the road. He looks at her. Now it's certain. He wants to go to bed with her . . .

Her hair is fluttering in the wind. She no longer holds it back, at high speed, the town flashes red and yellow around them . . .

It reminds her of when she first learned to drive – concentrating on the manoeuvre, the road straight ahead, foot on the accelerator, hands clenched on the wheel, eyes peering up into the rear-view mirror, and then to the left to overtake, and then straight on, a long triangle of energy . . . white black, white black, the motorway, fifth gear purring, *I'm driving, I'm driving*. Barriers. A car in front, a car behind. Safety distance. Stuck on the idea that she's driving. It starts to take up all the available space. A paralysing clarity, everything is continuing around me, but without me, the speed, tarmac, flashing lights, white lines, the long curve to negotiate. *I'm driving*, she's gripped, brutally assaulted by the idea. Amazed, not because she isn't driving, but because she's here. I was observing myself observing myself, sliding along the movement, having to go along with it, unable to escape – I missed the bend, one of those long, intelligent, motorway bends, and no way afterwards could she explain the accident, *I'm driving*, what can be said? That a sudden flash of light dazzled me? A noon sun in the rear-view mirror, chrome-plated bumpers? The bodywork folded around me, as though maternally warped to coincide with my body: an egg. And I was whole and yellow, the firemen cut open the shell with their massive scissors . . . my mother had to lie in bed for two weeks. Finally asked me if I was out to kill her. But as for *I'm driving*, how to explain that?

She leans on his thigh and kisses his neck, there, at the root of the clavicle, a smell of aftershave and toast. One of two possibilities . . . 1) either he thinks she's lovely, 2) he'll reckon she's drunk or luring him into a trap . . .

She guides him, right, left, she hopes he isn't hungry, that they won't have to go through the conventions, anyway there's nothing to eat in the house, swift dark trees bending, startled rabbits in the headlamps . . .

Anne

No, she doesn't need, doesn't want anyone to accompany her, they've left her all alone tonight, neither Laurent nor anyone else has phoned, left alone all evening, at the mercy of the first pick-up merchant, first pervert, the absolute zero of loving, affectionate care, she can't even remember what Laurent looks like. *ANOTHER VODKA PLEASE.* She tries to conjure him up, beside her, or behind the bar . . . WHAT THE HELL'S SHE DONE WITH HER VISA CARD? Ah, here it is. What does he, or did he, look like? *Mister Blue Eyes,* she remembers that his eyes are blue, Laurent the blue-eyed boy and sooooooo proud of it, imagine two eyes, blue ones, and a nose, a straight one, eyebrows, bushy maybe, he's got brown hair, that's right, with some white streaks round his temples, a mouth, no precise memories of that . . . For the moment, he looks like a Mr Potato, a spud face like they used to make when they were little girls, and if she closes her eyes and forgets the black and red shapes which are smoking and moving around her, she can see, what? The aura of a face, she's got his proportions recorded in her body, she raises her arms to embrace him, he's tall – but the face, nothing doing, she doesn't have it, an object she didn't look at long enough, being sucked in by his eyes at once. She doesn't know what he looks like, she's never taken him in, or else he hardly exists, she's oooverestimated him: two eyes, a nose and a mouth. The stroboscopic light beats on her eyelids, when she opens them, everyone looks the same: two black holes, a white crack, a red jostling face, death heads. May as well try and remember Jeaaanne, who she hasn't seen for God knows how long, or Jooohn, or Pierre, fat chance. Everybody looks alike, two dark blotches and a crack of teeth (fluorescent here, in the dark light) and the rest forming various ovals, a hint of a beard, lipstick, or the grime she discovered on her mother's elegant neck, everything's moving around with a distinct lack of reference points, one tooth darker than another, hairs in noses, warts, thwarts – there's Momo, of course, just over theeere. You should sketch everyone like with stickers to memorize them, trait by trait, mental snaps, immobilize them, EVERYONE REPORT HERE . . .

Dancing, first her feet, knees, hips, hands, arms, belly, close your eyes, down it goes, up it goes, it's clear, they've left her all alone at the mercy of one and all, of the first SERIAL KILLER, anyone out to slice her up, the opposite of TENDER LOVING CARE, she should have expected that, dropped here like a free electron – who cares – she'll make a deeevastating REPORT, she could make the most of the situation by escaping, vanishing, breaking all links with her CONTACTS, but she won't, she's conscientious, she knows from experience that *if one link snaps, JUST ONE*, then the entire p-pyramid comes tumbling down – *dancing*, it's a TRICK BY HER CELL, in order to spot the BEST ELEMENTS, on/off, field surveillance, make your mind up time, wide spectrum sweeps. In this nightclub, one of the local droids might be proceeding as vigilantly as she is. This is a favourable ground for contacts, infra-, inter- and super-linguistics, for capturing voices, receiving fleeting wavebands, stay vivivigilant while letting her ears range about; on/off, *dancing*, arms and belly. For instance, she can see N-Nore, that's just to warm up, a practice session, the immediate family attracts your attention at once. She can see Nore squirming with a man on her belly, mucous fluids activated mechanically, emotional charge low, a high level of impatience, while in the next room, the lounge, in their childhood home, beside the large green settee covered with a white sheet, there's another person, emotional charge high, bursting with impatience, mucous activity non-existent, energy aura SUPERPOWERFUL, this other person has been disturbed by Nore's arrival – *dancing*, she improvises, the bass lines shake her body, she concentrates on what she can see, racked by the music, the din, smoke, dances, vodka, she concentrates on the betweens of things, pulls herself together, can hardly make anything out, a vague face, imprecise traits, imprecise body, he passes through the fireplace, no, the wall, hesitates for a second above the garden, goes back, sits on the green settee, no, above the green settee, the night air gleams beneath his rump, his problematic body, he stands up, fidgets, looks bored, wipes a diaphanous hand across his ashen face, as though covered with talc – she's going to sneeze, she stops herself – *dancing*, he almost vanished, but she's got him, he starts up a strange dance in the garden, but he's also inside, on the green settee, and sitting on the edge of the bed where Nore and the other character are, and he's diffusing himself over all the points in her field of surveillance, of her security zone, crossing continents and oceans . . .

The Mother

Just as Dr Waterlot said, the fear was that he would come back. She thought she'd seen him, that's all, how stupid, she was going downstairs to let the cat in, because that idiot Nore had locked him out again. Momo's asleep, that's all, everything's normal, a reflection in the windowpane, the cat, her face, the moon, all is quiet. Sit down, pull over the chair, the kitchen is the warmest place, the most real, the most . . . I mean, really, to be afraid of a child, if he rang at the door, what could that possibly do to her now? Holding him in her arms is out of the question, finished, all is quiet and in order, the frogs are frogging and the toads are toading . . .

Little antennae were waggling above the eye sockets, water is worse than the earth, quicker, more alive, a heap of sea

168

maggots when the body came back – what if she had some hot milk? She'd trusted the girls, trusted them too much, Jeanne especially. They were supposed to be big, independent, according to John's theories. But if she hadn't let go of his hand, let him out of her sight . . .

In the end, the only one who really went mad is Anne, and the link isn't even there, in reality, she isn't John's daughter, it's that simple. Some milk, sugar and cinnamon. She had them like shelling peas – they say that kids understand everything, sense everything, like animals . . .

Why isn't she asleep? Twenty-six years now she's been counting, twenty-six years and the sum still doesn't add up. Make love, make love, it must be down to something else, a prayer she worded wrongly, a series of circumstances, and then it happens – a bulb planted skew-whiff, three dice falling on their edges, and behold the child. If she could just stop worrying for one second. Just one night would be enough, and the kids there, they soon sniff out what we're hiding from them. Always ferreting. Jeanne in the country everyone escapes to, then disappears. Anne in Paris. John down in his enclave, *de sa gwacieuse majesté*. And the two of them, the little one and the old one, Nonore and me, the last bastions, with Momo building the walls . . .

It's always at night, in the kitchen, when the numbness between her legs has gone, in the morning she can't say it, but there must be a link. Trying to come and only to come, the pleasure's the same, but the orgasm, throwing yourself upwards, grabbing it. To come, there must be a link, but tonight, tonight, what was there . . .

Jeanne

She's in time for the 19.10 boat, not too much traffic for a Friday evening. The session with her analyst has done her good – everything in good time. Family carpentry: a Basque-Anglo-Irish chest with French mouldings, and an inscription on the front: *I'm not guilty* in embossed letters. John on the left-hand panel, Mum on the right, everything in place, no one jutting out. Anne in the left-hand drawer, Nore in the right-hand drawer, and in the lowest drawer, the one with the false bottom, yet still clearly labelled, her brother. The four legs, her four grandparents. Central panel: Diego. A lid you can lower: a child. *Quizás*. File her work away somewhere in the rolls of paper in the large lower drawer. A few photos pinned on the cloth covering. Come to think of it . . .

The vague feeling of having had nightmares last night, a slight hint of anxiety in the larynx, a slight swelling, it's nothing, like an insect, she swallows, with lightness and elegance, she's driving the little Volvo coupé that Diego bought her, a folly, pure pleasure, raspberry-red nails on the leather steering wheel, it's not every day that she's so, how to put it? Jolly, pretty, what's it down to? The sun is shining side on. We're nearly at San Marco. Look, apparently there's a wedding, bells ringing, lots of cars and people dressed up to the nines – well, what the locals think of as being elegant – you can't miss the bride, what a big fat white meringue – with the hired limo too! San Marco's rather nice, in the end it's been a good day, except for Jimé, she could have phoned, I'm a worrier, she knows that, what's this cloud doing here? A mass of insects near the, what's it called? The canal, no, the *sound*, but round here you're never quite sure, it's October, the eggs have hatched, brand-new mosquitoes ready to pump out the first bag of blood they can get their hooks into, high-speed electric windows and what a slaughter on the windscreen! I must drop into the car wash, I can't stand this smell of synthetic lavender any more, I'll stop at the next garage and buy a new air freshener for the car, outside it smells of, what does it smell of? Honeysuckle, the red and yellow honeysuckle of the Tigre, the kind that's growing behind the house. Plants like that love water, this evening dinner with the Branconis, I could wear my green suit, unless Diego prefers . . . Or else we'll have a quiet evening on the veranda, listening to the lapping of the water. We must redo, have redone the coating on the shutters, it's the dampness that does it, and while I think of it, there's the grouting on the balcony in BA which is starting to . . . I noticed that this morning, I must tell him – apparently I've lost a bit of weight, my wedding ring is loose, unless it's got cooler, how hot is it? Twenty-eight degrees, but the electronics in this car always raise the temperature a bit. Yesterday, it went up to thirty-seven, it must work this time, another fortnight to wait if it's yes or no for my periods, it's no life being a woman, but I do ovulate, I've had tests done – we did it last night semiconsciously, it's better that way, without the brain butting in, when the body works without reason, the unconscious mind takes me straight down to the uterus, an egg, don't get carried away, *it's the story of the little red hen*, when I think Mum's taken up the tango supposedly so as to . . . I don't know, hold my hand, *dansez, dansez, vous avez chanté tout l'été* . . .

These clouds of insects are incredible, raised by the heat, the wind, the slipstream of the car, suddenly out of the lagoon, it reminds me of that lake in Africa, when those red puffy things came out of the water, like moss, and then the fish . . . we cooked them on palm leaves – Africa also smelt of honeysuckle, a white sweetish smell, dampness getting in your throat, it's rising distinctly between the lianas now, in springtime, up to the tips of the trees – how peaceful and green the canal is, a quarter to seven, I'm daydreaming, get a move on, I'll take that short cut that's so nice along the towpath.

Nore

She never knows when it's over, sometimes they spend hours labouring away, and the misunderstanding lasts and lasts, until they end up making a false move, slipping out and not being able to get back in, embarrassing, so she starts all over – builds up her respiration, makes him believe she's off again, these things happen – apparently, in *Marie-Claire*, moans getting closer and closer, glissades on the top notes, a simulated loss of control . . . the most difficult bit is to distinguish, to *make him distinguish*, the final cry from the preceding yelps, don't be afraid to act feline, to scratch, roll your hips, close your eyes, open them, stare wildly, grip him compulsively, your irresistible hair spread out, which he's run his fingers through after . . . have to wash it again – she cries out, don't overdo it either, it's an art, a measured art, she hopes she's already got him going enough so that he'll . . . how do other girls manage, yes, that's it, they always fall for it, whether they're fifteen or fifty, so incredibly credulous . . .

Afterwards, it's wet, it runs, even with condoms, how odd that the body produces so many substances, I hope he thought I was good, that I was his best yet, I give good head too, in any case, at my age, you should make love a lot, later the body ages, it's a question of health, of attention to your partner . . .

This bathroom, these jammed taps, Le Griffon, it's what happens when no one uses them, just to think, Mum even wanted to have the electricity cut off, so I told her, *j'y vais souvent dans cette maison*, my sisters want her to sell, but one day I'll make it my home, what on earth can a bobby girl be, he told me I was a bobby girl . . .

It's colder and colder, I was careful to put on an extra duvet, I hope he isn't cold, it's the best bedroom, my parents' one, *TU VEUX UN CAFÉ?* I'll make some coffee . . .

Nothing, a shadow at the window, that sensation of cold, a sort of frost which makes patterns on the glass with its breath. She hugs Nicolas's pullover and the feeling comes back, of wandering along an unknown corridor, she often gets panicky like that, in no matter which house, that impression of having died without being told, because that's what it's like, you die like that, the dead don't know they're dead and get up again after the impact thinking it was a trivial incident, a

172

false note, a drop in rhythm, while their body is lying there among the onlookers. Blindly, they continue on their way, left ignorant out of pity, they're so young, or because of consternation at such a stupid accident . . . then it's a question of organization, reintegrated in parallel universes identical in every respect to their original biotope, our dear ones as holograms and houses inhabited by machine-made images . . . Until, rounding a corner in a corridor, they accidentally walk off the set and fall in among the dead: nuts and bolts, obvious pulleys, the cogs and wheels all out in the open, hasty coats of paint, felt insulation . . . Or else, it's the seasons that change round, night falls at any old time, the thermometer goes crazy . . . Or else, Mum starts spouting a strange language . . . Or else, the lover's head spins round on his neck, faulty dummies, radiators, knick-knacks, this kind of detail, exorcists, you finally realize you're dead . . .

(She was sure she'd left more coffee than that in the tin. *Who's been drinking my coffee?* daddy bear asks.)

And if your entire life does pass before your eyes, what do you see? An objective, panoramic overview? Or a rewind of everything you've seen? Who does the choosing? Who's the narrator?

(She always leaves a packet in the left-hand drawer. Nothing there either.)

Leaning over the sink, to wash her hands automatically, varnish cracked already, as though days and nights had gone by in a few hours, and this colour was now old-fashioned, face facts, what interests her isn't so much making love, love, love, what interests her more is having a large number of lovers, as many as a young lady should have these days – what interests her is their style, her lovers' styles. Take this Nicolas, for example. The way he has of throwing himself forwards, then pulling back but only halfway, then a feverish reimpaling, gripping her hips, halfway, halfway at a time, like Achilles's arrow which will never reach its target, or was it the tortoise, in Arnold's lesson about *classical paradoxes* . . . The opposite of Thomas, with his long pelvic thrusts, to and fro, occupying the entire space with neither haste nor hesitation, without the slightest doubt that he had her in her entirety, pushed up on his hands, only touching her lower belly, a good job she dumped him – and that other one, last year, who was worried about her, if this was OK, or if she liked it this way, and *if he was hurting her*, what did he expect her to say? What do other girls say? – And Lucas, who asked why she wasn't moving. Thank God she's pretty, otherwise she'd have problems finding any . . . Problems changing men as often as necessary. How do ugly girls cope? And the ones that lick you for hours on end. It's hard to fake in such circumstances. They must see something, sense something, if there are women who really do *come* – their labia, for instance, must swell, vibrate, go blue, squirt or something . . . and then they come and kiss you afterwards, as sticky as a new-born baby, I wonder what Arnold's style is . . .

There's some Nescafé left, and water, what an idiot, she was sure she'd put it on to heat. It's as if the water-heater is . . . go down to the garage to check – no, it's too dark, too late, too cold . . .

Something at the window. Branches. A reflection on the pane – of her, no doubt. How white you look in evening reflections . . . when little, she played at scaring herself, seeing faces in the gaps between leaves . . . laughter or cries starting up, depending on the wind . . . It's like . . .

This steam is on the outside of the pane . . .

A nose pressed on the glass, the trace of a mouth . . .

She's already lived out this scene, suspected it, what with all those boys she brings back, some of them are practical jokers, would have a laugh making her believe that . . .

She hears her name. Someone is calling her, *Nore*, it came from outside, or maybe the living room, between the settees covered with sheets, one of which is rumpled, giving them away . . . a black column or a reflection in the air beneath the electric light . . . a vapour of particles, as though the air was . . . and now . . .

Now it's the cups that have disappeared, the cups she's just filled – the packet of coffee is brazenly back where it should have been, she'd looked everywhere . . .

Her name again . . .

She runs down the corridor . . .

He's surprised, he's dozing peacefully, no, he didn't call her name . . .

She curls up against him, if only he could love her as she is . . . and take away, remove (as you delicately remove a mosquito, a stain, fluff, dust from someone's shoulder without even mentioning it) . . . eradicate that panic which has taken her breath away nearly every evening since she was little, that breathlessness since she was born, nothing's happened, everything's normal, nothing at all, nothing's ever happened . . .

Anne

Her hair is . . . light, fragrant and smooth. Iris, she's called Iris, and she's English, she'd already noticed her in this club, and that mounting warm fragrance in her hair, scent of her skin, that odour that is obviously Iris, violet and gold, on a tall stalk . . .

She's sobered up a bit, calmed down, three vodkas are what she needs to get into this club, and now she's there, she's inside . . . in the pulp of the light, that woolly lucidity of the initial descent from alcohol, and Iris is here, the scent of her hair is an inch away from her and, in that inch, a third fragrant flesh has slipped between – a genie rubbed out from its lamp, which is embracing them . . . the whipped cream of their bodies on these divans of smooth leather . . . the waves of their bodies, of scent: their two bodies. Her teeth are small, white and crenulated, a childish grin below the cheekbones of a smiling thirty-something, the genie places Anne's hand on Iris's cheek, *you're not alone any more*, the singer whispers over the divans, boas, feathers and velvet. Iris leans over, the genie slips away, the singer fades, the club wavers beneath their breathing as their lips touch, a slight flash which makes them close their eyes, tongue to tongue, saliva to saliva, Iris's so sweet and hers of vodka, never mind. Such things won't stop Iris the messenger, because they're now together, because the club is drifting up in whorls around them as they kiss. Iris Anne, Anne Iris, a centrifugal effect through the cracks in space-time, and here they are at the little table, surrounded by divans . . . The club whispers, *who's that girl*, nervy, rare and beautiful, yes, as beautiful as Iris, with her hint of Gena Rowlands, both of them happy at the centre of the world . . . Anne floats down on to Anne and reintegrates herself – the second descent from alcohol, mind peeled bare, she's seen herself dancing in those irises, and no longer knows who was watching who, it doesn't matter, Iris breathes softly into her neck and laughs. These ten minutes of course make ten years, *what do you call a man with no arms or legs who's swimming in the sea?* . . . *Bob*, Iris is dribbling with laughter on her shoulder, she's known her for ten minutes and she can already tell her stupid jokes, violet-eyed Iris, a hint of Liz Taylor, a new arrival in the vortex of time . . .

The round magic lamp which contains them has shifted, has changed direction, a slow-down, smoke, incense, make a wish, my wish, my wish is that all of my wishes come true . . .

Looking for her keys on the landing, why is she babbling so much? The answering machine is flashing, oh, it's Laurent, then he can go and . . . She's at the top of the cliff and it's towards the sky that she . . . with Iris, who's surfing everywhere and hasn't yet mentioned transmission procedures and secret meetings and recruitment, because there's time enough for all that, Iris's brain is buzzing with receivers and bugs, and she knows that Iris knows that, and knows Anne's identity, she's another messenger – cooperation, coordination should be possible, teamwork, they've already talked about their families, problems, sorrows and all their well- or ill-buried dead, Iris/Isis and Anne/Osiris are counting on each other to stick it all back together again, age-old rites to keep the body intact, the brain removed through the nostrils by means of extremely fine needles . . .

To Anne's mind, it's obvious that the house, their childhood home, is haunted, and when she thinks that Nore (her little sister) has got it in her clutches, then it makes her flesh creep, maybe we'll go there, a house in the woods, *loup y es-tu, m'entends-tu?* But the worst of all is my sister Jeanne, how guilty she felt, of course she was the oldest, and was considered to have reached the age of *being responsible*, when we turned seven, our father used to *responsibilize* us, so where were our parents that day on the beach? And him, whoosh! Gone, vanished into thin air, thrown out into space, the fourth dimension, towards the other side of our world, and so you can just imagine it: Jeanne, my sister, left, has spent her life travelling, the perfect one, the absolutely perfect model daughter lost her war, her pedestal, her rightful heritage . . .

On the Chilean island of Chiloe, she saw an aurora australis flapping like a flag and spinning round the echoing sky . . .

In China, she ate beef stuffed with a lamb stuffed with a turkey stuffed with a pheasant stuffed with a quail, from stomach to stomach, all of it ending up in her own . . .

In India, she lit dozens of spirals of incense to, or so she claims, assure a good life for us all (Dad Mum Momo Nore and me, Diego came into her life later on) . . .

In Murmansk, she watched sailors dancing in slow motion to techno music in an underground disco decked with cretonne curtains . . .

In Africa, she admired the efforts made by men in the middle of nowhere to land their small but vital aircraft – a bamboo control tower, a runway of clay, a guide on the ground in blue overalls ironed for no one's attention, how space is distributed in wind-ravaged zones . . .

As for me, I went to the Texas Medical Institute in Houston, there's nothing to do downtown at night, so I slipped inside the Dubuffet sculpture and looked up to see the red, black, white and blue bodies looking up along with me and turning towards the skyscrapers, which were also doing the same thing – Jeanne was in Okinawa, a postcard illustrated by pen-and-ink calligraphy which gradually faded away, with different layers of ink which disappeared as the days went by, so that the figures changed, developed . . .

And in Africa, she saw cattle rustlers eating raw meat, huge slabs of bloody flesh, shedding clots, and the villagers forcing them to dispatch their booty with machetes and eat it there and then . . .

Nothing ever happened, she'd arrive, thinking that the post was vacant, but the previous volunteer would still be there and depressed, having failed to learn the language or impose his goat programme (one goat per family, to be paid back to the organization thanks to its milk and kids), his fridge was full of beer and villagers would pop in and out of his house without saying a word . . .

She replaced the Primus with water, packed off the old volunteer as far as the capital in the vet's old Jeep . . .

When she got back . . .

The vet, one of her few friends in the village, drank one of the remaining beers with her on her veranda. After having a good laugh at the goat programme, he said, *One day, you'll see someone having their head chopped off* . . .

At night, gunshots could be heard through the darkness, up in the hills, getting closer and closer to the village. The next morning, the people responded to Jeanne's questions with impassive faces and impenetrable skulls, in this country, they shaved their heads . . .

One day, two friends came to visit her in her backwater – she was alone, with no radio or telephone – and they went for a picnic in a borrowed pirogue on the long lake which forms one of the borders. They fried fish on an island under the eucalyptus trees opposite a yellow, peeled landscape, cultivated to death, its terraced slopes collapsing every time it rained and the earth forming small basins at their feet. Suddenly, as though igniting in a hundred different places at once, everything caught fire: the hills, the few remaining trees, the grasses in the basins, the entire horizon. Jeanne and her friends got back into the boat and paddled home, but the pirogue was old and leaky. When they finally made it, the fire was out, huge black swathes scarred the landscape. But at the village, everything seemed normal, the women were weeding, the men smoking in front of their huts and the children sleeping in the shade. A shower of fine ash fell down on their silent mouths . . .

Her eyes closed, Anne's hand between her legs, Iris rubs herself absent-mindedly. Her breasts, falling to one side, jolt a little as she breathes, a blue shadow of blood passes through them with each heartbeat. Her nipples are light pink. Anne leans down to an imaginary odour of milk, and yet, unstoppably, she has to tell her about Jeanne, all of Jeanne's life . . .

The peasant Jeanne was organizing the goat programme with had disappeared. His wife kept saying that he was there, not far away, would be back soon. Then the goats of the programme started disappearing too, only to return transformed into ancient nanny goats, as though several years had passed by in a couple of days. But in this country, time hardly ever accelerates, except in brief rushes before it stagnates again at

179

the bottom of the basins, as heavy as damp clay. In the village, a slight increase in prosperity could be seen every time a goat vanished – guns and machetes appeared, the nanny goats died, the guns and machetes were hidden away in the huts. Jeanne decided to leave. But the capital was five days away and her friends, on leaving, had warned her about the increasing number of checkpoints. The soldiers manning them were drunk all the time, but could still tell the difference between blacks and whites. For the moment, they were only killing blacks . . .

She started painting a huge fresco on the living-room wall, depicting all of us, the entire family, two-metre-high portraits in thick lines of black paint. It was only when she got back to France that she realized she'd painted a congregation of nuns. When there were no more goats, she almost went mad with boredom, the next volunteer was due to replace her in a year's time. Night fell at six o'clock. The women weeded and the men smoked. Days turned into weeks, making Jeanne's irrelevance increasingly obvious. One evening, the mayor's servants arrived with some trunks, which they put in her living room. More and more of them piled up. She ended up using them as tables and chairs and shelves. The mayor's house, which was next door, was now apparently empty. Then he suddenly reappeared: there was going to be an attack. Jeanne's house was the only one with shutters, if she locked herself inside, he'd entrust her with his possessions. Where was he going? What was happening? Every night now there was gunfire in the hills. An endless season of sun and showers. The village filled up with women and emptied itself of men. During daylight, Jeanne's house was invaded by children, who played inside her fridge and devoured her fruit . . .

When the phone rang in the mayor's house – the village's only line – it was now Jeanne who went to answer it. When her voice was heard, there was no reply, nothing, just the dot dot dot of the dialling tone. One day, there was no more dialling tone . . .

Go on, says Iris.

A hospital worker, a day's march away, came to fetch her so she could identify a dead white man. She learned that she was the only white left in the region of the lakes. The land on either side of the road was completely charred. There were birds lying on the ground, their wings burnt black as they flew. At the hospital, the patients were lying on the ground, the floor cloths were soaked in blood and lying by the doors, looking like huge sanitary towels. They weren't ill, they were wounded. They'd had their feet, arms or lumps of their heads cut off. The morgue was a sort of small, square cellar full of flies, with bodies stacked up along the walls, with a fresh pile in the middle of the floor. You had to slip in sideways. It was the first time Jeanne had seen a corpse. The face of the one she was shown, a white who had the privilege of having a slab, was black with decomposition, and there was no way she could possibly identify him. He was a volunteer based on the other side of the lake. He'd slit his wrists . . .

Later, she fled with the vet. She drove the Jeep, with him hidden under a tarpaulin. She got past the checkpoints, guns pressed against her belly, by handing out what little money she had left. The capital was deserted. The doors of the organization's offices were swinging on their hinges, the building was empty. Armed men were patrolling the streets. The shops had been pillaged. There were no whites to be seen. A smell of cooked sugar crept into the Jeep. She drove quickly, past the bodies on the clay pavements. In the residential district, the vet's parents' house was still standing, a key hidden beneath a pot of azaleas. The honeysuckle was flowering and the lawn had recently been mown. All around, they could hear rustling noises in the hedges, like deer escaping. Further off, there were gunshots. The vet barricaded himself inside. Through the windows, Jeanne could see men with machetes running from garden to garden. On the TV, CNN explained

181

that all foreign nationals had been repatriated. It took a while for that to sink in . . .

She got back into the Jeep, with the vet under the tarpaulin. At the Meridien Hotel, there were still some Belgian soldiers. They pointed to a helicopter. There was one place for her and it was now or never. She never found out what happened to the vet . . .

Life is life, says Iris.

Jeanne

How silly, why can't I concentrate, why do I suddenly lose touch with what I'm doing? As I was saying to Dr Welldon, concentration is the opposite of thought – you're afraid of being sidetracked by a daydream, so you assiduously read the backs of cereal boxes every morning, with their blatantly didactic advertising pitch: *to unite fitness and pleasure, Special K provides you with vitamins B1, B2, B5 and Folic Acid, ideal for mothers-to-be, did you know that 37 per cent of women are dissatisfied by their weight?* Meanwhile, I've got to get out of here . . .

How could I have missed the bend? Those clouds of flies surged up from the lianas or the water, like in the morgue in Barambé – and, splash, into the canal with me, *Jeanne tombe à l'eau*, how funny – Welldon's going to tell me that it's a Freudian slip and Diego that I've written off the Volvo he bought me, the leather seats, imported from Sweden, and Jimena will never believe me, and what shall I tell Mum? Meanwhile, I really must get this door open, it's stuck, it's the pressure of the water, I remember hearing about that, how calm I am, if anyone told me I'd be this calm . . .

Or else wind down the window, the water's still well below it, thanks to the boot, *capacious thief-proof rear boot*, which presumably makes a bubble, but the German or whatever motor is extremely heavy, the front's dipping down of course, and the electric window won't come down, why not? A handle like in my good old Austin, a good old crank system, like in the sets at the Biela, and I'd be safe . . .

The Volvo, Diego's present . . .

First undo your belt, that's still mechanical at least, clunk click before each trip, what can I remember someone saying? That you should let yourself sink and wait until the pressures are equal, with the car completely full, hold your breath, at the bottom, the door will open easily – but I'll never have the patience to wait till we hit the bed . . .

And no one on the bank as usual, a no man's land of lianas between two canal docks and Diego, I'm late, it was the speed, the bend, those clouds of mosquitoes, by the time he finds me . . . and the sun on the windscreen, I really don't want to . . .

I'll tell Diego that I didn't do it on purpose and, above all, don't say a word to Mum . . .

It won't budge, I can't believe this, what a stupid way to die . . . Try the passenger door – the boot, of course, the boot will open – but it's a coupé, I insisted on having a coupé – break the rear window with the heel of my shoe, but if I move, I'll upset the balance of the car, imagine if water starts coming in the back as well, this car's so small, a coupé, how long will there be air to breathe? – pressure versus pressure, will the doors then open? *Calculate your body mass index (BMI) by dividing your weight by the square of your waistline, waffles will be the death of you,* the predictions of doctors Waterlot and Kellogg . . . *But I have no sideways . . .*

Stop, find a solution, a solution to this puzzle, it's a test, a giant IQ problem . . .

If I break the windscreen and water only comes up to the wipers, then I'll have to – no sudden movements – how long have I been saying why not have a mobile phone, what's the point, does drowning hurt? I've already wondered about that – will I have time, for instance, to slit my wrists, suffer less, but what with the . . . Or even to hold my breath – much of a muchness – water in your lungs, pain – these heels are useless, Volvos are solid stuff, unbreakable windscreen, Anne finds them *bourgeois*, so much for the local goods, next time I'll buy some FRENCH shoes, all they manage to do here is to produce cow leather and shrinks, six years' analysis, for what? To die in the Tigre, don't say such things, a fortune down the drain and what if I'm pregnant – Princess Diana was, *lady dies* in her limousine in the Alma tunnel – don't even think about it, how long does it take to die? Two minutes? Ten minutes? When we used to play at sticking our heads under water . . . how long is it now? Three seconds since the car went splash, the circles in the water are only just closing – it's weird how the electric clock's still working, and the temperature gauge, thirteen degrees, the water's cold – if the electrics are holding up, why won't the windows work? *Breakfast like a king, lunch like a prince and dine like a pauper, drink a litre and a half of water a day and eat lightly in the evening because it's then that the body makes its reserves*, thank God I'm not digesting – and the four hours a week in the gym, the swimming pool, colonic irrigation, and the best years of my life thrown away with all those sodding blacks, TO END UP LIKE THIS – stop, calm down – someone's holding the windows shut – don't think about it – and the hell I went through to give up smoking . . .

It's a convertible, of course, lower the roof – an extra costing a grand, heaven and freedom – impossible to break as well, the sky's blue, no green, because of the tinted glass – *Emerit unbreakable*, it's written there, a necessity in Buenos Aires because of all the thieves . . .

Okinawa, Murmansk, Barambé . . .

The sky is green and shut off – watch out, the car's going to – don't move, easy does it – a good kick would do it, but how? It's as if someone was holding the car shut, pressed Tupperware air-tight cold meat – don't think about it – does your life pass in front of your eyes?

And that chemical smell of lavender, if I could at least smell the sky, water, honeysuckle, if you could smell them, you'd be free – it was because of the flies, you closed the windows and now they're swarming up in the sky, unless it's already the lack of oxygen – my God, the carpet, water's coming into the car from under the . . . near the . . . cold, temperature down to eleven degrees, when is it going to switch off? The time flashing away sarcastically at you, 19.06, the boat's motor purring away, black smoke, and Diego getting stroppy on the quay-side, stood up, *un conejo, on m'a pose un lapin*, Dad joking and translating the French word for word, *I was left with a rabbit, a big rabbit if you want to know*, time has lost its rhythm . . .

Like when Anne and I were on ether, so that was a training session, elastic time so fast and so slow . . .

In murder stories, the face of a smashed watch, the time of your death has struck, shut up and think, there must be some solution . . .

It's a quiz, a multiple choice, your students getting their own back, please tick the correct box or else . . .

I haven't marked my homework for Monday . . .

How deep is the Tigre?

Where the trees merge, the sky's a clear green, the Tigre is shaded, its arms quietly hold you, hug you, last tango in Paris, last trip to *don't cry for me, Argentina* . . .

God, this water's cold and the engine's tipping over, the bubble under the hood must have popped, I must . . . where to go? Heavy Swedish machinery . . .

Pull yourself together, do something, if Diego was here . . .
37 per cent of women . . .

You know he's waiting for you at the bottom, you know he's expecting you, laughing, covered with silt, it's been written since time immemorial, you knew that it had to happen, so stupid, at the bottom of the Tigre, sitting merrily playing with his toes in his little red trunks, a little blond Buddha, *je t'attends je t'attends depuis longtemps* . . .

Full fathom five my brother lies;
Of his bones are coral made:
Those are pearls that were his eyes
Nothing of him that doth fade . . .
Sea-nymphs hourly ring his knell
Ding-dong.
Hark! Now I hear them – Ding-dong bell.

Stop banging on the windows, it's pointless . . .

I must tell Diego that the grouting on the balcony's leaking . . .

He'll probably phone Anne first, then Anne will call Mum, I'll let her have the pleasure, then John, then Nore, if they know where she is. What's the time in France? To die in the middle of the night. Anne may well wait till tomorrow morning before she . . . It'll be the death of Mum, and you'll have been dead for hours . . .

How quiet and green it all is, an inside-out aquarium, air inside, water outside . . .

The water's rising more slowly than I'd have thought, by layers, a physical phenomenon to be studied on another occasion, maybe I'll survive for ages in the bubble, and no one, ever, takes this towpath, the sky's like a puddle, we're slowly slipping down the beams, down through the water, through the seeds of the trees and the pollen below the legs of the water spiders sitting on their little bubbles, one bubble per leg . . .

How beautiful it is, how lovely the sky, shifting away through the water in the beams pointing the way – let go, and relax, a green, calming relaxation . . .

Through the bedroom curtains, there on the far side of the sea, the air was as dense as water, in spring a creamy, fertile air, and Pierre always wanting to get into bed with me, Mum was already sleeping most of the time, not our fault at all . . .

186

À LA CLAIRE FONTAINE M'EN ALLANT PROMENER
J'AI TROUVÉ L'EAU SI CLAIRE QUE JE M'Y SUIS
BAIGNÉE
IL Y A LONGTEMPS QUE JE T'AIME
JAMAIS JE NE T'OUBLIERAI . . .

Okinawa Murmansk Barambé . . .

Tell them all I love them, do things as they should be done, nothing's in place, everything's a mess, knick-knacks and bits of string – you're supposed to say and then do certain things . . .

En las sombras de mi pieza
Es tu paso que regresa
Y es tu voz
Pequeña y triste . . .

It just isn't possible . . .
It isn't possible, I must be dreaming, it can't end like this . . .

This cannot be happening to me . . .

Not now . . .
Not fish . . .
How long will it last?

19.07 and nine degrees, oh, look, it's gone off . . .
Who would have thought that the Tigre was so cold?

All that wasted time . . .
Tell them I love them . . .
They could have told me too . . .

Not fish . . .
Emerit windows, there will be time enough before they get in, fish as curious as monkeys, like the apes in Reykjavik, a cloud of silt coming up – you know well no one's there, it's the car lifting up the silt and a few stray fish out to eat you . . .

DING DONG BELL, PUSSY'S IN THE WELL, WHO PUT HER IN? LITTLE JOHNNY GREEN . . .

Water . . .
　Water everywhere . . .
　By the roof, forming another bubble . . .

How stupid we are, needing air, why should we? One way of
organizing an organism rather than another, after all, foetus-
es have gills . . .

How long does the brain survive? All those things you don't
know, and when the moment comes, Mum always used to
say, *remain dignified in all circumstances,* her great victory over
Anne's sleepwalking, it's good to think about that for a
moment, will my life pass before my eyes? I'll find out everything they don't know, Mum, John, Anne and the others, so
much for that theory . . .

Maybe the glove compartment's airtight, there might still
be some oxygen in it, *la Mujer elegante* has sprung a leak, loose
pages, what a mess, you could have put away your mouth-
watering mint sweets, so that's what silt tastes like, you're
going to die looking ridiculous, *dignified in all circumstances,*
gulps of air up to the right, just below the vanity mirror, they
did tell me, *you've always been too fat and vain,* too this that and
the other thing . . .

I am . . .
　This is a joke . . .
　An awful joke . . .

It just isn't possible, a joke . . .

Tomorrow morning, a paragraph in *La Prensa* – *la esposa de
Diego Contrapuerta el famoso entrepreneur se noie dans le canal du
Tigre. Toutes nos condoléances à notre généreux donateur.* Will the
family come over? Money down the drain . . .

Diego will tell Anne, who will phone Mum, I'll leave her that
pleasure . . .

How sad Diego will be, may he get well and truly mad first, it will do him good, *I've been silly, you've been silly, let's start a family* . . .

37 per cent of women . . .

My God, it's burning, just let it be quick . . .

I'll be so fat when they find me, you shouldn't have gone off your diet, all puffed up and water swelling you, they'll see that I fixed my skirt with a safety pin . . .

Green and black, sparkling flies . . .

Underwater Bastille Day fireworks just for me, in my honour . . .

At last . . .

Here comes everybody . . .

They're all here, Pierre Mum John Anne and Nore, the plane tickets must have cost them a fortune, they shouldn't have . . .

Flies, spangles and that smile . . .

They've even hired a band, deary deary me, what extravagance . . .

Just pray that my panties and bra match . . .

A band . . .

Match . . .

Anne

Anne suddenly out of her sleep, out of her dreams, out of breath, opens the window on the daylight as it dawns and screams. Iris, hanging on to her waist, yells too, terrified, so that's it, the fits she was talking about – an inaudible gargling scream, spluttering tears, a word, sounds like *maman*.

189

The Mother

Someone calling so early scared me, after a night of struggling, and bad dreams – and Momo already out mixing his concrete, and then a bell rings, and I realize that it's the door. Immediately, before I even opened it, I checked to see if Nore's car was there, what a relief, and then, guess what? I can see – after putting on my glasses – the word Interflora *on a van. It was a delivery man who'd rung the doorbell and who was now coming up the steps with a bouquet, yes, that's right, she was still fast asleep, so young, you could see the child in her face, just exactly the same look about her as when she was little. So I woke her up, a bouquet, just imagine it. It's her first one, I think. Like a little sea calf, all puffed up with sleep, a baby's cheeks when it wakes up. But she just wouldn't surface – so I couldn't resist it. You're not going to believe this, but I opened the envelope, are you listening to me, Maïder? The poor boy was complaining about waking up alone in a* hostile *house, those are his very words, and, what do you know? He misses her already! Oh, I have a second call. I'll speak to you later – Yes, a wonderful bouquet. He really pushed the boat out. Roses as full as peonies, autumn roses, the ones that are so swollen because it's the end of the season, as if they were going to pop, still curled up, but as big as your fist, absolutely splendid, you know how much I like flowers – I'll talk to you later, I've got another call – splendid, magnificent roses . . .*

This book would not exist without Sam Francis, René Descartes, Dominique Fourcade, Cheney, H. G. Wells, Adolfo Bioy Casares, the 'Horizon' section of *Le Monde*, the horoscope in *Marie-Claire*, the fashion section in *Elle*, the local news in *Sud-Ouest*, Charles Perraut, Edouard Molinaro, Olivier Cadiot, Talking Heads, Denis Diderot, Alain Bashung, Bobby Lapointe, Barbara, Enid Blyton, David Bowie, Laura Kasischke, Blaise Pascal, Janet Jackson, Kenzaburo Oê, Stan Lee, The Cure, Oscar del Priore and Irene Amuchástegui, Philippe Sollers, Coluche, Svetlana Alexievich, Little Bob, Li Ang, Carmen Martinez, Valérie Bihan and Darian Leader.

M.D.